I0825397

Silent Justice

Scott Lawson

Published in the United States by Badge & Bell Publishing LLC
Dayton, Ohio

ISBN: 979-8-9931363-1-8

DEDICATION

To my wife Lora, my four daughters, and the grandchildren, who fill my life with love and purpose.

And to those in law enforcement who walk into danger, shoulder sacrifice, and quietly bear the burdens most will never see—

You are remembered and honored here.

ACKNOWLEDGMENTS

This book could not have been written without the quiet encouragement of my family. Lora, you carried me through every late night at the keyboard, and my daughters and grandchildren gave me reason to keep going when the words felt far away.

I am grateful as well to the men and women of law enforcement—those I served beside and those who continue the work today. Your courage, sacrifice, and resilience remain a constant reminder of what true service looks like.

A special thanks to my writing professor at Wright State University, who was the first to recognize that I had a voice worth putting on paper. That early encouragement planted a seed that has grown into this story.

Finally, thank you to the friends, teachers, and readers who believed this book could matter. Your voices carried me farther than you know.

Prologue
The Ghost in the Snow

"Not guilty on all counts."

The words hit the gallery as sharp as a backhand slap.

A murmur. Then a voice, rising above the others—

"You're letting a damn terrorist loose!"

Heads turned. A bailiff moved.

The judge banged the gavel once, twice.

But the damage was done.

At the defense table, Hassan Al-Khatib—a name he wore in Dayton, not the one he was born with—straightened his jacket, smoothed his tie, and smiled with the confidence of a man who'd always known he was walking out.

***

The black van sat in silence, legally parked along a snow-covered street. Its dark paint blended seamlessly into the shadows. The frost sealed the windows like curtains, and a thin crust of fresh snow on the roof and hood softened the van's silhouette. No one would ever notice another forgotten relic in a city that had long since given up on this part of town.

Inside, the shooter lay quietly on a custom-built platform, breath coming slow and steady. Every movement was deliberate; timing was everything. The narrow opening of a modified roof window framed the entrance to a crumbling warehouse two blocks away. The lonely glow of a single streetlamp cast pale light onto the sagging roof and rusted awning above the corroded panels of the dock door. To most, the warehouse was another decaying monument to the city's forgotten industrial past—silent and lifeless. But not to Hassan Al-Khatib.

To anyone passing by, it was nothing more than a run-down warehouse stocking incense, snacks, and imported goods for local markets. But inside were the horrors Khatib had long since brought to Dayton. Women and kids were commodities—no names, no guilt. Just bodies to sell and space to clear. Everything about this man made them sick. The shooter had studied his crimes, his routines, his movements, his habits. Vile and untouchable—but his victims had been failed by the system for the last time.

The shooter's gloved hand moved with precision, adjusting the Barrett MRAD rifle into position. A nearby streetlight reflected off the custom suppressor as it pushed through the opening into the night. Through the Vortex Razor HD LHT scope, they studied the warehouse door. The rangefinder clicked softly—230 yards. A routine shot under normal conditions. But tonight's bitter cold would sap the bullet's speed, dragging it down enough to matter. They adjusted the elevation turret two clicks—0.2 MRAD. Perfect.

They eased the scope left and right, looking for anything unexpected. Nothing seemed unusual, at least for this neighborhood. Snow was piled high along the curbs and sidewalks, with a faint trail of footprints leading toward the side entrance—a quiet clue that Hassan was inside.

The icy wind, speeding forward, a runaway train with no brakes, rocked the van as it funneled between the buildings. It tugged at the plywood covering shattered windows, rattling loose nails and scattering trash that had once filled the rust-covered dumpsters in every lot. Most sounds had been swallowed by the storm, except for the lonely wail of a siren in the distance—probably another shooting somewhere else in this godforsaken city.

They shifted their weight in the tight space of the van, searching for the right position on the hard wooden platform. The van was their den—safe, silent, invisible in plain sight, and self-sustaining for days if needed. Years of trial and error had built perfection—there were no excuses for failure anymore. Research, surveillance, execution—simple.

The waiting was always the worst part. The shooter had been in place over an hour. It was one of those Sunday nights when the city seemed to forget itself. Time crawled by, like molasses in a blizzard. The street remained deserted except for a rat scurrying between dumpsters, its paws leaving tiny tracks in the snow. A raccoon darted across the cracked pavement, claws scratching the asphalt as it vanished. "Weren't they forest animals?" the shooter thought. Maybe once, before they discovered garbage. An old friend used to call them trash pandas—the thought brought the faintest hint of a smile, there and gone as if it knew better than to stick around.

Off in the distance, the headlights of an occasional car or bus passed, but nobody ventured down this way. This part of town was long forgotten, snowdrifts swallowing the curbs and wind piling white over potholes deep enough to drown the tires.

Then, right on schedule, the dock door creaked open on its weathered, rusted hinges. Hassan stepped into view, shivering in the cold. He paused, lit a cigarette, and checked his phone—completely unaware that he was already dead.

The shooter exhaled slowly, aligning the crosshairs with the center of Hassan's chest. In their mind, the scene had unfolded a hundred ways, but the timing was always exact. There would be no appeals tonight. No mistrials. No bribes. No more victims. A suppressed crack. Inside the van, the sound disappeared—gone as quickly as it came. Hassan folded to the pavement, limbs slack and life gone. His cigarette dropped from his hand and hissed in the snow.

The warehouse door remained open, exposing the crates and debris inside, but no one came. Somewhere in the bowels of that dilapidated old structure, Hassan's acquaintances might not have even noticed yet—or maybe they had. Maybe they were already huddled in some dark corner. Terrified. Silent. Wondering if they were next.

The shooter waited, listening to the silence, watching the dock door, knowing that eventually someone would call the police—maybe. A body on the sidewalk draws attention. Hassan's body lay limp, his phone resting a few feet away in the snow, the screen casting a weak glow. No one would pick it up. No frantic footsteps. No shouts. Nothing but silence.

The shooter needed to close the window before the police arrived, but quickly scanned the area one final time. Snow was falling once again and had already begun filling Hassan's footprints. Soon, they'd be gone—erased by nature itself, eliminating one of the only clues to the time of the shooting.

They closed the hatch with a faint click, sealing out the

winter air, then slid the rifle back into its foam-lined Pelican case. The faint scent of gunpowder lingered, mingling with the smell of insulation. The shooter leaned back against the platform, exhaling slowly as the tension drained from their muscles—a practiced ritual, as familiar as the shot itself.

Climbing down from the platform, they reached for a thermos and took a much-needed sip of coffee laced with bourbon—merely enough to knock back the chill of the van.

They had done their part.

Every motion was smooth, practiced, and deliberate—completing in seconds what the courts had failed to do in years.

They switched on the van's heater and sat in the small folding chair in front of the warm air. The power station was one of the van's most expensive additions, but on frigid nights, it proved worth every cent. As the heat began to flow, they settled into the seat, letting the weight of the mission sink in. The heater ticked softly as the van came alive—plastic, wiring, and old steel breathing heat for the first time in hours. The heat revived the once-frozen chemical tang of bore cleaner and something sharp and sour that always lingered after a job.

The first time, too many years ago to recall, had been the hardest—hands shaking, stomach churning with the significance of what they'd done. The cold sweat, the deafening silence afterward, and the doubt creeping in through every pore. But now, it was different. The process had become a series of precise steps, each one carefully designed to achieve a specific goal. Efficiency over emotion. Logic over doubt.

Damn, that was too easy. When the plan was hatched, it was all about Hassan. Human trafficking infuriated them like nothing else ever had, and when he walked on a ridiculous technicality, his death warrant was signed. While researching Hassan, they were shocked by how many other despicable criminals were escaping punishment for so many different reasons. A list of those worthy of death began to grow. Could they strike again? Should they strike again? The question lingered for only a moment. After all, justice hadn’t only failed once—it had failed countless times. Someone had to do what the system wouldn’t. Not out of vengeance. Not even out of anger anymore. Just a cold understanding: if no one stands in the gap, more bodies stack up. That’s the deal.

They retrieved a small, worn notebook from a side panel.

Inside was a list of names, carefully gathered from public records, news reports, and a few blogs that didn't mind naming names. Some names had been crossed out, others were circled in red ink. These were the best targets according to their research. Looking at Hassan's name, written neatly at the top of the page, they drew a dark line through his name, marking the mission's success.

Would there be another mission? The choice wasn't hard. The fate of someone on this list had been sealed. Flipping to the next page, they studied a grainy surveillance photo—a man in a suit mid-handshake, his partner mostly out of frame, face lost to the blur. Another catastrophic failure of the system. Would it be him?

The shooter closed the notebook, pausing on the handwritten words across the cover: *For God will bring every deed into judgment, every hidden thing, whether good or bad. Kohelet 12:14.* They closed their eyes for a moment, then slid it back into its compartment.

There would be time tomorrow to decide. Shivering a little, they took another sip of the spiked coffee. The warmth didn't chase the chill, but it gave the illusion of comfort. That was enough.

A muffled radio transmission crackled through the police scanner mounted underneath the shooting platform. The shooter smirked slightly, as the dispatcher's voice came through: "112, start for the 900 block of Pruden Avenue on a man down—possible DB. Respond Code 3."

The shooter removed their gloves, flexing their fingers and allowing the weight of the mission to settle. Police would be arriving soon, and silence was essential. They killed the volume on the scanner and let the quiet return. No celebration. No regret. Just the steady rhythm of a mind that had done this before—comfortable in the silence.

The planning for the next target would begin soon, but for now, rest.

They pulled the blanket to their jawline. A yawn. Eyes closed. The waiting had begun.

Another predator, another night. But snow was falling again. And this time, someone was watching.

Chapter 1
It Begins

I wasn't asleep, but I wasn't awake either. These days, I mostly dozed on and off for a few hours.

I sat in my ratty old recliner to eat and never made it to bed. The TV was on, though I couldn't tell you what I'd been watching. The glow flickered across the bare walls, casting shadows that played tricks on a tired mind.

A few empty Coke cans and a couple of stale slices of pizza littered the coffee table. I usually had beer with pizza, but I hadn't been to the store in weeks.

The house was quiet—the kind that settles in when your wife and daughter have moved on. Never peaceful. Just lonely and sad, as though silence had unpacked a suitcase and planned to stay.

And the nights were the worst—probably why I couldn't sleep. They pressed in from all sides, thick and shapeless. Dark, even with the lights on.

You don't realize how loud and happy a home once was until it's nothing but the hum of the fridge and the creak of a sagging floorboard. And by then, it's too late.

I needed sleep.

Buzzzzzzz. Buzzzzzzz.

I glanced at my watch—1:30 a.m. I didn't need to look. I already knew. There was only one reason my phone rang this time of night. Nevertheless, I looked—DISPATCH SERGEANT.

I answered the call. "MacLaren."

The voice was all too familiar these days.

"Detective MacLaren, this is Sergeant Kline. We've got a shooting on the east side. Are you available?"

"Yeah," I muttered, rubbing my eyes as I reached for the spiral notebook I kept close for these calls. "What is it?"

"We've got a shooting in the 900 block of Pruden Avenue. One victim, DOA—no removal," Kline said. "Your brother's en route. Coroner too."

Dropping the notebook back on the table, I picked up the TV remote instead.

"Alright, thanks, Sarge. I'm about thirty minutes out."

I didn't rush. Nothing good comes fast in this job. Besides, dead's dead. He wasn't going anywhere.

I switched to the weather channel to see what kind of hell I was heading out in. Ten degrees. Twenty-five mile-per-hour winds. Snow. I grabbed the notebook and pen and jotted down January 20th and the weather, then got dressed.

A few minutes later, I was in the car, the heater barely making a dent in the cold. I pulled out of the drive, shaking my head. Warehouse district. Early morning. Didn't add up.

With the streets nearly abandoned, it only took about ten minutes to get over to Pruden, but I didn't approach the scene right away. I sat in the car, observing. I noted the nearest intersections and made mental notes on lighting, camera angles, line of sight—little habits drilled into me from a decade of crawling through other people's worst nights.

I also asked myself questions. Did anything seem strange? Any people around that shouldn't be, or maybe a little too interested? It took a few seconds for me to realize these were stupid questions tonight. The weather was terrible—nobody would be lurking around. And besides, I hadn't been on this block in years. I had no idea who or what belonged here, so I pulled on my gloves and opened the door.

I zipped up my heavy winter coat—my call-out coat—and stepped into the wind. It whipped down the abandoned street, slicing through my layers like paper. It slammed into my face, breath-stealing and sharp as the reaper's hand. The winter didn't care who it claimed next—maybe me.

I moved toward the body, where Graham and a couple of patrol officers I didn't recognize stood behind the scene tape snapping in the wind. The air reeked of exhaust from idling cruisers.

It hung there, thick, mixing with winter's bite—a silent warning that something was wrong.

The neighborhood was silent. If not for the flashing reds and blues and a single dim streetlamp near the body, it would have been total darkness. Most of the streetlights had vanished long ago—along with everything else that once called this street home. All that was left was the wind, and the occasional squawk from a radio. No headlights. No night-shift wanderers. Not even a stray dog. Just stillness, as if death had settled over the whole block.

What the hell happened here?

I used to shag calls in this neighborhood when I was a rookie—back when this part of town had life. The blocks were alive with night crews, truck horns, coffee shops open at 3 a.m. Everywhere you turned, the dockhands were hauling crates under sodium lights, the nearby bars full of guys blowing paychecks. This was a place that never really slept.

Now? The trucks are gone. The docks are sealed. Fences sag under drifts. Pavement cracking after years of ice forcing its way in.

This city used to mean something. Dayton gave the world the airplane, the pop-top can, microfiche. Now? No more than another rust-belt relic. The factories were ghosts—corroded skeletons standing over the neighborhoods they once fed. These days, all we produced was poverty, overdoses, and crime stories nobody beyond the county line even read. The city was dying, and most people didn't see it.

I shook my head and moved closer to the body. My breath curled around me—pale, weightless in the cold.

The scene was eerily frozen; the only movement was the faint steam rising from blood seeping into the slush. The snow, once white, was now a crimson smear. The streetlights flickered, casting weak cones of light that barely reached the dead man. Snow crunched behind me as an officer passed by without a word. There was nothing to say. Another night. Another name on the city's long list of forgotten dead.

I knelt down on the stoop, the cold biting through my pants as I searched for wounds. Brown-skinned, not Black. Middle Eastern, maybe—I couldn't be sure in the dark. Mid-thirties. Well-dressed in a dark wool coat that probably cost more than my car. One shot. Center mass. Cops and soldiers are trained that way. No signs of a struggle, no scattered belongings. He probably never saw it coming.

Probably stepped out for a smoke and dropped before he could take a drag. A clean, efficient kill—as if death had stepped in and vanished before he could blink.

Graham crouched beside me and flipped open his notepad, shivering in the early morning cold.

"Hassan Al-Khatib. No warrants. A few FIs in the system. Vice stopped him on Keowee and N. Main. No convictions yet, but I'll dig deeper when we get back."

I scanned the dim street. A few lights glowed weakly in windows. Most sat dark. Nothing moved but the slow drip of melting snow from awnings.

"So far, we've got nothing," Graham muttered. "No casings. No prints. No tracks."

"Do we have anything?" I asked. "Please tell me we at least have the bullet."

"The E-crew's on it," Graham said. "It's stuck in the doorframe."

I looked past the body to the splintered hole—black against chipped white paint. Mangled or not, it'd tell us something.

Could we be looking at a pro?

My phone buzzed. I let it ring. Graham smirked.

"Sarge?"

I nodded and slid the phone back into my pocket. "He can wait."

He didn't argue. Jenkins always called before there was anything to report—before the evidence was bagged, before the puzzle was even dumped out of the box.

"Chris our E-crew tonight?"

"Yeah. Hasn't found much though."

I shook my head and looked around. Whoever it was—phantom or not—someone had to see them. Nobody vanishes in this city. Even the pros slip up. A missed camera. A nosy neighbor. A trash can rolled a few feet out of place. The city leaves marks on all of us, whether we mean to or not.

I took my old, reliable Canon PowerShot camera from my coat pocket. I started grabbing images of everything I saw, and that was when I realized something was wrong. The untouched snow. No casings. No scuff marks. A body and a dark stain. None of this fit the usual Dayton homicide scene.

One shot. No overkill. That wasn't luck. That was experience. A street shooter would've emptied the mag. This was deliberate. Controlled. Not a junkie. Not a random disagreement.

Something else. Something worse.

"You planning to open a gallery?" Graham asked.

I didn't look up. Just kept snapping photos through the scratched viewfinder of my old camera.

"When we get back, I'll study these. Sometimes a picture catches what the eye misses."

"You'd get better pictures with your phone."

I laughed. "Yeah, and then my whole phone gets subpoenaed. Some punk defense attorney digging through baby photos and vacation shots? No thanks."

Graham chuckled but kept his comments to himself. He knew I wasn't joking.

I continued taking photos as Chris walked up with a huge smile and held up the mangled bullet.

"Pretty damaged, but I think the lab can ID it."

"Good," I said, rubbing some heat into my hands. "What about trajectory?"

Chris glanced down the street. "Barely any angle—street level. If it came from a building, no higher than a first floor."

I frowned. "Any ideas from where?"

He exhaled and pointed down N. Irwin Street. "Somewhere down there. The shooter may have been standing, or even elevated, but not by much. Maybe from a truck bed or something."

The thought hit my gut, a stone dropping hard inside me. A shooter lying in wait was cold. Intentional. And that was the terrifying part.

This wasn't rage. This wasn't a deal gone bad. This was a hit.

I let out a slow sigh. The night was unnervingly subdued, as if the city itself was hiding from its demons. No sirens. No murmurs. Just the hum of engines and the occasional radio squawk.

I turned toward my car, chasing the promise of warmth. We'd done all we could tonight. We needed lab work. Traffic cams. A gun.

But one thing was already clear. Whoever did this wasn't lucky.

They were good.

I ducked under the crime scene tape. "Hernandez!"

The uniform turned. "Yeah, Detective?"

"Check the parked cars on this block."

"Anything in particular?"

"No idea, whatever stands out."

He nodded and moved off, flashlight sweeping windshields.

I didn't expect much. Whoever did this wasn't sloppy. But nobody's perfect. If they used a vehicle, they parked it somewhere. Maybe someone saw something. Maybe a camera caught a flicker. Maybe there was a roof with no snow where there should be.

Graham was already on the phone, finding next of kin. Somebody out there loved this man—and might know something worth hearing.

I turned back one last time, memorizing Al-Khatib's frozen face. His eyes were open. Locked in permanent shock. My gaze dropped. The blood had stopped spreading, frozen into the slush beneath him. His coat hung open enough to reveal a crisp white dress shirt, now ruined by one perfect shot.

Maybe that's the worst part of dying out here—not the bullet, not the cold—but the simple fact that the world keeps turning as though you were never even there.

He never saw it coming.

Neither did we.

But we would.

Chapter 2
Investigation Begins

After I left the scene last night, I went home for a couple of hours of sleep—not that it did me any good. I should've gone straight to the office and gotten paid for three hours of chasing my own tail. By 7:00 a.m., I accepted that sleep was as likely as winning the lottery. The case already had its hooks in me, and that was never a good sign this early, so I got dressed and headed downtown. But first, I needed coffee. Lots of strong, black coffee.

I hated squad room coffee. It was more used motor oil than beverage—thick, bitter, so strong my grandma would say it would walk if it had legs. So I stopped by UDF for a cup of Highlander Grogg, black, of course, and a Krispy Kreme. The donut and coffee combo was as classic as a badge and a sidearm—a cop's version of a morning prayer.

I pulled into the rear lot of the building around 8:15 a.m. The parking lot was alive with movement. The first relief guys lingered—some finishing up paperwork in their cruisers, others shivering in the cold as they made plans to head to the pub. These days, most guys favored The Brass Shield in Belmont. I shook my head. I missed those days—nothing better than beer and wings at 8:30. I kept moving—I wasn't one of them anymore, not really. As I walked toward the door, the wind cut through my coat chilling me to the core. January didn't care if you were a cop, a killer, or something in between.

Second relief had wrapped up roll call and they were already debating where to grab breakfast as they headed to their cruisers. I chuckled—some things never change.

I walked through the back door and headed to the ancient prisoner elevator—a relic of past abuse more than a ride to the upper floors. If this thing could talk...

I stepped off the elevator—its gears groaning like a beat-up old detective chasing a kid through an alley—and made my way down the hall to the office. The place was half-lit, stuck in that early morning limbo—night shift lingering, day shift not fully settled in. I flipped on a few more lights, something more suitable for actual work. Detectives from other squads drifted in, and the stench of strong coffee followed. Nobody would admit it, but it was probably the same coffee from yesterday. Maybe three days ago.

Graham wasn't in yet, but Sergeant Jenkins was at his desk, flipping through paperwork with the same dead-eyed look I'd seen on him for years. He glanced up as I walked in.

"MacLaren! Why the hell didn't you answer my call?" His voice cut through the squad room—loud, grating, and distorted by irritation. "I need to know what's going on."

I thought about explaining. Thought about making up something halfway decent. In the end, I didn't have the energy.

"Good morning to you too, Sarge," I shot back. "I must have left my phone in the car. Anyway, there was nothing to tell, last night or now. So far, we've got nothing."

I dropped into my chair—probably the same one that had been here since the Johnson Administration—and powered up my desktop.

The photos I took last night were on my camera's SD card, so I plugged it in and downloaded the images to the hard drive. I pulled a fresh manila folder from my drawer, scrawled Hassan Al-Khatib — 900 Pruden on the tab, and grabbed a few sheets of printer paper.

A few minutes later, the first image began to appear from the ancient office printer—a black-and-white reminder of the precision hit on Hassan. It was slow as hell—slow enough you could grab a UDF coffee and be back before it spit out a page.

I leaned back and closed my eyes. Damn, I was tired. I didn't hear Graham come in. Must've dozed off. He took care of that when he kicked my chair. Kicking a 60-year-old office chair is no safer than slapping a sleeping bull—you might get away with it—or knock someone on their ass.

Cracking one eye open, I looked up at Graham as I tried to rub some life back into my face. Graham stood over me, his hands stuffed into the pockets of his cheap suit pants, the same damn pants I was wearing. Our circumstances were different, yet somehow the same. Graham had three kids and a stay-at-home wife; I had an ex-wife and a daughter. Neither of us had a dime for luxuries, including nice clothes.

Graham looked down at me with a face I had seen a hundred—hell, a thousand—times before. A familiar mix of irritation and mild amusement. It was the same look he gave me when we were kids and I "borrowed" Dad's .22 without asking. That day ended with a hole in the rain barrel, a lecture from Mom, and Graham smirking in amusement.

"Rough night?"

That was the thing about Graham—he never missed an opportunity to remind me when I looked terrible.

I sat up in my chair, yawning as I rubbed my eyes. "You could say that." I nodded toward the printer, which continued wheezing out the last of the crime scene photos. "Not that it did me any good."

Graham pulled up a chair and sat down with a groan, leaning forward to grab the first photo from the tray. He studied it, his mouth tightening into a thin line.

"Hell of a shot." He flipped the photo onto my desk and looked at me. "Classic whodunit," he said, looking at the photo a beat longer than usual. "You think he was targeted for a reason? Gang hit maybe?"

I picked up the photo and studied it for a moment before shaking my head. "I don't know, Graham. Maybe. But what if it was random? Remember those guys in D.C. who were shooting people from their trunk?"

"Damn," Graham muttered, sorting through the photos as they came off the printer. "We need a place to start. Lab send anything yet?"

I grunted in agreement and stood to stretch. My back's shot—no different than any cop with thirty years on the job. "Nothing back yet—too early for that."

I kept looking at the photos, spreading them across my desk. Adjusting the angle of the old desk lamp, I killed some of the glare. Hassan lay dead center in the frame, limbs twisted, a discarded marionette frozen in the last moment of his life. One hole, right in the chest—almost too exact to be real. Clean. Quick. Efficient. I'd seen hundreds of bodies, but this one unsettled me in a way I couldn't quite name.

I was struggling to find a starting point. A man, dead in the street. No witnesses. No casings. Not even footprints. Just silence and snow.

This wasn't a typical Dayton homicide. This was professional.

Graham leaned over my shoulder, eyes flicking over the images. "Unbelievable," he muttered.

I nodded. "Whoever pulled the trigger knew exactly what they were doing." I tapped one of the wider images, showing the full length of N. Irwin Street. "The shot came from this direction. This wasn't close-range," I said. "It could have been from anywhere between the warehouse and the tracks—maybe farther."

"High-powered rifle," Graham said, not even bothering to phrase it as a question.

"Has to be." I studied the image, my finger hovering over the small entry wound. "Small entry, significant exit damage."

Graham exhaled, shaking his head. "Not a street shooter, then."

I didn't respond. I didn't have to. The lack of evidence and the precision said it all. This wasn't some thug settling a score. This was methodical. A calculated assassination. Whoever did this was surgical—sharp, fast, unforgiving. And methodical killers didn't usually show their hand unless they wanted to be noticed.

Graham turned to his computer and started typing. The antiquated records database crawled slower than rush hour traffic in the rain before finally spitting out Hassan Al-Khatib's file. The screen flickered, reminding me of a dying neon sign in an old TV detective show.

The file wasn't thick, but every detail was worse than the last.

"Now this is interesting," Graham muttered.

I leaned over his shoulder, squinting at the screen like an old man reading a prescription bottle. Where were my damn readers?

Hassan Al-Khatib, a forty-five-year-old male from Syria. He entered the U.S. legally years ago, arriving in Dayton to work in the family markets.

"Suspected trafficker," I said, scanning the notes. The screen revealed that the vice squad picked him up three months ago while serving a search warrant at an apartment complex on N. Main Street.

Graham continued to scroll through the records, brow furrowing. "Damn," he said. "Vice located several missing, underage girls in that apartment. They charged Hassan with kidnapping, but something went wrong. The charges were dropped."

I exhaled, rubbing a hand over my jaw. "Of course they were."

We both skimmed the case summary, looking for the answer we already knew would piss us off. Sure enough, there it was. The warrant was faulty. The defense had filed a motion to suppress, arguing it was an unlawful search. The judge agreed, and the case was tossed. Hassan had likely been right back to business, but somebody stopped that permanently.

Now, I almost hated to find out who. But I would. It was my job.

I believed in the law, and while some people may deserve to die, killing them can never be condoned. And yet, even as I thought it, a part of me wondered if that belief was enough.

Graham let out a bitter chuckle, shaking his head. "Guy gets caught with multiple underage victims but walks on a technicality."

I didn't say anything right away, just stared at the screen. I'd seen it too many times before. Bad warrants. Sloppy procedures. Good cops doing the best they could but getting outmaneuvered in court. Excuses didn't make it any easier to stomach.

"A dangerous human trafficker who should've been behind bars but wasn't," Graham said, stretching back in his chair. "The list of people who might've wanted this guy dead will be pretty long."

I nodded. "Yeah. Fortunately, the skill needed for this hit should shorten that list a lot."

I started listing them off. "First possibility—business deal gone bad. Traffickers don't work alone. Maybe he pissed off the wrong guy."

"Possible," Graham admitted. "But if it was a cartel or mob hit, why make it look so clean? They usually go for spectacle. This wasn't a message, this was a hit."

I nodded. He wasn't wrong. Those groups always sent messages. This was clinical.

"Second possibility—one of his victims' families."

Graham exhaled through his nose. "You ever seen a grieving father pull off this kind of long-range shot?"

I didn't answer, but I had to agree.

Graham tapped his fingers against the desk. "Could be a vigilante."

I scoffed. "One body doesn't make a vigilante."

"Maybe," Graham said. "But if it was, and they had the skill to pull this off, then Dayton has inherited a problem it wasn't built to handle. And these type of people don't stop."

I didn't argue, but a thought kept chewing at the back of my mind—if this was the start of something, we might already be too far behind to catch up.

"Alright, detective, what's next?" Graham asked.

"We find out who was investigating Hassan before the case got tossed," I said. "See if Vice has anything they never got to use."

"And we check for cameras," Graham added. "Anything that might've caught the shooter or their vehicle."

"Call the lab," I said, glancing at the clock. "If we're lucky, they've identified that round—or can at least tell us when."

Graham turned back toward his desk as I grabbed my coat. "I've got to go to court," I said. "I'll see you after lunch, and we'll make a plan."

Graham nodded as he started to dial his phone. I grabbed my notebook for court and headed down the hall. Sitting in court for some random street shooting seemed such a waste of time.

Chapter 3
The First Clue

"Firearms, this is John."

"John, Graham MacLaren from Dayton. We were hoping you had something for us on the bullet recovered on Pruden last night."

John didn't respond right away, and Graham could hear some shuffling in the background.

"Yeah, your property clerk got it to me about an hour ago. I haven't had time to do much more than take some measurements, but from what I'm seeing, it's definitely unusual."

"How's that?" Graham replied.

"Class characteristics and diameter put it in .338 caliber—very likely .338 Lapua Magnum," John said. "I haven't seen one of these come through here before. It's a specialized long-range rifle cartridge, originally developed for military use."

"Damn!" exclaimed Graham. "Are they even legal?"

"Legal, but expensive—several dollars a round."

"Yeah, I don't see gang-bangers spending that kind of cash," Graham said. "Thanks, John. Get that report to us as soon as you can."

Graham turned back to his computer, opened Google, and typed ".338 Lapua" into the search bar. A list of results appeared—retail availability, specs, long-range shooting forums, military usage. He clicked on the first link and began reading through the technical details. Developed in the 1980s for military shooters, the .338 Lapua is for extreme long-range precision—capable of hitting targets over a mile away. Its stopping power and accuracy made it a favorite among elite marksmen. Civilian use was legal, but rare, thanks to the cost of both the round and the rifles chambered for it.

Graham dug deeper. Few rifles could even chamber the .338 Lapua—Barrett MRAD, Accuracy International AXMC, Sako TRG-42. All high-end. None of them cheap. Even entry-level models started around five grand—and that was before optics or suppressors. Most ran more than ten grand.

And then there was the ammunition. Clicking through a few retailer sites, Graham discovered that rounds started around $100 to $150 for a box of 20, but could exceed $200 per box for premium loads.

Availability also seemed to be an issue. This wasn't a rifle or ammunition that just any dealer stocked. Only a handful of high-end dealers carried .338 Lapua, and even fewer stocked the rifles themselves. Every local shop required the .338 Lapua rifles and ammunition to be special-ordered, often with long wait times. This was not an impulse buy, nor was this a heat-of-the-moment purchase.

"Son of a bitch," Graham muttered softly. He rubbed his temples, staring at the screen. Maybe the numbers would change if he looked hard enough. This wasn't some gangbanger settling a score or a botched robbery gone bad.

Whoever fired that round had planned it, trained for it. This wasn't merely someone with a high-end rifle—it was someone trained to kill with it. Ex-military, law enforcement, maybe a professional marksman. Calculated. Patient. Lethal. Not a shooter who guessed where a bullet might land—but one who already knew: wind speed, humidity, even the earth's rotation. Whoever had this kind of weapon wasn't some thug pulling the trigger in a fit of rage. This was worse.

The deeper Graham dug, the worse it got. Every rifle chambered in .338 Lapua had one thing in common—precision. These weren't drive-by guns bought at a gun show, and they sure as hell weren't the kind picked up cheap from a pawn shop. Graham scrolled through long-range shooting forums, reading posts from guys debating bullet weights, suppressors, and trigger pulls. These were men who didn't need an anemometer to tell you the wind speed. Graham read every post, every argument, and looked at every image—hoping someone would leave a clue. Nothing.

Yet Graham knew—one of those people in the forums probably pulled the trigger on Hassan Al-Khatib. Maybe not bragging. But watching. Graham leaned back in his chair, eyes narrowing. This wasn't random, and it sure as hell wasn't accidental. Someone had planned it. And that meant someone had a reason.

***

I left the third-floor courtroom and hurried toward the elevator, running in as the doors closed. As we descended, I checked my watch and grumbled to myself—12:30 already. Nearly three hours wasted. When it was all said and done? A continuance. The whole morning had been spent running on a treadmill—exhausting, but I hadn't gotten anywhere.

When I reached the ground floor, I retrieved my Glock from the deputies at the door, gave them a nod, and stepped out onto the sidewalk. The cold smacked my face—snow was falling in lazy flakes, crunching underfoot as I cut through patches of salted slush. A clerk from upstairs hurried past, muttering about the heat not working in half the building.

I pulled out my phone and dialed Graham.

"MacLaren," he answered after a couple of rings.

"Hey, I'm leaving the courthouse, and I'm starving," I said. "I'm grabbing something to bring back. You want anything? Or are you still on that weird fasting thing?"

There was a pause on the other end, followed by the faint clicking of computer keys and a heavy sigh.

"I'm good, man. Already ate," Graham said, his irritation clear.

"Black coffee and vending machine food don't count."

"Doritos, actually—and I was working while you were lounging in court, probably creeping on that new prosecutor. What's her name again? Kaylie? Callie?"

"It's Carlie," I said. "And I assure you, I wasn't 'creeping' on her, whatever the hell that means. Anyway, court was a waste of time. It's been continued. Again."

I exhaled, shaking my head. "Oh, and Carlie wasn't even there."

I was walking through the Safety Building toward the rear door when I remembered the real reason I had called Graham.

"Did you hear back from the lab?" I asked.

"Yeah," he said. "And it was weird. That bullet was a .338 Lapua."

".338 Lapua?" I repeated. "What the hell is that?"

"Expensive, specialized long-distance round," he replied. "Not something you pick up at the local gun shop on a whim."

I unlocked my car and slid into the worn driver's seat, tucking the phone between my ear and shoulder as I turned the key in the ignition. "Legal?"

"It's legal," Graham said. "But as I said—unusual."

I let the news sit for a moment, forgetting I was on the phone with Graham as I stared through the windshield at the back of the county jail. I glanced up at the rooftop basketball court hiding behind rusted chain-link and razor wire. Inmates used to play there and I always wondered how they dealt with that. Sweating under the sun, the clang of the ball echoing over the parked cars below. Freedom so close. And yet out of reach.

"Angus! Angus! Are you still there?" Graham yelled through the phone.

"Sorry, bro," I responded. "I must have nodded off for a second."

"Maybe you need some rest," Graham said.

"Yeah, but not today," I said with a smirk. "I gotta get some food."

"Get me a black coffee."

I snorted. "Of course."

***

I walked back into the office about forty-five minutes after I spoke with Graham—gone a lot longer than I expected. Hopefully the burgers were worth driving halfway across the county. Graham was sitting at his desk, hammering at his keyboard like he was trying to break through a locked door, convinced the FBI's most wanted was on the other side. Most guys handwrote their reports before calling them in, but not Graham. His handwriting was so bad that even he couldn't read it, he typed everything.

Graham looked up, smirking. "Well, look who—"

His phone rang. He frowned, glanced at the screen, and answered. "MacLaren."

He listened for a few moments, his expression shifting from boredom to something closer to interest. "You said Miami Valley Crime Tips?" he asked. A pause. "Alright. Yeah, send it over."

He hung up and turned to me, a rare flicker of interest breaking through his usual deadpan.

"A tip line lead came in," he said. "Someone called after

seeing Hassan's murder on the news."

I arched an eyebrow. "And?"

Graham clicked his pen against the desk, the soft tap the only sound in the near-empty office. "Caller didn't give their name—just said we should be looking at the father of one of Hassan's victims. The guy was in court the day Hassan walked. When the judge dismissed the charges, he lost it—stood up, shouting that it wasn't right, that someone should put Hassan down before he hurt another girl."

I exhaled. That was motive. Rage that didn't fade overnight.

Graham glanced at his notes. "The caller said they didn't know his name, but it was that Callahan girl's dad."

That made me sit up. "Callahan?"

Graham nodded. "Yeah. That mean anything to you?"

I didn't answer right away. I was already reaching for my keyboard. If this was legit, we could pull court records, find out exactly who he was.

"Pull everything we have on Callahan's case," I said. "Find out the father's full name, where he lives, where he works. If he's got any history with guns, I want to know yesterday."

Graham was already typing. "On it. And it's a good thing you decided to come back," he said with a laugh. "I'd have had no idea how to proceed without you."

I tossed the bag of burgers down on my desk with a thud and handed Graham his coffee. "Traffic was terrible," I said, knowing the truth was, I'd driven fifteen miles to get them. "Anything new?"

I sat back, flipping open my notepad. A dad didn't forget. And if he hadn't let it go, maybe he hadn't stopped at wishing for Hassan's death—maybe he'd made it happen.

Graham took a sip of coffee and leaned back in his chair, exhaling. "Nothing new. The lab hasn't sent the report over yet, but really, what else can they even tell us? I spent the last hour knocking out my supplemental report."

I nodded, reached in, and pulled out a small hamburger from the once-white paper bag, now nearly transparent with grease. I took a bite, enjoying the simple pickle, onion, salt-and-pepper flavor the little cart was famous for.

"Jury selection started today for the homicide at The Purple Circus last year," I said, rubbing the back of my neck. "I'll be sitting in with the prosecution during the trial, so I'm going to spend the rest of the day prepping—trial is probably going to run a week, maybe longer. We'll pick this back up when it's over."

Graham gave a slow nod before taking another long drink of what had to be cold coffee. His eyes were heavy—he hadn't slept much either. "What do you need me to do in the meantime?"

"Reach back out to Hassan's family. Find out everything you can about his life," I instructed. "I want it all—family, friends, business partners, criminal associates, anyone he ever knew. If someone's connected to him, have their name on my desk by the time I'm back."

Graham nodded, fingers already back on the keys. He didn't need any more direction than that. Digging through people's lives—dead or alive—was part of the job, and he knew how to do it well. I watched him for a second longer than I meant to, the way his fingers moved faster when his brain caught on something. Quiet as he was, Graham noticed things other guys didn't—and right now, that mattered.

I finished my first burger and grabbed a second. I also took the last couple of sips of my coffee. It wasn't hot, but caffeine was caffeine.

The case had already wedged itself into the back of my mind, waiting to push forward the second my focus drifted. My shoulders were tight. Pain that came with every unsolved homicide, every victim left without justice. I couldn't go home, couldn't relax. Somewhere out there, a cold-blooded shooter was on the loose. And if we didn't get a lead soon, this case would fade into cold storage along with too many before it. I refused to allow that to happen.

The energy of the morning had ebbed, leaving the squad room quiet except for the muted clack of Graham's keyboard and the hum of the lights overhead. Snow tapped faintly against the windows, a reminder that winter had settled in for the long haul.

I closed my case file, pushed my chair back, and stood. "Alright. I think I'll head home. I'm too tired to focus on this right now. I'll study the details tomorrow—assuming jury selection hasn't wrapped up."

Graham looked up from his keyboard. "And what about Callahan?"

"We'll find him," I said. "Soon as I get a break from trial."

"Sounds good," Graham said. "I'll let you know if anything earth-shattering comes up."

Chapter 4
A Father's Fury

It was Thursday morning before I finally got a break from the trial. Graham and I used it to chase down the courthouse threat tip. We knew we had to identify this guy fast, so we pulled up the records from the original search warrant packet when Hassan was first arrested. The names of the girls had to be there. If we were going to find him, this was our best shot.

I was scanning witness statements when Graham let out a sound of a wolf catching the scent of wounded prey—quick, hungry, ready to chase.

I glanced up. He was studying the screen; he couldn't believe what he was seeing.

"What?" I asked, though I already had a feeling.

He turned to me with a huge grin.

"I found her," he said. "Erin Callahan."

"And the dad?" I asked.

"Yep," he said, voice tight with excitement. "Joseph Callahan—listed as her legal guardian. Has to be him."

A few keystrokes later and Graham was printing everything we had on Joseph Callahan—which wasn't much. No arrests. A couple traffic tickets. He wasn't exactly shouting, "I'm an assassin."

"Not much to go on," I said, looking through the printouts. "We'll never get a warrant."

Graham nodded in agreement. "Yeah, but we can go talk to him. Those threats are all the reason we need for a knock-and-talk."

"Okay," I replied. "Get an address. Maybe we can at least find out if he has any guns."

As Graham tracked down Callahan's last known address, I called an old friend at the Sheriff's office.

"Detective Benson."

"Jimmy," I responded. "It's Angus, brother. How you been?"

"Great to hear from you, buddy," he replied. "I've been doing great. How about you? You finally calling about that fishing trip you owe me?"

"Wish I was. But it's work. Need a favor," I said.

"Anything, Angus," he replied. "What can I do for you?"

"I need to know if a guy we're looking at has a CCW permit," I answered.

"No problem. What's the name?"

"Appreciate it, Jimmy! Name is Callahan. Joseph Callahan."

Jimmy was quiet for a moment. "Yeah, he's got a CCW permit. He's had it for years. Renewed it last fall."

I nodded to myself. CCW permit holders weren't typically criminals, but that didn't mean Callahan wasn't the guy.

"Anything else on him?" I asked.

I heard keys clacking in the background, then Jimmy exhaled. "Nothing major. But… there's an old report here. There was a neighbor trouble call from last year. No charges filed, but the officer noted that Callahan was 'extremely agitated' and 'mentioned something about if the cops wouldn't take care of it, he would.'"

Graham shot me a look. That sounded a hell of a lot like a guy who'd say, 'Someone should put Hassan down before he hurts another girl.'

I exhaled as I leaned back in my chair. "That's not a smoking gun, but it's something," I muttered, scratching the top of my bald head.

Jimmy had sent the report to Graham's email, and he had already opened the file. "Callahan's neighbor called it in," he said. "Apparently neighbor's kids were having a party that got out of hand. He claimed Callahan came to the door with a bat, yelling, cussing him out about the noise and kids sitting on his truck. When officers got there, they noted he was furious, wouldn't let it go."

I exhaled. Not a hardened killer, but it strengthened the temper argument.

"The bat the only weapon mentioned?" I asked.

Graham shook his head. “Nope. Well, the bat is the only one seen by the neighbor, but he told the deputies that Callahan was always carrying guns.”

I nodded, tapping a pen against the desk. “Alright. He has a CCW, so that doesn’t mean much.”

I sighed as I looked at my watch. “Let’s go talk to him. Maybe he’ll give us something we’re missing.”

Graham grabbed his coat and headed for the door. “We taking my car or yours?”

“Mine,” I said, standing up and stretching my back. “I’d rather walk barefoot through broken glass than ride with you.”

Graham smirked. “Haven’t killed you yet.”

I ignored him and pulled on my coat. The cold outside was going to be brutal, but I couldn’t worry about it. Winters in Ohio didn’t care if you were ready for them or not.

We climbed into my car and I cranked the ignition. The Crown Vic’s engine turned over with a reluctant growl before settling into a steady rumble. Graham pulled up Callahan’s address on his phone.

“Harrison Township,” he said. “Little house at 3888 Yellowstone. Not a bad area.”

I nodded, pulling out of the lot. “Good. Maybe he won’t answer the door with a shotgun.”

“Maybe,” Graham said, “but if he really is our guy, he won’t be too surprised to see us.”

We drove in silence for a while, the city moving past us in flashes of dim streetlights and old brick buildings. We were on a quiet drive where thoughts creep in—unwanted, but persistent. I kept thinking about the tip that got us here.

Tip line calls weren’t always reliable. Most tips were noise. But this one? This one felt different. It had a ring of truth to it.

We pulled onto Callahan’s street—small, modest, mostly well-kept houses, with the occasional boarded-up eyesore. Graham double-checked the address and pointed toward a single-story home with a covered porch, two houses up on the left.

“That’s the one,” he said, nodding.

A truck sat in the driveway, dusted with the thin layer of snow that had fallen overnight. Lights were on inside.

“He’s home,” I muttered, killing the engine. “Let’s see if he invites us in.”

We walked up on the front porch slowly, eyes scanning the windows and the side yard for movement. If this was our guy, what was stopping him from taking a shot at us?

Standing on opposite sides of the heavy wooden door, I used the end of my flashlight for the classic cop knock—loud, obnoxious, unmistakable.

"Dayton Police!" No response. I yelled again. "Dayton Police, open up!"

I knocked again. Yelled again. No response.

Graham gave me a look. "Definitely someone's home. Think he's avoiding us?"

I was about to knock a third time when I saw it—movement behind the curtain. A shadow and slight ruffle of the curtains caught my eye before the door creaked open.

A white male, late 40s or early 50s, stood in the doorway. Joseph Callahan.

Short brown hair, graying at the temples. Eyes worn, tired. So tired he'd given up.

He didn't speak at first. Just stared at us, one hand on the door as if he might slam it in our faces.

I pulled out my badge. "Mr. Callahan? I'm Detective MacLaren, Dayton Police. This is my brother, Detective MacLaren. We need to ask you a few questions."

His eyes flicked between us. "Two MacLarens?" He didn't wait for a response. "This isn't Dayton. What do you want from me?" His voice was low and wary.

"We want to ask you about Hassan Al-Khatib," I answered.

His grip tightened on the door. It was subtle, but I caught it. A half-second delay before he answered.

"I've got nothing to say about him," he muttered.

Graham snorted. "Yeah, you might want to reconsider. You were overheard threatening him in the courtroom when he walked free."

Callahan's jaw tensed. "So. I was pissed. That bastard hurt my baby girl."

"I get it," I said. "But now he's dead."

His breathing changed. Slightly.

"That was anger talking," he muttered. "People say things when they're angry."

I nodded. “They do. But here’s the thing—Hassan was shot last night. Clean. Precise. Whoever did it knew what they were doing. And then someone called Miami Valley Crime Tips with your name, and now we have to ask questions. I’m sure you understand.”

Callahan’s expression didn’t shift. No flinch, no surprise—only a long, measured look. The kind that told me he was thinking about every word before he said it.

“That’s a hell of a coincidence,” Graham added.

Callahan exhaled slowly, rubbing a hand over his face. For the first time, he looked exhausted.

“Look,” he said, voice lower now. “I was furious. I won’t lie about that. But I didn’t kill him. I don’t even own a rifle.”

I let that sit for a moment. “Anyone who can vouch for that?”

He scoffed. “You think I had an alibi lined up for a murder I didn’t commit?”

I didn’t answer. The silence did the work for me. After a long pause, Callahan sighed.

“I didn’t do this.”

Graham folded his arms. “Maybe not. But you’ll stay at the top of our list. So don’t go anywhere.”

Callahan shook his head, muttering something before stepping back. “Do what you gotta do.”

I studied him for another second, then nodded. “We will.”

We turned back toward the car, the cold cutting deeper now. Callahan didn’t slam the door behind us, but he didn’t wait long to shut it either. Halfway down the walkway, Graham glanced at me.

“You buy it?”

I exhaled through my nose. “No. But I don’t think we’ve got enough to make a move yet.”

He grunted in agreement. I leaned against the hood, thinking it through.

I looked at Graham but didn’t say anything right away. After a couple of seconds, he gave me a look.

“What?”

“I’m not sure,” I said. “Did you catch that he mentioned a rifle?”

“Yeah. So what?”

“We never mentioned the weapon. I know it’s not a secret, but I haven’t seen it reported in any of the news coverage I’ve caught.”

"Huh." Graham rubbed his jaw. "I'm sure it's been broadcast somewhere, so maybe it's nothing. But it does tell us old man Callahan has been following the story."

I nodded and stood up, heading for the driver's side.

"So what now?" Graham asked.

I stared at the windshield for a beat—watching our reflections in the glass, both of us worn thin.

"We wait," I said. My voice was steady, but my gut was tightening. "And hope to hell we're not already behind."

Chapter 5
Unexpected Company

I smacked the nightstand as I fumbled for my phone. It was Saturday, 7:00 a.m.—too damn early. I finally shut off the alarm, knocking a half-empty cup of coffee onto the floor. I slowly dragged myself out of bed, a groaning corpse crawling out of a shallow grave. Didn't crash until after 2:00 a.m. I was trying to refresh my memory on The Purple Circus murder, but all I could think about was Hassan. The trial starts Monday, and if I don't get my head straight today, I'll be as lost as a rookie on his first shift alone.

I wandered into the kitchen to make some coffee, only to discover that along with everything else, I was out. No coffee. No sleep. No chance of winning this battle in my head. I was running on fumes.

I sighed and rubbed my eyes as I leaned back against the counter. "Maybe I should go to the woods." I ignored the doubt.

The sky was clear—a perfect day. A few hours and a dozen miles—exactly what I needed. The courtroom was rigid. The woods cleared my head. The Orange Trail at Germantown MetroPark beat any liquor for easing my stress.

***

Thirty minutes of cracked sidewalks and boarded-up storefronts soon fell away to farmland and deep woods.

I stepped out of my truck, stretching to force a little life into my stiff body. The woods seemed too quiet. Something felt off. Maybe it was me. I almost turned around. But I didn't. Instead, I shook it off, grabbed my day pack and headed for the outhouse. Old habits. Every old cop knows you never pass a restroom.

A few steps into the woods and I knew this was where I should be. The tightness in my shoulder, the pain in my neck, the cloudiness in my head—all fading more with every step.

The first couple of miles were as rugged as the Appalachian foothills. Steep—not Everest steep, but enough to get the heart and lungs working. I loved chasing that burn. A good climb makes you feel alive. I had walked about an hour and my breathing had settled into a steady rhythm when a flash of color caught my attention.

A woman was standing motionless in the middle of the trail. At first, I thought she was taking a break, but something about her made me slow down and watch. She didn't appear to be resting; her stance was deliberate, as if she heard me coming and expected danger. As I moved closer, she looked up—dark hair, sharp eyes, effortless confidence. Stunning. Then she spoke. "Detective MacLaren?"

How did she know my name? Suddenly, that dark feeling returned, settling over me like a cold hand on the back of my neck. She looked harmless. Too beautiful to be a threat. But I couldn't be sure. I approached cautiously, my right hand resting innocently on my lower back. I was in the woods, but I was still armed. I'd seen too many things. Had I sent her boyfriend to prison? Her husband? Her dad? I couldn't be sure, and that made me a little uneasy.

"I'm sorry," I said, trying to recognize her. "Do I know you?"

She laughed, glancing down at herself. "I guess I do look different. I'm Daniella—the court reporter in Judge Ferrell's courtroom."

I couldn't believe what I was seeing. I knew Daniella—but she seemed different. The woman I'd spoken to in the courtroom wasn't the same one standing in front of me now. That Daniella was refined, composed, professional. This version was wild, untamed, stunning. She belonged in the woods, and suddenly, I wanted to know why.

"I'm so sorry I didn't recognize you," I said, shaking my head. "You look—so different."

She smirked, tilting her head slightly, her voice low. "Different good? Or different bad?"

I stared blankly. My brain stalled, frozen in time. Flirting never came easy for me. I imagined a dozen different responses in my head, but none of them made it out. A bomb squad was under less pressure than I was. "I wasn't expecting to see you out here," I managed to mumble.

Daniella put her hands on her hips and looked at me with a grin. "Detective MacLaren, that's not an answer."

"Sure it is," I said, fumbling with the straps on my pack. "Where the hell did that stupid drinking tube go?"

Daniella crossed her arms, tilting her head with a playful pout. "MacLaren, I would expect a big city detective to handle pressure better."

"I'm Angus, and I love pressure," I muttered, finally yanking the damn drinking tube free. "When it involves violence."

Daniella laughed, shaking her head. "Relax, MacLaren—I'm messing with you. But nice try."

I smiled, giving a small nod to acknowledge her teasing. Daniella adjusted the straps on her pack before turning back toward me.

"I thought I was the only fool to come all the way down here from Dayton," I said.

"Oh, I live in Germantown—takes about five minutes to get here."

"I didn't know that," I replied. "I assumed you lived in Dayton with the rest of us."

Daniella turned and started moving down the trail. "You didn't know because you didn't ask." I stood there again, stuck in place as she moved ahead as if she owned the trail and I was just passing through. "Hey, hold up a sec," I called, jogging to catch up with her. "If you're staying on the Orange Trail, mind if I walk with you?"

"I'd love that, MacLaren," she replied. "I'll stay with you until trail marker 4; I'll have to split off onto the Green Trail to get back to my car."

"That works," I said, matching her pace as we moved along the narrow path.

We moved swiftly along the trail, even through the floodplain, where mud was several inches deep in places. The trail narrowed significantly, and I had to drop behind her. I couldn't ignore the strength of her legs. They were incredible—she moved as graceful as a deer, effortlessly navigating the hills and weaving through the forest's obstacles.

"You're fast," I said, pushing to keep pace with her.

She glanced over her shoulder with a smirk. "I hike with a purpose. Gym's good for some things, but for legs and cardio? The woods can't be beat."

That made sense. Watching her move, I could tell she wasn't out here for the fresh air or to watch the birds. She was working. Hard. Every step was efficient; every climb met with power. She didn't even slow down on the steeper hills.

"You out here often?" I asked.

"Depends," she said, stepping easily over a windblown tree. "I hit the gym a few times a week, but I must get in at least one long hike on the weekends. Nothing builds endurance as fast as elevation gains and rough terrain."

I nodded, stepping over the same tree, but with much less grace. "Makes sense. I keep moving, but I wouldn't call it training. I come out here maybe once a month. The rest of the time, I walk in my neighborhood to stay loose."

"Neighborhood walking, huh?" She sounded amused. "You sound like an old man, MacLaren."

"Hey, not all of us are fitness gurus," I shot back. "I enjoy hiking, but I do it for the peace, not the workout."

Daniella hummed in response. "That's fair. I appreciate the quiet, too. But I love feeling strong more."

We hiked in silence for a moment, the sounds of our boots crunching against dirt and squelching through the thick mud, filling the space.

"So, you always lived in Dayton?" she asked.

"Yeah," I said. "Born and raised in the city. Can't imagine anything else."

"You ever think about leaving?"

I hesitated before answering. "Sometimes. Small-town life is… interesting. Not sure if I could handle the slower pace, though. Could get boring."

She laughed, ducking under a low-hanging branch. "You get used to it. But yeah, if you need constant noise and flashing lights, it's probably not for you."

"I don't know if I need all that," I admitted. "But having options isn't horrible."

Daniella glanced back at me with a knowing look. "Yeah, you'd be banging your head against the wall in about two weeks."

We'd been walking for a while—sometimes talking,

sometimes settling into a silence that felt like we'd been hiking together for years. We had climbed above the floodplain, and I knew the Green Trail was coming soon. Ahead, I could see the trail curved slightly and split into two. A wooden post with the number 4 carved into it marked the split in the trail.

Daniella paused briefly to allow me to catch up.

"This is where I get off, conductor," she said with a laugh. "I'll see you in court."

Then she was gone, moving swiftly onto the Green Trail and up the steep grade toward the top of the ridge. Her strong legs carried her up as effortlessly as a mountain goat scaling the slope. I watched as she moved deeper through bare trees. She never looked back, never hesitated. Just kept moving forward, her path set.

I smiled as I turned back toward the Orange Trail, pulling my phone from the nylon pouch strapped to my chest. Almost eleven, and I needed to get moving. Nowhere to be except home with that case file, but that couldn't wait long. Monday was coming fast.

I dropped my phone back in the waterproof pouch and took a long drink through the tube over my shoulder. I had been so focused on the conversation with Daniella that I had barely touched my water. I should've been drinking more, but I had a couple of liters left. I adjusted the straps on my pack and started walking.

The Orange Trail had flattened out, allowing me to pick up the pace. Soon, I was across the prairie and back into the woods for the final push to the dam.

Suddenly, a large shadow swooped down from my left, cutting across my head before landing in a tree straight ahead, maybe fifty yards up the trail. An owl. Nothing moves through the forest with such grace and beauty. The sight stirred a memory—someone else moving that way, deliberate yet effortless. As I got closer, I could see it was a large barred owl, dark against the branches, and it was staring right at me.

Beautiful, but not harmless. Barred owls can be fiercely territorial, striking without warning if they feel threatened—same as many things in the woods. I was in no mood to fight an owl, so I moved slowly, never taking my eyes off the bird. We watched each other with suspicion until I was out of sight, but I kept looking over my shoulder. The woods were silent again, but that didn't mean I was alone—you're never alone in the forest, even in Ohio. If it wanted me, it could be on me before I even knew it was coming.

Fifteen minutes later, the trail widened, and the trees began to thin. The dam was about a mile ahead, and my truck was another quarter mile through the forest. Soon, I was standing beside my truck, boots muddy, mind clear.

I dropped my pack and drew in the forest scent. The crisp afternoon air felt incredible filling my lungs. This was perfect. The stress, the endless hours searching for clues, the trial looming over me—everything had been pushed back, at least for now.

I also thought about how the day began.

Daniella.

Seeing her out here was unexpected, as was the ease of conversation with her. And the difference in her behavior was remarkable. In the courtroom, she was all business, all composure. Out here? Something else entirely.

Everything about her said she belonged. And she did.

I chuckled and shook my head. I thought I had known her for years, but today I realized how wrong I was.

I slid into the driver's seat, stretched once more and started the engine for the drive home. Muscles loose. Mind clear. Happy. I was finally Detective Angus MacLaren once again.

Time to get back to work.

Chapter 6
Precision & Preparation

Glancing cautiously down the broad aisle, ensuring no one had followed, they entered the storage unit and pulled the metal door down with a loud clang. The lock clicked into place, sealing them and their secrets inside, as lost as treasure swallowed beneath the ocean floor. After listening briefly for footsteps, they moved past the van, striding toward the back of the unit with the quiet precision of a predator in the dark.

After shooting Hassan, they had headed out to Trotwood's forgotten business district, leaving the van hidden and safe. The place was perfect—climate-controlled, drive-in storage units, open 24 hours. Few security cameras, and no staff watching monitors. No nosy employees. After they'd backed the van into its designated space, they shut everything down, and slipped away into the dark.

By Friday morning, after a week of silence, the lull was over. It was almost comforting to be back preparing for the next mission.

The warm, familiar scent of Hoppe's No. 9 lingered in the air, clinging to the metal shelves and the folds of the rubber gun mat, a memory of the last cleaning. There was little time to enjoy it, but they paused—letting the memories settle before moving on. The overhead light buzzed faintly, its cold glow turning every sharp edge into a shadowed outline. Even with climate control, the concrete floor held the day's chill, creeping through the soles of their boots.

A large folding table sat beneath the harsh overhead light. Covered in court records, photographs, maps, a laptop, and a compact printer, it held the keys to the entire operation. Metal shelves lined the walls, meticulously stocked with ammunition, gun-cleaning supplies, dehydrated food, and survival gear. In the back corner sat a second table holding a custom rack, ready for weapon maintenance, calibration, and cleaning.

There was much to do before they could leave, but first—the tools. A clean, well-maintained rifle was the foundation of any mission. On this, there was no compromise. They set the Pelican case on the table, unlatched it, and lifted out the Barrett MRAD, placing it carefully into the cleaning rack. At nearly $10,000, it cost more than two months' salary—but for a mission of this importance, it was the only choice.

The MRAD was a masterpiece, and to its owner, cleaning it required the same patience and devotion as restoring the Mona Lisa. But this wasn't all about cleanliness or preservation, this was about details. In the field, even the smallest flaw could mean failure.

With all of the needed supplies arranged on the table, they began as they always did—opening the Scriptures to Kohelet 12:14. The verse lay waiting, stark against the page. Fingers brushed the lines, moving slowly, deliberately, as if touch alone could bind the words to memory. Nothing was spoken. Only the silent prayer, the same one every time, slipping into the stillness between thought and action.

It was time. They pulled on nitrile gloves, keeping the metal free from skin oils. Removing the magazine, they checked the chamber to ensure it was clear, then pulled back and lifted out the bolt assembly. Next, the upper and lower receivers were separated, and the barrel module was removed.

With a bore brush, cotton swabs, and plenty of solvent, they meticulously worked through each component, ensuring every surface was spotless. This wasn't simple maintenance—it was ritual. Muscle memory. Every pass of the brush, every drop of oil, was an act of control, an assurance that the rifle would never fail them. Every part was scrubbed, oiled, and carefully reassembled with practiced precision.

The ritual complete, it was time for the function check. They pulled back the charging handle and let the bolt glide smoothly into position. Cycling the action a few more times, they listened for any hesitation, any inconsistency. The rifle was operating as intended.

Next, the trigger. The Barrett's two-stage trigger was a thing of beauty—clean, predictable, a lifeline when fractions of a second determined everything. Inserting a snap cap to protect the firing pin, they pulled back the charging handle and pulled the trigger. It snapped quick and crisp, just as designed.

Satisfied, they inserted a laser bore sight into the chamber and raised the rifle to their shoulder. Looking through the optics to a target hanging at the front of the storage unit, the laser was hitting a bit low, but that wouldn't cut it. This mission demanded perfection. Zeroing had to be done outside—at least two hundred yards.

Finally, the suppressor. Threading the AM338 onto the barrel, they secured it with a smooth, practiced motion that ensured a perfect fit. The rifle, silent and deadly, slid into the Pelican case, where it would remain safe until needed. But there was more work to be done.

They turned toward the second table, where photographs, court documents, and handwritten notes lay, organized as precisely as a surgeon's instruments before an operation. A tightly framed telephoto image, clipped to a redacted case file, showed the face of their next target.

They picked up the manila folder and flipped it open. Printed transcripts. Surveillance images. A dismissed indictment.

Malik Walker. Local gang leader. Career predator. Luckiest thug in the city. He should have been locked up a half dozen times.

The charges this time had been serious—aggravated robbery, felonious assault—both with firearm specifications. But same as always, nothing stuck. Witnesses vanished. Paperwork got "lost." A judge's ruling made sure he never saw trial.

They studied the photo, no doubt in their mind—Malik was next. This one was careful. No social media. Rarely in the same place twice. But mistakes had been made—there were always mistakes. They had followed several times, and there was one place he always came back to—Paco's Liquors on Rosedale. Malik was there every night, drinking and smoking with his boys on the front sidewalk. He thought the crowd made him untouchable. He was wrong.

They picked up the map and studied the Dayton View neighborhood. The liquor store sat on the corner of Lexington and Rosedale, its entrance facing south.

The map was useful, but not enough for a mission of this scale. They turned to the laptop, opened Google Earth, and entered Paco's address: 801 Lexington Avenue. The liquor store had a brick front, with a noticeable hill directly behind it. That virtually eliminated any risk of collateral damage from over-penetration—or a miss.

Only one streetlight stood near the entrance, casting uneven pools of light across the cracked sidewalk. Enough illumination to see… but not enough to be seen.

The satellite images offered possibilities. A drive-by would be necessary to confirm, but with numerous vacant lots in the area, they could park a couple blocks away—near Superior. Few houses remained on this block, and most that did were abandoned shells with sagging porches and boarded windows—the kind of street where no one looked too hard at a stranger.

Getting in and out quietly wouldn't be a problem. They could park right past the alley entrance, allowing a quick escape without turning around should something go wrong. The range finder put the distance at about 240 yards—ideal.

All the surveillance and preparation were solid. These were things they could control.

But the weather was going to be a problem. *Snow was in the weekend* forecast with temperatures in the mid-20s.

No wind, though. That helped.

If Malik showed up, it would be simple. Clean.

Leaning back in the chair, they exhaled slowly. The plan was set. Every angle considered; every variable accounted for. No more than a few minor details remained—restocking the van, zeroing the rifle at the farm, and doing a daytime drive up Rosedale.

The van came first. Supplies had to be replenished—food, water, extra layers for the cold, wet wipes, painkillers and emptying the camp toilet—little things that made long hours in the confined space tolerable.

Then, Rosedale. Seeing it in daylight was critical. The map and satellite images provided a layout, but nothing replaced being there—standing on the pavement, watching the angles, feeling the space. A slow, unnoticed pass from the driver's seat. No one would notice another delivery van, one of a hundred that passed through daily—not stopping, not lingering, just absorbing details. The liquor store's front sidewalk, the closest streetlights, the alley they'd disappear through when it was over.

They closed the laptop, stacked the papers, and rose from the chair. Everything was set. Now, it was just execution. Taking a final glance around the room, they gathered the files, photos, and map, sliding them into the van's side pockets. There could be no mistakes. The target had to be confirmed—on the street, in real time—before the shot. They locked the van, pulled on a heavy winter coat, and adjusted the balaclava over their face. Caution was everything. They eased the overhead door open, stepped out, and locked it behind them. Soon, it would be time.

Chapter 7
Hiding in Plain Sight

I stepped through the back door of the Safety Building. The sharp, chemical foulness of insecticide was thick in the air—much the same as a crime scene hastily scrubbed but never quite clean. First of the month—pest control day. A necessary evil in an old building riddled with leaky pipes, a ventilation system that coughed more dust than air, and enough hidden corners to make even the most skittish cockroaches feel at home—some of them probably had seniority over half the department.

The farther I went, the heavier it became, clinging to my nostrils like the stench of death in a house sealed tight in July. That smell you taste in the back of your throat when last night's cheap whiskey is haunting you. It lingered on desks, chairs—hell, even the stale, recycled air pumping through the ancient ducts.

Entering our office, it smelled of printer ink and old paper, with that faint river-damp mustiness you get in any building this close to the water. Besides Graham and me, our unit has two other guys—Det. Jeffries and Det. Koski. They were at their desks, deep in conversation as I walked in—Koski leaned back, hands behind his head, that lazy smirk making it impossible to tell if they were discussing a case or last night's hookup. His polished wingtips were propped on the desk edge, a Styrofoam coffee cup in one hand, a pen balanced between his fingers—where you knew he wanted a cigarette. Jeffries—always wound tight and never short on words or criticism—sat studying him, probably dissecting every detail. Graham hunched over his phone, scowling at whatever half-assed tip he was chasing. It was rare to see all four of us in the same place at once. The city must have been quiet last night.

I don't think Graham even knew I was there, so I patted him on the shoulder as I walked toward Sergeant Jenkins' office. He looked up, nodded, then went back to his call. He sounded frustrated. Jeffries and Koski were still wrapped up in something, so I didn't acknowledge them. We'd catch up later.

I knocked lightly on Jenkins' doorframe. He was on the phone but motioned me in. He raised a finger, mouthing, "Give me a minute." I shrugged and dropped into the chair left of his desk.

It took him about five minutes to finish his call and finally acknowledge that I hadn't walked away.

"Welcome back, MacLaren," he said. "I was starting to think you quit."

I chuckled. "I thought about it, but then I'd miss your lovely personality."

He smirked. Around here, sarcasm and ball-busting was how we showed respect.

"Trial finally over?" he asked.

"Yeah," I said. "Had me sweating for a bit. Thought the jury was going to hang, but they convicted on all counts."

"Fantastic." He leaned forward. "You ready to get back on this Pruden case? It's attracting some unwanted attention from the first floor."

"I would be if you hadn't spent half the morning on the phone." I grinned. "You're worse than my ex-wife."

"Get out of my office, MacLaren." He flipped me off. "Go arrest somebody—preferably not your brother."

"Of course, boss." I smirked, stepping back into the squad room. Normally, I'd toss out some smart-ass remark about going home sick, but not today. Today, I wanted to work. That was either a sign I was coming down with something or a warning that this case was different—bigger.

Jenkins was a great sergeant. Lord knows I've had worse. But he could only keep the first floor off our backs for so long. Protecting our squad from the whims of the brass was like bailing out a sinking boat with a shot glass—no matter how fast he worked, the tide of nonsense kept pouring in.

We needed to make progress—fast.

Pressure from the chief's office was ramping up, and no one knew why. Homicides happened every day in Dayton, but none had drawn this kind of attention. The first floor was breathing down Jenkins' neck, barking about press inquiries, department transparency, and why we didn't have an update yet—I guess we were holding something back for laughs. The media had jumped on this case from the beginning, but even they didn't seem to know what they were looking for. It's not as if the shooter's hiding in our supply closet—we barely had a case. We had a dead man and a vague sense that something bigger was happening, and a lot of questions. But that wasn't the answer the brass wanted to hear. They wanted sound bites and progress reports—proof for the public that we were competent. They had no interest in the truth—that we were as in the dark as they were.

It wasn't about stopping the threat—it was about controlling the narrative. The chief didn't care who pulled the trigger, only that we looked in control. Homicide was slow, messy, and unpredictable. But that didn't fit the story they wanted to sell. They needed a suspect—cuffed, booked, and paraded for the cameras before the evening news. Problem was, we weren't any closer than day one.

Bottom line? We had nothing. And the vultures weren't making it easier. Every hour without an update, the media dug deeper, twisting scraps of information into their next headline. It wasn't about Hassan anymore—it was about the spectacle. A murder turned into a public event, headlines outpacing the investigation. And we were caught in the middle, forced to pretend we had control while chasing shadows.

As I left Jenkins' office, I pulled my phone from my pocket, half-expecting a message from Daniella. Nothing. I shoved it back in my coat and looked up to see Jeffries and Koski were gone. But Graham was at his desk, staring intently at his screen. His call was over, but whatever he'd found had his full attention.

"Hey," he said, barely glancing up. "You need to see this."

I walked over, squinting at the screen. "What is it?"

Graham exhaled sharply, running a hand through his hair. "Hassan wasn't our typical Dayton dirtbag. This guy was a genuine international villain."

I frowned. The name on the screen wasn't Hassan Al-Khatib. It was Tariq Al-Mansour. "Who the hell is Tariq Al-Mansour?" I asked, pointing at the screen.

Graham exhaled, shaking his head. "That's Hassan. No idea which one is real. After what I've read so far, they're probably both aliases."

"Hezbollah?" I muttered, reading further.

"Hezbollah," Graham repeated. "And that's not all. This guy has intelligence reports flagged by agencies that don't even know Dayton exists—Mossad, Shin Bet, MI6, DGSE, even the CIA, and an Interpol Red Notice out of Lebanon."

I felt sick. My stomach dropped as it would if I was stepping into an unfamiliar room and realizing too late the floor was gone. I read the name again, sure it was a mistake. But there it was—Hassan Al-Khatib was a mask hiding Tariq Al-Mansour—the man underneath. And that man was wanted by some of the most dangerous agencies in the world.

How the hell had he ended up here, slipping through customs, then blending into Dayton with all the other immigrants? A guy with this background doesn't simply vanish into a Midwest city for the quiet life. Either he thought no one would come looking, or someone had placed him here. Either way, we were dealing with a hell of a lot more than a body on a loading dock.

The crimes weren't new—human trafficking, smuggling, drug distribution. But the affiliations? That was the real shock.

"We have to call the FBI," I said, grimacing. I hated working with the feds. Most of the Dayton agents were fine, but they had that arrogance that came from being federal—their nationwide jurisdiction somehow made them superior to the people actually working the case. Last time they got involved, we wasted two weeks chasing ghosts. Pretentious, uptight jackasses who swooped in with big talk and vague threats, strutting as if they were the only ones who knew how to do the job—so long as they didn't have to be in the inner city after dark. The real cops did the work; they did the press conferences and took the credit—even spelled my name wrong in the release.

Graham nodded. "Yeah, I'll take care of it." He headed off to fill in Jenkins.

I kept scrolling through the files. Hassan—or Tariq, or whoever—had been part of a trafficking pipeline moving people, drugs, and weapons through Syria, Lebanon, and Israel. He'd even been flagged by Israeli intelligence years ago.

And he'd been right here in Dayton.

The more I read, the more irritated I became. "How the hell was this missed when he was arrested?" I muttered.

"They'd have needed to check deeper than local databases," Graham said, walking back toward his desk. "Sarge is on the phone with the LT. He'll notify Major Trammell, then the FBI. This is spiraling out of control, brother."

But it was worse than that. It was exploding—fast. And we were standing there as lost as rookies, watching the wreckage pile up faster than we could track it.

I knew what came next. Special Agent in Charge Vaughn, or some other stuffed shirt from the FBI, would stroll in with a counterterrorism badge and an agenda thicker than our case file. They'd want access to everything, and give us enough back to keep us on a leash. If the feds decided this was theirs, every lead we had could dry up overnight.

These types of cases were hard us old street cops. The kind more at home searching a rat-infested basement than making nice with anyone above sergeant. And now the feds were coming, ready to stomp in with their boots and briefings, complicating things, same as they always did. We needed something—some direction—before this case got away from us completely.

I'd seen it before. When cases got too big, too messy, too many people wanting their piece, they turned into monsters. The kind that didn't bury cases—they buried the cops who worked them. And this? It had all the markings.

Graham hesitated, then clicked on another file. "I think I figured out how he slipped through," he said. "Tariq Al-Mansour entered the U.S. legally years ago, got fingerprinted as any visitor from Syria would. But a few years later, he became a wanted terrorist and disappeared. Then, suddenly, a man named Hassan Al-Khatib, a Turkish citizen, enters the country on a tourist visa."

I stared at the screen. "No fingerprints?"

Graham nodded. "Exactly. Turkey's a visa waiver country. Years ago, no prints required for U.S. entry. He probably used a fake identity, slipped back in before they tightened biometrics. After getting in, disappearing in Dayton was easy."

I exhaled, shaking my head. "Damn. So when his prints got run after the arrest, there was nothing on file? No one thought to check deeper?"

"Nope," Graham said. "But I did. And that's when I found the match."

I sat back, absorbing it all. Hassan—or Tariq—had made it look easy. How many more were out there?

"Unbelievable," I muttered. "How the hell did he end up in Dayton?"

"That's the thing." Graham leaned back, rubbing his jaw. "I think he chose Dayton for the same reason we can't believe he was here. It's not exactly a hotspot for international terrorism. Who would look for him here? No FBI counterterrorism units. No Homeland Security pressure. No NSA. No CIA. Just low-key law enforcement dealing with drugs and violent crime. He was hiding in plain sight."

I exhaled, processing that. "So, is this what it appears to be? Did someone from his past find him?"

"Maybe," Graham said. "Someone with the right knowledge, someone who knew who he really was. Maybe a rival. I wouldn't rule out a foreign government hit."

I nodded slowly. This wasn't some turf feud. It was professional. An execution.

"Alright," I said, standing up. "We need to pull everything on him—contacts, travel records, financials. If someone came looking, they left a trail."

And if the feds tie this to a broader op, they'll be camped in our backyard for weeks—running their own playbook, while sidestepping ours. Either way, the "terrorist angle" isn't going away. It's one more storm rolling in, and we're already knee-deep in water.

If someone had finally come for Hassan after all these years, they weren't done. If he wasn't Dayton's only secret, another body would fall.

Chapter 8
Threading the Needle

Skipping their usual Sunday morning 5K to get an early start, they had arrived at the storage unit by 0630. The van was prepped and loaded, ready to pull out by 0700. At that time of the morning, nobody was around the facility—or anywhere in this part of Trotwood—making it easy to get on the road unseen. The morning was hushed, the world half-asleep, and they moved swift as a shadow through the quiet.

After a brief stop for fuel and coffee, they headed toward an abandoned farm in the next county. They had stumbled across it last summer while riding their motorcycle and, after digging through property records, discovered it had been caught in probate for years. A contested will, multiple heirs, and unpaid debts had left the land in legal limbo, a place no one visited, let alone cared about. The farmhouse sagged under years of neglect, its windows empty sockets, and the fields stretched at least a mile, wild and untamed. At nearly 1,000 acres, it was the perfect place to slip in, disappear, and zero the rifle without a soul in sight.

Zeroing in a .338 rifle is an exercise in patience and precision—and money. Each round cost several dollars, so the fewer fired, the better. Back at the storage unit, they'd used a laser bore sight to get it close—adjusting the scope until the laser hit four inches below the crosshairs at thirty feet. That should put it nearly on target at two hundred yards, ideally three or four shots away from perfect.

An hour after leaving town, the van turned down the overgrown lane, swallowed by trees and weeds that had taken over the neglected farm. It was the farthest point from any neighbors, shielded by unkempt timber and the skeletal remains of forgotten outbuildings. They parked inside a dilapidated pole barn, its rusted metal siding clanging in the light morning breeze, hinting at the approaching snowstorm.

The shooter moved efficiently, retrieving the rifle, a box of .338 Lapua Magnum ammunition, and two paper targets and stands from the rear. The barn smelled of dust and decay, the air thick with the scent of rotting hay, old fertilizer, and oil stains long forgotten. A perfect place. Quiet. Isolated.

The open side of the pole barn faced a wide-open, flat pasture where they placed a target—200 yards out. Perfect concealment to fire from in the scant chance someone came nosing around.

Placing a tarp on the ground behind the van, they removed the Barrett MRAD from the safe confines of the Pelican case and lay prone on the ground. Through the optics, the targets were visible, and there were no signs of any hazards in the field beyond. The grass barely stirred, and nothing moved on the horizon. It was safe to fire.

Carefully opening the bolt, the first live .338 round was inserted into the chamber with a crisp snap. The weight of the rifle settled against them, solid and unmoving. Lining the crosshairs up with the center of the target, they fired.

The suppressed crack of the rifle reverberated against the metal walls of the pole barn like a wrench dropped in an empty oil drum—muffled, but unmistakable. The sharp scent of gunpowder mixed with the stale air inside the barn, the faint vibration of the shot lingering in their chest.

Looking through the spotting scope, they noted the first shot hit the target less than an inch below dead center. A quick calculation in their head, a .50 MRAD adjustment on the elevation turret—the scope gave a faint, satisfying click.

Opening the bolt, the empty shell was ejected, landing softly on the tarp. A fresh round was inserted, the bolt closed, the crosshairs centered—fire.

Once again, they peered through the spotting scope. Dead center.

That was easier than expected. But then again, perfection should be.

After returning the rifle to the case and retrieving the targets and tarp, they eased the van out of the barn, the tires crunching softly over frozen dirt as they headed toward the road. It was going to start snowing soon, and they wanted to be parked before it hit full force. A nice layer of snow over the van was a great way to stay hidden.

The drive to Lower Dayton View gave them plenty of time to run through the mission again, step by step. This one would be harder—too many people around. There was never room for mistakes. But this shot carried even greater risks.

The snow had begun to fall as they turned onto W. Grand from Salem, but when they spotted heavy police activity ahead, they continued another block, turning onto Superior. They knew they were completely under the radar, but caution was everything.

They glanced in the mirror as they continued to move, putting distance between themselves and the police. Careful to follow every traffic law, they covered the one mile to Rosedale, turning right to get back to W. Grand.

A few days ago, they had decided the best place to park was in front of the abandoned apartment building at 926 Rosedale, just south of an alley. This provided a clear shot of about 240 yards, with an easy escape route down the alley to the west.

When they arrived, they were relieved to find everything as it had been earlier. After taking a slow drive around the block and through the alley, they were comfortable they could park without being seen—easing to a stop and switching off the ignition.

It wasn't quite noon yet. Snow had begun falling earlier than expected, but that only helped. Based on his habits, Malik wouldn't show up until sometime between 10 p.m. and midnight. It would be a long day, but it was the safest way.

There were no windows in the van, but using a small camera mounted in the front grill, they could see the snow was falling heavily now. Soon, the van would disappear beneath a blanket of white, blending in as if it had been abandoned for days.

It was also starting to get a little cold. There was a heater, but they couldn't risk running the batteries down too early. After eating a bit of lunch, they pulled on gloves and a hat and climbed up into the hammock with a heavy down blanket. A few hours of sleep would help pass the time.

Sleep came easy, but by 7 p.m., the vibrating alarm on their watch signaled it was time to get up and prepare. Now that darkness provided some cover, they had to open the hatch and confirm the line of sight was clear. They turned on the heat and climbed up onto the shooting platform to open the window. Looking out with the spotting scope, they were satisfied that they were parked in a suitable place.

By the time they sealed the opening and climbed down, the van was warm again. They ate a sandwich and drank some water before opening the file to study Malik's face and features. With an unknown number of people in front of the liquor store, they had to be sure—Malik's face needed to be burned into their memory.

The time dragged by, slow as a melting icicle, each minute seeming longer than the last. As the clock reached 9 p.m., the rifle was removed from its case and carefully inspected. It had worked flawlessly at the farm, but a professional always ensures the tools are up to the task. Satisfied that nothing had shifted since the earlier zeroing, the rifle was placed on the shooting platform with a single .338 round next to it. This mission was the same as setting a mousetrap—you had one chance, and if you missed, the target scattered. There would be no second shots.

Malik's routine was simple. He would arrive at the liquor store in a black Escalade, which would continue on after dropping Malik off. He would go inside for 10 to 15 minutes before exiting to the front sidewalk. The plan was to take the shot within a couple of minutes of the exit.

Watching through the monitor, they observed the Escalade drive up at 10:15 p.m. Malik stepped out and walked into the store. As the Escalade pulled away, they silently climbed up onto the shooting platform, brought the rifle into position, and carefully opened the drop-down hatch. The Barrett settled into position, heavy and solid; an anchor securing them to the moment.

The line of sight was clear—the front of the store perfectly aligned, with no obstacles in the way. Scanning the front of the store and up Rosedale, they saw no other bystanders—the snow was working in their favor tonight.

Patience.

10:27—The door opened, spilling light onto the sidewalk. For a moment, Malik was illuminated, followed by two other guys they didn't recognize—but that didn't matter.

After double-checking the photos, they opened the bolt and inserted the single round into the chamber, easing it closed.

The three men moved to the left of the doorway as expected and opened their bottles. While studying the target, Malik always stood in the middle—tonight was no different. The other two men on either side, shoulder to shoulder, but not quite touching.

Taking down a target in such close proximity to others was not ideal, but it had been done before. Tonight, it had to be done.

They'd rehearsed it a hundred times—angles, wind, bullet drop. But theory and execution were two different things. There was no amount of training and preparation that could replicate the weight of the moment before a kill. And experience whispered that one day, it wouldn't be this clean.

Pausing a couple of minutes to ensure the men had settled into their spots, they silently released the safety and brought their glove-tipped finger to the Barrett's two-stage trigger.

They adjusted the bipod and tucked the stock into their shoulder, lowering their head until their eye aligned with the optics. The rifle was a beast—steady in their grip, obedient. From this view, the world was smaller, confined to crosshairs and calculations.

Perfectly aligning the crosshairs with Malik's chest, they slowly depressed the trigger through the first stage. Malik laughed, raising his beer for what would be his last sip. Still on target, they inhaled deeply, held it—like a diver bracing before plunging into deep water—and pressed through the second stage.

They stared in silence as Malik dropped, lifeless before he hit the ground. The two men beside him flinched, amusement flashing across their faces as they seemed to think he had slipped on the ice.

Both men extended a hand to help him up—then froze. Instead of the laughing face of their friend, they saw the dark stain of blood spreading through Malik's coat. Looking around wildly, their minds not yet catching up with what their eyes had seen, they hesitated only for a second before they began screaming for help.

No one had heard the shot. No one ever did.

For a brief moment, the street remained silent, the snowfall softening the scene, a muted canvas. Then, as the men's frantic voices cut through the night, chaos erupted.

With the mission complete, the roof hatch was softly closed, and the shooter climbed down from the shooting platform.

Two down. Six to go—though each number left carried a little more weight now.

Too early to move. Too many eyes out there. The van would be their shelter tonight.

Settling back into the van's dim interior, they listened. The streets outside were alive now—flashing lights, sirens wailing in the distance, frantic voices and panicked cries cutting through the snowfall. A dog barked somewhere down the block, startled by the sudden energy in the air.

The snowfall muffled it all, turning the night into an eerie blend of urgency and silence. The chaos was close, and it was growing, but it wouldn't reach them. Not tonight. They pulled a blanket tight around their shoulders. It was going to be a long night.

Chapter 9
Surgical Precision

The first patrol cars arrived on scene within minutes. Officers were never far from this neighborhood—one of the busiest in the city. The wail of sirens cut through the cold air like a rusted blade, sharp and unforgiving. Snowflakes swirled in the flashing red and blue, turning the night into a shifting canvas of light and shadow. Officers moved fast, stretching crime scene tape across another dead man's last steps, their voices sharp as they cleared the street.

Medics were on the way, but the officers had seen enough shootings to know this guy was dead.

A gust of wind sent a ripple through the yellow crime scene tape, threatening to rip it from the stop sign holding it in place.

As officers arrived, a crowd was gathering, eager as moths to a flame. Too many shootings had dulled their compassion, leaving only the thrill. They weren't witnesses—just spectators. Their eyes and cell phones stayed fixed on the body. Some whispered, some laughed; most didn't know the victim, none of them cared. A few stood there, unmoved. Somewhere in the back, an old woman shook her head, muttering to herself, her hands tucked deep into the pockets of a worn-out coat. She tightened her scarf and turned away, mumbling to whoever would listen, "Another shooting—can't even get groceries in this damn city."

Reaching for his shoulder mic, the first officer on scene radioed dispatch.

"534 dispatch, we need a supervisor."

A moment later, the response crackled through. "530, are you clear?"
"530 clear and en route."

This was a homicide. Detectives were needed, but it wasn't the patrol officers' job to make that call. A supervisor would take care of that. Right now, they focused on maintaining order and identifying any potential witnesses.

***

I was home—alone, as usual—half-watching a movie, the police radio crackled in the background. With a sniper loose in the city, I'd been listening more than ever, waiting for something—anything—that might break the case open. When I heard the patrol officer request a supervisor, I didn't wait for the call. I slipped on my shoes, grabbed my gun, and was out the door.

The dispatch sergeant finally rang about ten minutes later. I told him I was almost there and asked who else was coming. He advised Jenkins was on scene; Graham was on his way.

When I arrived, I pulled right up to the scene tape, parking dead in the middle of the intersection. The clock on the dash read 10:42 p.m., the temperature hovering below freezing. I jotted this down in my scene notes and stepped out into the steadily falling snow. Sergeant Jenkins was talking to the field lieutenant, so I made my way over to the body sprawled outside the liquor store's front door.

This looked like another drive-by shooting in a city ravaged by gang violence. It wouldn't move our case forward, but we still had a job to do. I figured it would be routine—another name added to the office body board.

But I was wrong.

This was surgical—a scalpel was slicing through the city's underbelly.

"Gentlemen," I said, nodding to the two officers next to the body. "What do we have?"

"Hey, Detective," responded the older of the two—a guy who was probably chasing calls since before I was born. I knew him, but could not remember his damn name.

"It's the strangest thing I've ever seen," he continued. "Three guys were standing here in front of the store, and suddenly, this guy drops dead—single shot, straight through the chest. Nobody heard or saw a thing."

I snapped my head toward the officer, my eyes narrowing. "What did you say?"

"Yeah," he replied. "I think a ghost pulled the trigger."

My initial assessment crashed. Another body on the pavement. The suspect kept working in silence and leaving nothing but questions. We weren't closing in; we were falling farther behind, one corpse at a time.

A serial killer in Dayton. The thought felt ridiculous. This wasn't New York or Chicago—just another town where murder was common, but never this clean. A lover's quarrel, a gang beef, a robbery—typical urban crime. But this? This was different. It wasn't desperation, it wasn't sloppy—it was controlled. Calculated. The kind of shooter who worked in silence, removed from the heat of the moment.

The corner liquor store's neon sign buzzed and flickered in the falling snow, casting a sickly glow over cracked sidewalks and boarded-up shops. A gust rattled the metal sign of a shuttered diner down the block. Streetlights gave off more shadow than light, pooling over empty pavement.

"Where are the witnesses?" I asked.

"They're in cruisers—both have warrants."

I exhaled sharply. "Perfect," I muttered. "Take them both to the second floor. We'll talk to them there."

"Yes, sir," he responded and moved toward his sergeant.

I turned to the officer beside me. "Anything else?"

Nothing he said surprised me—no evidence, no sounds, and two "witnesses" who swore they hadn't seen a thing. He gave me the victim's name, Malik Walker, while looking at me as though I should know who he was. I didn't. Maybe I should have, but the name meant nothing to me. I thanked him and went to see Jenkins, who was now talking with Graham. They heard me coming and turned, shaking their heads. This gunman was making us out to be fools—watching as we were chasing shadows in a city that didn't care who lived or died.

We knew nothing about the victim, which meant we couldn't begin to connect him to Hassan—if there even was a connection. All we knew was that a second target had been shot once, from long range, with near-perfect placement. We had to get back to the office and start connecting any dots we could find.

I told Jenkins and Graham I'd sent the witnesses to the second floor, and I was heading up to get started with them. I asked Graham to find some patrol officers to canvas the neighborhood and check with the E-crew before heading downtown. Maybe they could at least tell us if it was a high-caliber rifle round. I turned back toward the car when Graham stopped me.

"You okay brother? You're quiet tonight," Graham said, smirking. "Don't tell me you're daydreaming about that lawyer you met."

"I'm great," I replied with a smile. "She's a court reporter and we had a fantastic dinner tonight at that new steakhouse downtown."

Before I could leave, Frankie Calloway walked up to us. "Hey, guys," he called. "Could I get some sound?"

Frankie Calloway had been around forever, a veteran cameraman for the local news. Most cops respected him—he had a job to do, but he wasn't pushy, and we helped him when we could. He also knew protocol: detectives weren't his sound bite guys. He was hoping we'd slip and give him something the patrol sergeant hadn't.

"Sorry, Frankie," Jenkins replied. "Not our job. Go see Sergeant Phillips—he'll give you what you need."

"Worth a shot," Frankie muttered as he walked away.

I was in the office within fifteen minutes. After putting on a fresh pot of coffee, I headed to interview room two to speak with the first witness.

"Tommy?" I asked as I opened the door.

He nodded, fidgeting in the hard chair.

"I'm Detective MacLaren," I began. "First, I'm sorry about Malik. And I'm sorry to drag you down here, but we need to get some things sorted out, okay?"

Tommy tipped his head in agreement.

"Tommy," I said, leaning forward slightly. "I know you told the officers at the scene you didn't hear or see anything. Is that still the statement you want to make?"

"Yes, sir," he replied.

That was something—a little more respect in his tone. Maybe he was starting to relax, which meant he might actually be helpful.

"Okay," I said. "That's fine. Let's talk a little about Malik, then. How well did you know him?"

Tommy hesitated, then said, "I been knowing Malik for a couple years now. Since I moved here from Columbus."

"What can you tell me about him?" I asked. "I can pull his criminal history, but tell me what I can't find in a file. What was he into? Who did he run with?"

Tommy's jaw tensed. "Malik was good people," he said. "Yeah, he done some shit, we all have, but nothing to deserve getting shot down like a dog."

"Anything new or unusual been going on with Malik?" I asked.

Tommy hesitated, shifting in his chair. He wasn't sure if he should say what was on his mind. Finally, he spoke.

"You know, Malik just Malik, but ever since he got out of those charges a couple months ago, dude been acting weird."

"Weird?" I pressed. "In what way?"

Tommy exhaled, rubbing his hands together. "I don't know, bro," he said. "He was always talking about Palestine, Hezbollah, the Taliban—crazy shit. One night, he straight-up said he wished somebody would do another 9/11."

That made me sit up a little straighter.

Malik was talking about Hezbollah. Hassan WAS Hezbollah. Could be nothing. Could be everything.

I left Tommy in the interview room and went to speak with Carlos. I didn't waste time asking about what he may or may not have seen. I wanted to know about Malik's fascination with Middle East terrorists.

"Carlos," I said, leaning forward. "We've been talking to people in the neighborhood, and it sounds like Malik was leaning into dangerous behavior. You said he was talking about 9/11. Was he planning something? An attack? Was he working alone? With you?"

Carlos's eyes went wide—big as frisbees. "Man, I ain't no damn terrorist! And I don't know what the hell Malik was into, but he was always linkin' up with them dudes out front of that Islam house on Broadway."

"A mosque?" I asked.

Carlos shrugged. "I don't know, man. They got a sign out front with words in Arabic or some shit, and they all be wearing robes and towels on they heads."

I had Carlos write down everything he told me, thanked him for his help, and had an officer transport him to the jail so he could post bail. Then I went back to see Tommy.

"Tommy," I said, stepping into the room. "I was on the phone a minute ago with a citizen who said Malik had been spending a lot of time at the mosque on Broadway. Did you go there with him?"

"Not me, hell nah. But Malik? Every day since he got outta jail," Tommy admitted. "Me and Carlos told him to stay away from them freaks, but Malik ain't listen. He just kept goin'… gettin' more weirder every day."

"So he converted to Islam?" I asked.

"Nah," Tommy said. "He said they rules too tight, but he still wanted to support they work."

I shook my head and handed him a notebook.

"Write down everything you know," I said. "Then we'll get you to the jail so you can post bail. And thanks, Tommy—you've been a big help."

I got back to the office as Graham and Sergeant Jenkins arrived from the scene.

"Nothing!" Graham muttered, shrugging off his coat. "As clean as Pruden."

I was about to agree when Jenkins added, "Although… there is one thing." He reached into his coat pocket and pulled out a folded slip of paper. "One of the uniforms got a hit from the exterior camera at the market across the street. Grainy as hell, but it caught an old, beat-up brown sedan blowing through the intersection about five seconds after the shot."

I frowned. "Plate?"

"Too blurred," Jenkins said. "But the car's distinctive—one headlight dim, passenger side fender dented in. Loud exhaust you could hear even over the tape flapping in the wind. The store clerk said it backfired twice as it passed."

"That's not nothing," Graham said.

I wasn't convinced. In this neighborhood, half the cars fit that description. I ignored my doubt and jotted it in my notes. It was something to chase, even if it went nowhere. I'd make a broadcast. You never know, sometimes a dead end still shook something loose.

I nodded, having expected nothing less. "A little better news here," I said. "Our witnesses revealed some fascinating details about our victim."

That got their attention. Jenkins and Graham both stopped and looked at me.

"Well?" they said in unison.

"He was obsessed with Muslim terrorist organizations," I replied. "Hell, I'm not even sure he wasn't part of one."

Both of their mouths dropped.

I continued. "He'd been hanging around a local mosque every day, praising terror groups—including Hezbollah. Sound familiar?"

Sergeant Jenkins let out a low groan and dropped into his chair, rubbing his face. "Damn," he muttered. "Terrorism in Dayton? That's a huge problem."

Graham shook his head, moving toward the coffee pot. "With Hassan having confirmed Hezbollah ties, and now this guy—even if he was just playing the groupie—we have to consider the possibility." He poured himself a cup, his hand steady, but I could see the gears turning in his head.

"If someone's cleaning up a mess, we're gonna see more bodies."

"I agree," I said, glancing toward Sergeant Jenkins. "Sarge, we have to let the FBI know what happened tonight. I guess we can wait until morning, but if we sit on this, they'll be pissed."

Jenkins was already moving toward his office in the back corner of the squad room. "I'll call now and leave a message," he said. "I'll try again in the morning as well."

I checked my watch. Not even midnight yet.

"Hey, Graham," I said, stretching my back. "It's still early. Why don't we go knock on some doors—see if any of our snitches know anything?"

"Sounds good to me," he replied. "I definitely want to get out ahead of the FBI on this."

We both grabbed our coats. As I zipped mine up, I stepped into Jenkins' office to let him know we were heading out to make some contacts before calling it a night. Sometimes he rode with us, but tonight, he just shook his head.

We'd see him in the morning—if another body didn't turn up first.

Chapter 10
Working the snitches

The snow was falling again as we left the office, heading out to find some answers. As I turned right onto W. Third Street, the falling flakes caught in the streetlights, glittering like a million tiny diamonds. The city is beautiful when it snows—soft, silent, almost pure. A white shroud over the streets, masking the rot beneath.

We continued into the belly of the west side, making our way more from muscle memory than from what we could see. The defrost was cranked up high, fighting a losing battle to keep the windshield clear. The wipers slid across the glass with the sound of a soft breeze, leaving a narrow strip of clear view, only to be covered again before the blades swung back. Driving this old car in the snow was harder than riding a polar bear—heavy, unpredictable, and liable to spin out if I so much as breathed wrong. The rear tires fought for traction at every turn, the steering wheel giving just enough resistance to remind me I wasn't steering the car, the ice was.

Graham sat beside me, trying to scroll through his phone with his gloves on. I let out a low laugh, watching him fumble with those so-called touch-sensitive fingertips while trying to text a few trusted snitches—guys who hated cops but hated everyone else a little more. Throw them a few bones, and they'd tell everything they knew, as long as nobody was around to hear it.

"Take those damn things off, Graham, or we'll never get the info we need."

Graham sighed, yanking off his gloves and tossing them on the dash. “How am I supposed to text with frozen hands?” He jabbed at the screen with his bare fingers, squinting as his breath fogged up the glass.

I shook my head, easing the car forward through the snow. “Yeah, well, nobody said it’d be easy.”

Graham grinned sideways. “It’s better than when you used to make me write your book reports in eighth grade because your hands were ‘too cold’ from basketball practice.”

I snorted. “And you never fail to remind me about it twenty-five years later.”

“That’s because you never paid me back.”

“Anything?” I asked as I turned left onto N. Broadway, slowing briefly as a couple of kids in dark hoodies darted across the snow-covered street. Heads down, hands stuffed in their pockets. Probably not looking for trouble tonight—but I kept my eyes on them. I watched the way they moved, the quick glances over their shoulders. That’s the curse of the job; you’re always reading people, whether you want to or not.

I watched until they disappeared into the alley behind the old bank, swallowed by the night.

Distracted by my phone buzzing once, I let them go—Daniella checking if I’d survived the snow. I shot back a quick thumbs-up before Graham noticed. Not something I wanted to explain.

Hopefully, Graham could get something from his snitches, but if anyone in the hood knew what went down, it’d be De’Andre Carter—Biggen, as he was known around here. Biggen was as connected to the shadows of West Dayton as roots were to the earth. He had an old garage at the corner of W. Fifth and S. Broadway, and he was always there. He wouldn’t be happy to see us, but honestly, that’s what made it fun.

“Nothing,” Graham grumbled. “Everybody’s heard about it, but if they know anything, they’re keeping quiet. Looks like the streets aren’t giving us anything tonight.”

As I pulled into Biggen’s lot, I noticed Graham was calling someone—unusual for him.

Graham tapped his phone’s speaker.

“Tommy? Hey, it’s Detective Mac. You got anything on that shooting up on Lexington? How about Pruden?”

Static crackled on the line—muffled voices, a hesitation. Longer than usual. Graham frowned, then shook his head. "Alright, Tommy. Thanks anyway."

"Who was that?" I asked as I stepped out into the snow.

"Tommy Mullins," Graham said, slipping his gloves back on. "He's an east side guy, but he's been mixed up in some stuff on the west side lately. I got his kid brother out of a jam a while back, and he's been helpful since."

I nodded. "Well?"

Graham stepped out and looked at me over the roof of the car. "Nothing. Says nobody in the neighborhood is claiming it." He threw his hands up. "I don't know, bro—had to be a demon, man. Nothing else makes sense."

I didn't know about ghosts, but something wasn't adding up. If this was a gang hit, someone, somewhere would be running their mouth. Gang shootings always have a purpose—and they want everyone to know it. So, if it wasn't the gangs, who the hell was it?

Desperate for a lead—anything—I pounded on Biggen's garage door with the end of my thirty-year-old MagLite. Man, the stories this thing could tell. I'm just glad it can't.

"Dayton Police!"

Biggen was unpredictable. If he was sober, maybe things would stay peaceful. You never really knew. It was impossible to predict how he'd react when he saw the police. Graham and I each stood off to the side with our hands on the grips of our Glock 19s, ready to respond to whatever Biggen might have in mind. We stood silently as the large metal garage door began to rise, revealing a set of huge feet in well-worn, oil-stained Timberlands. Yep, that was Biggen. I've never seen feet as big as his—those damn things were at least size 14.

The guy was huge—an absolute tank. Easily 6'7" and pushing 350 pounds. His shoulders strained the seams of his filthy T-shirt, his thick hands big enough to crush a man's skull. Tonight must not have been bath night. The stench of sweat and cigarettes clung to him, the kind of grime that wouldn't wash off in just one shower. His T-shirt might've been white once, but between the food stains and who-knows-what, those days were long gone. His jeans were so dark and greasy, as if they'd been washed in motor oil.

Biggen spotted me and scowled. "MacLaren! I'm busy." He jerked a thumb toward the garage.

I looked past his massive torso and saw a woman sitting on a ratty couch shoved into the corner.

"Hey, Biggen," I said, flashing a smirk. "Nice of you to get cleaned up for us."

Biggen scowled. "What do you guys want?" he snapped. "I can't have nobody seeing you guys hanging around here."

Nodding, Graham chimed in, "We won't take much of your time."

"But we do need to talk," I added.

He ushered us inside and let the metal door crash shut behind us. The air inside Biggen's garage was thick; a nauseating blend of motor oil, cigarette smoke, and something else—old and stale, like rotting wood soaked in cheap liquor. The fluorescent ceiling lights seemed well past their prime, flickering enough to make the shadows crawl. The place was a mess. A workbench covered in rusted tools, half-stripped engine blocks, and the guts of a disassembled motorcycle. It wasn't how I'd keep my shop, but Biggen had his world arranged the way he liked it.

"Alright, guys," he said, rubbing his hands together. "What brings you to my garage in the middle of a snowstorm?" I shot a glance at the woman on the couch, raising an eyebrow at Biggen.

"Oh, don't worry about her—she cool."

"Okay then," I started. "We caught that shooting over on Lexington earlier tonight." I watched as he pursed his lips and nodded. Biggen leaned against the workbench, arms crossed over his barrel chest, his expression unreadable. "Damn shame about Malik. Y'all think this some gang shit, don't you?" he asked, his voice carrying the weight of someone who knew more than he was letting on.

"We have to consider it," Graham replied. "But we also know Malik wasn't always running with the same old crowd."

Biggen let out a slow exhale, shaking his head. "Man, Malik was my boy, but he been actin' different these past couple months. Not just weird—paranoid. Kept talking 'bout how people was watchin' him. Said he had 'bigger things' to focus on. Ain't wanna be in the streets no more. He was deep into some shit, but it wasn't dope or hustlin'."

I shot a glance at Graham. "What kind of shit?"

Biggen hesitated. He wiped a hand over his face, looking suddenly weary. "Some of the boys said he got religious, but like, not—church. He was talking about overseas shit. Hezbollah, Palestine, all that. Said America had blood on its hands. Now, I ain't saying he was in no terror cell or nothin'… but he wasn't some corner hustler no more."

Graham set his coffee down on the edge of the workbench. "You ever hear him talk about making moves? Not just talking—real plans?"

Biggen shrugged. "Not directly. But I know he was meeting with people outside the city. Dudes nobody recognized. Ain't from here. He was always running his mouth about how 'real change don't come from elections'—said some crazy shit about how people gotta 'take it to the streets.'"

"Sounds a lot like radicalization," I muttered.

"Malik's murder was eerily similar to the Pruden shooting two weeks ago." I let that hang for a moment, watching Biggen's face. "Word on the street says this isn't a gang hit." I paused, waiting to see if he'd react. No response, so I pressed on. "We know the guy on Pruden was connected to overseas terror groups. We need to know what happened, Biggen.

He glanced over his shoulder at his friend, then back at us. His jaw clenched. His tongue ran over his teeth. Finally, he exhaled, shaking his head. "I really don't know, MacLaren, but this one scares me man."

Holy shit. I'd known Biggen for years and never seen him afraid of anything.

"What do you mean?" I asked.

"That hit was clean, man," he whispered. "One shot. No mess. No witnesses. Two other brothers standing right there, and they didn't see a thing. C'mon, MacLaren—who does that?"

I looked at Graham, and his eyes were wide. Mine probably were too. Biggen had shared details no one outside our two witnesses and the police should know. My stomach dropped. The streets were talking—fast. But did they know what we needed to know?

Biggen plopped down next to his friend, who we could now see clearly. I didn't recognize her, but she was a looker—maybe 25, silky black hair, sharp features. Clean, well-dressed. She appeared to belong anywhere but here.

I caught Graham's glance—he was thinking the same thing I was. We both shrugged and smiled. Good for Biggen.

"Go on," I said. "You've clearly heard things about tonight. What do you know about Pruden?"

"I don't know, guys," he muttered. "Nobody knows. But it's got everybody freaked out." He leaned forward to grab a bottle of water. "We survive out here 'cause we can always see what's coming. We read the streets, feel the shifts—know what I'm sayin'? But this? This ain't normal, man. It's different. It's wrong." He looked at Graham, then me, then over at his girl. "Everybody scared, bro."

We thanked Biggen for talking to us, and I handed him my card. I've given him a hundred of those over the years—old habits die hard. But if he hears something, he'll call.

"Call me if you hear anything else," I said as I headed toward the door. "You know I got your back, Biggen. But only if you share what you know."

The wind outside had picked up, rattling the old sheet-metal door like something trying to get in. Biggen shifted, no longer the confident master of his block but a man terrified of what he couldn't see.

"You hear anything else, you let us know," Graham said.

Biggen let out a bitter laugh. "I'll try MacLaren."

He nodded as he lifted the garage door, and we stepped back into the cold. As we slid into the car, I cranked the ignition to get the heat going and turned toward Graham, "Well," I said. "I guess we can rule out gangs."

But something wasn't right. If this wasn't gangs—if it was terrorism—where was the manifesto, the grand speech? Real terrorists don't work in silence.

But this one did.

Taking out targets in the dark, no warnings, no claims of responsibility. Too controlled. Too precise.

I was starting to sense this was just the beginning.

Someone else was next.

And we had no idea who—or when.

Chapter 11
Borrowed Time

Graham and I had chased leads all over the city, and I hadn't made it to bed until 3 a.m. What we learned didn't tell us who the shooter was, but we had a good idea of who it wasn't. Whatever was going on in the city, it wasn't gang-related.

I woke up around 8 a.m. to a beautiful Monday morning, and I wasn't going to waste my day off worrying about the case. I had taken some much-needed PTO to spend time with my daughter. Today, I was going to be Dad, although for a second, I thought about texting Daniella — see if she wanted to join us. But I wasn't ready for that overlap, not yet. Penny was my whole world today.

Penny was five, and she meant the world to me. Her mom, Lena, and I split a couple of years ago. We tried, but it didn't work, but we stayed close. I see Penny whenever I want—Lena too.

Lena lived in the house we bought when we were married—a nice two-story on a quiet cul-de-sac in the far northeast corner of the city. It gave me comfort knowing Penny could play in the yard without worrying about cars speeding by. Back when we moved in, city employees had to live in the city limits. This little suburban oasis was once packed with cops and firefighters—everybody called it Cop-Land, a nod to that old Stallone movie. Those were great days, but no different than anything else, they had passed. Most cops fled the city as soon as they could—some of us didn't.

I called Lena to let her know I was coming, then stopped for donuts. Some cops avoid them to dodge the stereotype. Not me. The damn things are worth the punchline.

I had a key, and Lena always told me I could come and go. But I hadn't lived there in a while, and it didn't feel right—so I tapped lightly on the front door. I didn't want to wake Penny if she was sleeping, but I shouldn't have worried.

When Lena answered the door, Penny came flying down the steps like a tornado made of giggles, spinning straight for me right as I sat down our breakfast.

"Daddeeeeee!"

She must've jumped from the fifth step, launching straight into my chest. She wrapped her little arms around my neck as tight as glitter on glue, her legs wrapping around me for good measure. Wrapping my arms around her, I kissed her on the forehead.

"Good morning, Princess!"

Lena giggled as I stumbled back from the impact.

"Somebody's excited to see you."

Lena picked up the donuts and drinks and headed toward the kitchen, with Penny and me right behind her.

"Daddy," Penny began, "can we play in the snow?"

Lena chuckled, pulling out plates. "Penny, honey, Daddy just got here—give him a few minutes."

Lena set out the plates and mugs for the coffee. She always did the little extras when I was here. I would've been happy eating my doughnut off a napkin, but I appreciated the effort.

Lena slid the coffee across the counter, her fingers lingering on the rim for a second too long. I caught the look in her eyes—something between nostalgia and amusement. We'd come a long way from the fights and slammed doors. Some days, I wondered if she ever missed what we had. Some days, I know I did.

Penny talked a mile a minute as we ate, bouncing in her chair, her little hands flying as she described everything from her best friend's favorite color to the *biggest, scariest* book in the classroom reading corner. Kindergarten was her whole world, and I loved hearing every detail.

I let Penny's words wash over me, nodding at all the right moments, but somewhere in the back of my mind, the case lingered. Something wasn't adding up. The pieces were there, but out of reach. But not today. Today was about her.

She suddenly gasped, eyes wide. “Oh! Daddy, I made you something!”

She darted up the stairs before I could say a word, her footsteps pounding like a tiny stampede.

Lena smirked, sipping her coffee. “Brace yourself. It’s covered in glitter.”

I chuckled, wiping powdered sugar from my fingers. “Of course it is.”

A few seconds later, Penny came barreling back down the stairs, clutching a lopsided piece of construction paper with enough glue and glitter to blind a man. She held it up with both hands, beaming.

“Ta-da! It’s for you, Daddy!”

I took the masterpiece carefully, shaking off a bit of loose glitter. It was a crayon drawing of the two of us—me with long, spaghetti-thin arms and legs, and Penny right beside me, holding my hand. A giant yellow sun was in the corner, and above our heads, she had scribbled in her very best five-year-old handwriting: "I LOVE DADY".

I ran my thumb over the crayon lines. Kids always press too hard when they’re really trying. It hit me how fast she was growing up. Someday, she wouldn’t squeal in excitement when I showed up, or throw herself at me from the stairs. She definitely wouldn’t cover everything in glitter. But today, she was still my little girl, my baby girl, and I wasn’t going to waste a second of it.

I swallowed the lump in my throat and smiled. “This is incredible, Baby Girl. I’m framing it.”

Penny squealed, hopping in place. “Really?”

“Really,” I said, tapping her nose. “I’ll hang right above my desk at work.”

Lena snorted. “That’s gonna look real professional.”

I grinned. “It will look perfect.”

Penny clapped her hands, smiling as big as a kid on Christmas morning. “Mommy, did you hear? Daddy’s taking my picture to work!”

Lena smiled, looking at me with a smirk. “I heard, sweetie. That way, he can always remember how much you love him.”

Penny looked at me with a grin, “Yeah! In case he forgets.”

I chuckled, reaching over to ruffle her curls. “I could never forget my favorite girl.”

She giggled and reached for another doughnut, but Lena moved the box away. "Nope, one's plenty," she said with a shake of her head. "Otherwise, daddy won't be able to stand you today."

Penny puckered her lips, pouting as kids will do. But she let it go and turned back to me, eyes big as an owl's, "Soooo… can we build a snowman now?"

I took another drink of coffee, stretched my arms and pretended to shiver. "You sure it's not too cold?"

Penny gasped as if I had told her it was nap time. "No way! I've been waiting to play outside all week! Mommy bought me new boots and gloves, and I got a new sled for the hill."

I glanced at Lena, who arched an eyebrow. "Good luck. She's been talking about that hill nonstop."

I chuckled, finishing my coffee as I stood up from the table. "Alright then, let's go!"

Penny squealed, jumped from her chair and ran for the stairs. "I gotta get my snow pants!"

Lena giggled as she watched Penny run up the stairs. "She's going to keep you out there all day, you know."

I laughed as I grabbed my coat from the chair, "That's the plan."

By the time we got outside, the snow was fresh and untouched except for a few bunny tracks in the yard. Penny dashed out first, immediately flopping onto her back to make a snow angel. "Look, Daddy!" she called, swishing her arms and legs back and forth.

"I see it! That's a good one."

Shc grinned, then hopped up and pointed to the middle of the yard. "Let's build the snowman first!"

I knelt down and started packing a ball of snow. "You got it, boss."

We spent the next half hour rolling snowballs, stacking them, and decorating the snowman with whatever we could find—sticks for arms, a carrot Lena brought out, and an old scarf she didn't mind sacrificing. Penny insisted he needed a hat. All I had was a wool toboggan, so I ran back to my car and grabbed it from the trunk.

"There!" Penny shouted, stepping back to admire our work. "He's perfect."

"He's something, alright," I teased, adjusting the hat so it wasn't completely lopsided.

Penny giggled as she brought her hand from behind her back. Before I could duck for cover, the snowball she had been hiding smacked into my chest, exploding in a puff of white powder.

I stared at her in mock horror. "Oh, you're gonna pay for that."

Penny shrieked with laughter and took off running, already scooping up more snow.

Lena watched from the porch, arms crossed, smiling as she watched us play. "Try not to let her bury you alive," she called.
"No promises!" I shouted, launching a snowball of my own.

Penny ran behind the snowman, laughing as she peeked out from behind its lopsided head. I crouched, packing another snowball, giving her a playful smirk.
"You better run, kiddo," I warned.

She shrieked and took off, her pink snow boots kicking up snow. I tossed the snowball—it landed behind her, sending a puff of snow into the air.
Penny turned and grinned. "You missed!"
"Oh, did I?" I scooped up another handful of snow, but before I could throw, a snowball smacked me right in the shoulder.

I turned and saw Lena standing on the porch, trying, unsuccessfully, to appear innocent. She was giggling as she said, "I think it was the neighbor."

I shook my head, as I scooped up a handful of snow. "Oh, so that's how it is?"

She laughed and ran back into the house, my snowball smacking the door as she slammed it closed

Penny was laughing so hard she could barely breathe. "Mommy's the winner!"

I knocked the snow off my coat and turned toward Penny. "Alright, Princess, I think it's time for that sled hill."

Her eyes widened, and she gasped dramatically, like I'd told her we were going to Disneyland. "YES!"

I picked up her new plastic sled from the porch, and Penny grabbed my free hand, pulling me behind her toward the small hill in the neighborhood park. It wasn't much—just a gentle slope, but it was perfect for a five-year-old learning to sled. Penny thought it was the best place in the world.

Other neighborhood kids were already there, bundled up in coats and scarves, their laughter carrying on the crisp morning air. A few parents stood at the top, watching, laughing, drinking coffee, and maybe a little something else, from trendy travel mugs.

Penny suddenly let go of my hand and ran ahead of me, and sat down on her new sled at the top of the hill. She turned, her cheeks rosy from the cold, her eyes shining. "Push me, Daddy!"

I gave her a big push, sending her flying down the hill. Her arms waved in the air as she screamed with joy. She hit a small bump near the bottom and went tumbling into a pile of snow. I started to run toward her, but she popped up immediately, laughing so hard she could barely stand.

"Again!" she shouted, already dragging her sled back up.

I laughed, as I took the sled from her. "Alright, but this time, I'm going with you."

It was tight, but we managed to squeeze onto the sled. Penny sat in front, her tiny hands gripping the sides.

"Ready?" I asked.

"GO!"

Using both hands, I shoved us over the edge, and we raced down the hill, laughing like hyenas as we sped toward the bottom. Penny's laughter filled my ears, and for a moment, nothing else in the world existed. Not the killer, not my bosses, not the media. Just me and my baby girl, sledding on a snowy hill, her giggles shaking her entire body.

When we hit the bottom, the sled flipped on the same bump that got her before, sending us both tumbling into the snow. I landed on my back, Penny sprawled across my chest, laughing uncontrollably.

I stared up at the sky, snow falling on my, and realized something—I needed this. I needed this more than I even knew.

Penny rolled off me, breathless from laughter. "Again?"

I groaned playfully, pretending I couldn't move. "I think Daddy's too old for this."

"Noooo," she said, climbing on top of me and pushing at my shoulders. "You're not old, you're lazy."

I grabbed her, rolling her onto the snow beside me, tickling her ribs until she squealed.

"Say 'Daddy is the greatest!'" I demanded.

"Never!" she shrieked between giggles.

"Say it!"

"Nooooo!"

I tickled harder, and she finally caved, gasping out, “Daddy is the greatest!”

I let her go, but we were both out of breath. We lay there motionless as we stared up at the clouds floating by. The world was quiet, except for the occasional squeal of another happy child on a sled, and the rustling of tree branches in the cold breeze. Far off, a siren threaded the cold air and faded—a reminder that peace never holds in this city.

For the first time in a long time, I felt… peace.

Penny turned her head, looking at me with love in her eyes that only a child can share. “Daddy?”

“Yeah, Baby Girl?”

She reached over and took my hand, squeezing it tight. “I love you the most.”

I swallowed hard, squeezing her little fingers. “I love you the most, too.”

We lay there for another minute, the snow under us cold but not uncomfortable. Eventually, I sat up, brushing off my coat.

“Alright, one more run, then we head inside,” I said.

"But, Daddy!" Penny grumbled.

“It's getting late, sweetheart,” I said. “Daddy has to get home soon, and I have a feeling Mommy’s already got hot chocolate ready for us.”

Penny’s eyes lit up. “With marshmallows?”

“Only if we hurry and you don't crash us again,” I said, laughing as I stood up and reached for her hand.

She jumped to her feet, grabbing her sled. “Come on, Daddy, it'll be okay!"

So we hauled the sled back up the hill and flew down again, Penny’s laughter cutting through the cold, keeping us warm a little longer. I knew she wouldn’t always be this little and let me sled with her, but for now, I cherished every second.

When we finally skidded to a stop, sprawling onto our backs, we didn’t move. We stayed where we were, our chests pounding with laughter and cold.

Penny lay beside me in the snow, her little mittened hand holding tight to mine.

“Daddy?” she whispered, staring up at the sky.

“Yeah, Baby Girl?”

She squeezed my fingers. “I wish you could stay with me.”
I kissed her forehead and smiled. “Me too, baby.” And I meant it.

We stayed on the ground a little longer, watching the clouds thicken as they drifted across the sky—another storm was coming. The sounds of kids laughing and sleds scraping against packed snow were the only things we heard. Soon, I realized the cold was creeping in, and I knew Lena would have hot chocolate waiting.

I sat up, pulling Penny up with me. “Alright girl, it’s time we head inside.”

Penny didn’t complain. I think she was finally getting cold too. We picked up the sled and ran toward the house, pretending we were running from the police. We didn’t slow down until we hit the driveway. Lena, of course, was already expecting us. She was waiting with two steaming mugs of cocoa, tiny marshmallows floating on top. She shook her head as Penny bounced into the house, kicking off her snow boots without a second thought.

“You get all the fun, and I get the mess,” she said with a smile as she handed me a mug.

I took it with a grateful nod. “Perks of being the cool parent.”

Lena rolled her eyes but didn’t argue. Penny had already climbed onto a chair, cradling her cup in both hands, the warmth seeping into her little fingers.
“Best day ever,” she declared between sips.

I smiled, taking a slow drink of my own. The rich chocolate, the warmth of the house, the way Penny’s face practically glowed with happiness—it was one of those moments I wanted to lock away and keep forever.

But moments don’t last.

I glanced at the clock. It was getting late.

I set my mug down and ruffled Penny’s curls. “Alright, Princess, I gotta get going.”

Her face fell, but she nodded. “Okay.”

I knelt beside her chair. “You be good for Mommy, you hear?”

She threw her arms around my neck, squeezing tight. “I love you, Daddy.”

I closed my eyes, breathing her in. “I love you more.”
She pulled back, grinning. “Nope, I love YOU more.”

I laughed, standing up. “We’ll continue that argument next time, okay?”

Lena walked me to the door as Penny ran back to the table, humming a song from school. Lena hesitated for half a second before speaking.

"You good?"

I exhaled, as I pulled my gloves on. "Yeah, I'm fine."

She didn't look convinced, but she let it go. "Be safe, Angus. You know I worry about you."

I nodded. "Always."

As I stepped outside, the cold air bit at my face, and reality settled back in. The shooter. The bosses. The media. The city waiting beyond this quiet street.

I climbed into my car, placing Penny's glitter-covered drawing carefully on the passenger seat. I ran my fingers over the crayon lines once more before starting the engine. The glitter caught a stray beam of winter sun, bright as cartridge brass.

For a few hours, I'd had peace. But peace never stays long. It was time to get back to work.

Chapter 12
Pressure Points

Starting the week on Tuesday always threw me off balance, but I wasn't complaining. I'd had a great long weekend. I spent several hours with Penny and Lena, clearing my mind of the violence of the city, and I felt refreshed—ready to stop this sniper. For the first time in weeks, I'd fallen asleep without replaying bullet trajectories and crime scenes in my head.

I was whistling as I walked into the office, excited to be back on the hunt—until I saw Graham and Sergeant Jenkins.

Graham's fingers were already gripping his collar, his usual tell when things were overwhelming him. Jenkins had that thousand-yard stare, the one I'd seen on guys who knew they were walking into a no-win situation.

"What's up, guys?" I asked, eyeing their forlorn faces. "You both look like someone ran over your dog, then got out and kicked it."

Sergeant Jenkins exhaled. "Assistant Chief Carpenter just called. All three of us have been summoned to an emergency command staff meeting."

He glanced at his cheap Timex. "In the War Room. 8:30—sharp."

I stared at my slightly nicer Timex. "That's five minutes!" I exclaimed. "How the hell are we supposed to prepare?"

Graham was running both hands through his hair. Anybody with a rank above sergeant made him nervous on a good day. Having to present to all of them unprepared was worse than going to Internal Affairs with no idea what they wanted to talk about.

Sergeant Jenkins threw his hands up. “I don’t know, Angus,” he exclaimed a little too loud. “Tell them what you can. It’s time—we gotta go.”

We took the stairs. It was much quicker than waiting for the ancient elevators in this tired old building. We reached the ground floor and made our way down the hallway to the War Room.

The War Room—really an old conference room—was exactly what the name suggested: a place where major decisions were made, high-profile press conferences were held, and sometimes, careers were built or buried. A long, rectangular conference table dominated the center, surrounded by high-backed leather chairs that had seen better days. Large whiteboards lined the far wall, the paint behind them faded from what was once a bright blue.

At one end of the table stood a wooden podium, scuffed and worn from years of use. Anyone called to provide information—whether a detective, a supervisor, or some poor patrol officer caught in the crossfire—would stand there, delivering their findings to the expectant eyes of the brass. That podium was what scared Graham the most. To him, it wasn’t wood and screws—it was a firing squad post where careers took their last breath.

The whiteboards were usually covered with crime scene photos, maps, and suspect profiles—anything tied to the latest major case. Today—nothing. That alone told me why we were here. A projector hung from the ceiling, its lens aimed at a blank screen at the front of the room.

The air was stagnant and stale. Whoever designed this place hadn’t thought much about ventilation. It smelled faintly of burnt coffee, old cigar smoke, and tension that hangs in rooms where bad news is routine. A faint hum from the overhead fluorescent lights buzzed in my ear, adding to the uneasy quiet.

When we entered, it was apparent we were late. All of the department leaders were already seated, quietly awaiting our arrival.

Not exactly an entrance that inspires confidence for me.

Carpenter pointed us toward three empty chairs along the wall. “Sergeant Jenkins,” he began, “we want to thank you and your detectives for accommodating our last-second request.”

I chuckled under my breath. Request.

Chief David Robertson waited as we took our seats, his face unreadable. Even in silence, he commanded the room, his presence settled over us with the weight of a lead vest. He was an outsider who never let anyone forget it. A retired NYPD captain, he carried himself with that New York swagger, spoke with a deep, unmistakable Brooklyn accent, and had the build of someone who spent more time in the gym than behind a desk. His salt-and-pepper hair was always perfect, his suits tailored, his expression frozen between disinterest and disdain.

Unlike the rest of the brass, who had come up through the ranks of DPD, he had been handpicked by the mayor to "fix" the department—not that anyone had asked for his help. The other commanders, at least, were familiar faces. Graham and I had worked with most of them when we were all patrol officers. I'd even gone through the academy with two of them, including Carpenter. That didn't mean they'd go easy on us, but at least we knew what we were dealing with.

The chief was different. He didn't want answers—he wanted control. Once we settled in, he got straight to it. "Gentlemen, I'm not going to sugarcoat this. You know why you're here, and we need those answers now. Sergeant Jenkins?"

Jenkins glanced at Graham, then at me, before starting to rise from his chair.

Robertson waved his hand and shook his head. "Sit down, Sergeant. We don't need the formality today—just tell us what we need to know."

Jenkins lowered himself back into his chair, flipped open his notebook, and looked up at the chief. "This is a tough one, Chief, but we'll do our best," Jenkins said. "What do you want to know?"

Robertson let out a short chuckle. "We want to know what the hell is going on—and how you're going to stop it."

Sergeant Jenkins coughed before speaking. "We began this investigation under the belief that Hassan's murder was tied to his connections with Middle Eastern terror groups. Hassan was operating under an alias and was in the country illegally. We turned over everything to the FBI, and they're pursuing that angle."

He paused to pour himself a glass of water from the plastic pitcher in the center of the table, took a small sip, then continued. "Last week, we learned that a parent of one of Hassan's victims threatened him in court. Angus and Graham were working this lead, and it looked promising—until Malik was killed. Now, we haven't ruled him out, but we haven't found a connection either. At this point, he seems unlikely to be our shooter."

Carpenter, who so far had just been listening, lifted his eyes from his notes and fixed them on me. "Angus," he began, "If there is no connection between the parent suspect and Malik, how about between Malik and Hassan?"

"Nothing concrete yet," I replied. "We've been told that Malik has been radicalized by an Islamic group. Along with the FBI, we are working to determine if Malik had any contact with Hassan through this group, or any other known terror organization."

Looking at me over the top of his reading glasses, he asked, "And?"

"Too early to say," I replied. "The FBI is digging as well. If they were connected, we'll find it."

Robertson looked at Jenkins. "Anything else you want to add, Sergeant?"

Jenkins flipped through the pages of his notebook. None of it was relevant to this case—but it looked better than showing up empty.

"At this time, Chief," Jenkins began, "we believe we'll find that Malik and Hassan were killed by the same person because of their terrorist ties. With the pressure the FBI is putting on radicalized networks in the city, we are confident the shootings have stopped. We also believe the shooter has fled the city, placing it in the FBI's jurisdiction to find and arrest."

Robertson checked the time, the bezel of his Rolex Submariner clicking softly as he rotated it with precision. Even his watch—iconic, expensive, built for performance—was a reflection of the man himself. Not at all like the department store Timex watches most of us wore, which reflected more of an everyday, working-class kind of reality.

"Okay, Sergeant," he began. "Let me be blunt. This has to end—today. I do not intend to wake up tomorrow to hear of another shooting. Am I making myself clear?"

"Yes, sir," Jenkins responded.

"Good," Robertson continued. "The mayor, the media, hell, even two local gang leaders have called this morning demanding answers. I do NOT enjoy those calls!"

He paused, scanning the three of us. We all nodded in silent acknowledgment.

"Sergeant. Detectives," he said. "I really can't make this any clearer. If this continues—if I'm awakened in the middle of the night to hear about another shooting—all three of you will be back in here before you can even finish saying the word *fired.* And you'd better have a hell of a good reason why I shouldn't."

His tone sharpened, but I knew the edge wasn't just for us—it was for whoever might be listening upstairs.

"This is a headache for all of us, gentlemen. The mayor's office is on me every morning, so I'm going to be on you. Council's whispering about budget cuts. I can't give them excuses to slash us at the knees."

Robertson's phone buzzed. Without another word, he stood and walked out to take the call, leaving the room in tense silence.

Carpenter looked at us with a slight frown. "Sorry about that, fellas. He's getting hammered by his bosses. The mayor's breathing down his neck, and now we've got city council members calling, expecting us to believe they suddenly care about gang violence. You know that's going to find its way to you."

We nodded. We had all been around long enough—we knew how it worked.

"You guys know he can't fire you over this," Carpenter continued. "But he can make your lives hell. Find something—anything—he can take to his bosses, and you'll be fine. The next CompStat meeting is Tuesday. I need you guys there. Hopefully with news the shooter is locked up. If not, be prepared to tell us why."

"Yes, sir," we all said in unison as everyone stood to leave.

What we didn't say—what didn't need to be said—was that somewhere out there, someone was already lining up their next shot. And we were three steps behind.

Not even 10 a.m. on a Tuesday, and I was already over it. If this was how the week was starting, we were in for a hell of a ride.

Chapter 13
Citizen Dorsey

It had been three days since we were called on the carpet in the staff meeting, and we weren't any closer now than we were then. At least the sniper hadn't struck again. Small victory—but short-lived. If we showed up to CompStat empty, Chief Robertson was going to gut us in front of the entire department.

Two more workdays. That was all we had. And right now? We had nothing. Graham and I had chased every lead we could, grinding through interviews, surveillance, and dead-end tips. Nothing to give Robertson. Nothing to give the mayor. Nothing to stop the clock from running out. And instead of being out there working the case, we were stuck wasting another morning on admin nonsense.

Firearms qualification time. Every cop's least favorite bureaucratic hoop to jump through. Because apparently, proving we could hit a paper target was more important than stopping a killer terrorizing the city. And I could always hit the target—100% was my norm—but the threat of failure was always there. One bad shot, one mechanical issue, and I'd be stuck on administrative duty until I could requalify. I clenched the wheel a little tighter as we drove. This was time we didn't have to waste. But rules were rules.

I parked in the far corner of the range lot, killed the engine, and sat for a second. Graham didn't say anything, just stared through the windshield thinking he may be able to will the day to be useful.

"Let's get this over with," I muttered, grabbing my gear bag.

Inside, the air was thick with gunpowder, lead, and Hoppe's No. 9. Cops in various states of boredom shuffled through the motions—loading mags, checking sights, signing in with that glazed look we all get when we're here to check a box. The instructor barked reminders about safety in case we hadn't all heard them a hundred times before.

We took our places in lanes five and six. Graham went first. Tight groupings, quick rhythm, no wasted motion. Same as always.

I stepped up next. My mind wasn't in it. I could hit center mass without thinking—muscle memory—but every shot was a distraction from what we should be doing.

Halfway through my second magazine, Graham's phone buzzed. He checked the screen, then stepped back with a muttered, "Gotta take this."

He disappeared behind the soundproof divider, and I kept firing, trying to block out the tingle in my spine—the sense that the real action was finally starting somewhere else.

"Detective MacLaren," Graham said as he answered the call.

"Detective MacLaren, this is Tobey," the voice paused – maybe expecting recognition – before adding, "From Dayton Tactical."

"Hi, Tobey," Graham replied. "What can I do for you?"

"Yeah, listen, I know my boss said we couldn't help you, but...."

Graham didn't let him finish, "What is it, Tobey?"

"Uh, well...a guy just left here with two boxes of .338 Lapua. I thought you should know."

Graham's eyes opened wide, as if the prom queen had said yes. "That's incredible. Did you get his name?"

"No," he said. "I'm so sorry, but I did see his van and the plate."

"You're kidding?" Graham said. "Tobey! This is amazing! "What did you see?"

"He left in a full size van, pretty sure an old Chevy. Maybe mid-90's, and it was dark purple," he paused, "The plate was Ohio XZQ9812."

"Tobey," Graham said as he looked at me and grinned, "You are the citizen of the year in my book, buddy. Thank you so much!"

"Of course Detective," he replied. "You know I've always got your back."

"Thanks again Tobey. We'll talk soon." Graham ended the call and looked at me like he had won the Powerball.

"What the hell was that about?" I asked as we walked back to the firing line. We still had to qualify with the shotguns that lived in the trunk and never saw daylight.

"That was exactly what we've been waiting for. Our shooter!" Graham said with the excitement of a kid at Christmas. "We got him!"

Graham was a solid detective—thorough, methodical—but he had a habit of getting too attached to early leads. I'm the opposite – a complete cynic. We balanced each other out, and I knew this was one of those times. No case gets solved on the first phone tip—and we weren't breaking that streak today. No matter, we had to pursue it. I was about to bust Graham's bubble when the range officer called us to the line. It would wait.

Each of us picked up an 870 Marine Magnum 12-gauge and three shells from the table, then walked back to our lanes and waited for instructions. At the range officer's command, we raised the shotguns, racked the rounds into the chambers, and fired in unison—three targets, three shots. One more rack ejected the final spent shells, and we returned the 870s to the table.

Simple. Quick. Stupid.

If you miss from three yards with a shotgun, you have no business with a badge—or a gun.

Graham was nearly running as we headed back to the car. I was a little excited too. I didn't expect much from the tip, but it gave us something to do—something to keep us moving forward, instead of stuck in wet cement up to our knees.

We grabbed sandwiches and made it back to the office after noon. Graham didn't even wait to eat before logging in to the LEADS terminal in the back left corner of our office.

"Let's see who this asshat is," he muttered, typing in the plate number.

The information came back quick. Looking over his shoulder, I saw that Ohio XZQ9812 was registered to a 1994 Ford Econoline, owned by a Keith Alan Dorsey at an address on Smithville, over on the east side. Tobey swore it was a Chevy. Eyewitnesses always screw up the details—hopefully this time it was the make, not the plate.

If the plate is correct, our guy was a forty-two-year-old male with a valid license—and no wants or warrants.

"That's rather unremarkable," I said, scanning the screen. "Call Carol down in Records. See if she can find anything on this guy from outside the department. I'll check our database for anything local."

I sat at my computer and entered Dorsey's name into the search bar. I could hear Graham talking with Carol, but I wasn't listening. The information coming back on this guy was concerning—a giant red flag had been raised right in our office.

Dorsey's record could have been a Greatest Hits album for Dirtbag of the Year. He'd been a suspect in unlawful possession, felonious assault, disorderly conduct, trespassing, and who knows what else—but somehow, I didn't see a single record of local arrests.

He'd walked on everything.

"Thanks, Carol," I heard Graham say as he hung up the phone.

"Anything?" I asked, turning toward him.

"Nope. Not one damn thing of use," he replied. "Although this was interesting—couple years back, the guy sued the city and county for violating his Constitutional rights during multiple traffic stops. Claimed they had no right to see his license. Classic Sovereign Citizen."

Of course he is," I said. "A government-hating, YouTube-educated constitutional lawyer."

We pulled his BMV photo. Dorsey looked exactly as you'd expect—square jaw, long beard, dead eyes. I didn't trust the picture. I wanted to see him in person. We had nothing but a hunch on this guy. We couldn't stop him, but nothing was stopping us from watching him. We didn't know if he had a job—Carol was working on that for us—but even if he did, maybe he worked nights.

We were going to his house anyway. Might get lucky.

We made it down to the car and out onto W. Third St. right at three o'clock, heading toward Smithville. What should've taken ten minutes was taking forever. Traffic was heavy, like the whole city was fleeing a hurricane. But we finally got there, turning left onto N. Smithville and, at last, out of the jam.

"It's 243," Graham said as we crawled up the street. "Should be up ahead on the left."

And it was.

I was a little surprised it was a house. This part of Smithville is the armpit of the east side. Most people lived in one of the ratty apartment buildings that lined these blocks. Dorsey, though, had gone one better—a ratty house.

There were junk cars in the yard. The roof over the porch was sagging—looked ready to collapse any minute. Plastic sheeting flapped in the wind where windows used to be, and two large pit bulls were chained to a tree in the front yard. And right next to the porch sat a ragged, rust-covered purple 1994 Ford Econoline.

With its dark-tinted windows, rust and oxidation spreading across every surface, the flapping and tattered Don't Tread on Me flag hanging from the back door, and its mud-covered tires, it couldn't belong to anyone other than Sovereign Citizen Dorsey.

I wanted—no, I needed—to see this guy. But it wouldn't be easy. We couldn't just knock on his door, so we had to wait.

But where?

Dorsey's house sat across the street from a wooded lot, and there wasn't any good place nearby to park and watch him for a while. So I made a U-turn at the next intersection and went back to a church about half a block the other way.

It wasn't ideal, but we had a decent line of sight through binoculars or the telephoto lens on the camera—and he definitely wouldn't be suspicious of a car parked that far down the block. The whole area looked forgotten—snow chewing at the edges of tarps where siding should've been, a block held together by cable wire and stubbornness.

We sat in the church lot and watched that crumbling house until nearly 1800 hours.

"Graham," I said, "we're going to have to call it, buddy. They're not going to pay us OT to watch a hunch. We'll try again Monday."

Then the front door creaked open.

Dorsey stepped out as a cliché: camo pants, flannel jacket, combat boots. His beard was thicker than his BMV photo, and he carried a battered green duffel, held close, never leaving his side.

He looked both ways before walking to the van. Not paranoid—practiced.

Suddenly, I couldn't care less if they paid me.

"Tell me this isn't a guy who's used to stalking prey," I said.

Graham lifted the camera and snapped a few photos through the telephoto lens. "Or one who's about to hunt someone else."

I nodded quietly as I studied him through the binoculars.

Dorsey moved from the house to the van multiple times, carrying some things out and some things in, but we never saw anything resembling a long-gun. I really hoped he'd get in the van and go somewhere, give us a chance to learn more about his movements—but he stayed put.

After about an hour, Graham looked over and said, "Brother, I think he's in for the night. Let's go home and get back on his tail Monday."

I hated to admit it, but he was right. Dorsey would have to wait.

We certainly weren't going to lose him. He was entrenched in his house like a rat in a NYC sewer. He wasn't going anywhere.

We'd find him again Monday.

We pulled out of the lot and headed back downtown. Graham called Sergeant Jenkins to fill him in. We'd forgotten to let him know we were working something, so he wasn't too happy about that—but once he heard the details, he calmed down. We finally had something for CompStat.

He thanked Graham for the update and said he really hoped he didn't see us again until Monday.

I couldn't agree more.

Because if someone else died before Tuesday morning, this hunch wouldn't mean a damn thing.

And we'd be right back to explaining a body to Robertson—with nothing to show for it.

Chapter 14
Donuts and Dorsey

I yawned. What was I doing up so early on a Saturday? Saturdays were for sleeping in—peaceful rest, black coffee, maybe the crossword if I was feeling ambitious. But not today. I hadn't slept well. I couldn't stop thinking about Dorsey. What were we missing about this guy?

Anyway, here I was—7:30 a.m., eating bacon and eggs, and reading yesterday's newspaper.

I was about halfway through my second cup of Devil's Tears Pitch Black—more tar than coffee, but I loved it—when the doorbell rang, slicing through the stillness like a blade.

"Who's ringing my bell at this hour?" Dropping the paper, I pushed back from the table and shuffled toward the door in socks and a faded Dayton PD T-shirt from the academy.

DING-DONG!...DING-DONG!...Dammit. I yanked the door open, ready to knock whoever was interrupting my morning coffee back to the curb.

I was so irritated, it took a second to realize it wasn't some guy wanting to trim my out-of-control elm tree—it was Graham.

"Graham?" I said with a shake of my head. "What the hell, man? It's the middle of the night."

"It's 7:30," he said, grinning. "Technically morning."

Graham laughed, holding a huge Donut Kingdom box, the glittery purple logo practically glowing in the morning light and taunting me with its artificial cheer.

"Morning, Bro!" he said. "You look dead."

Graham pushed past me with his box of sinful pleasures and headed for my kitchen. I glanced briefly out into the street for any other surprises before closing the door.

"Those donuts are the only reason I didn't slam the door in your face," I said, grabbing another coffee cup from the cabinet. "Why are you here so early?"

I poured Graham a cup of coffee and set it on the table in front of him.

"Dorsey," he replied. "I can't stop thinking about him. Didn't sleep a bit."

I reached over and opened the donut box. "Blueberry?"

"Two," he said.

Blueberry. Really, the only legitimate donut a man can eat. Dense. Warm. The sugar glaze cracked, intricate spiderwebs on glass, and inside, violet blueberry flecks burst with flavor that lingered slow and steady on your tongue.

Graham took a drink of his coffee, wrinkling his nose with the same disgust he showed at the stench of a week-old corpse. He glanced into the cup, as if checking to be sure it really was coffee, then took another sip.

"Good coffee," he said, coughing. "A little strong."

I laughed as he set the cup on the table.

"Something about Dorsey bugs me," Graham said. "You want to go sit on him for a while?"

I sighed and rubbed the back of my neck. "It's Saturday."

He gave me a look of confusion.

I had no plans—I could admit that much. Didn't mean I wanted to spend the day parked across from a meth-stained porch watching a wannabe militiaman pick his nose. Still…

"I guess I've got nothing better to do today," I said.

"So… you're in?" Graham interrupted before I could finish.

I stood up and started down the hall. "Give me five minutes."

I dressed quick—jeans, boots, a black zip-up hoodie that made me look more construction crew than cop. I shut off the coffee pot and grabbed another donut before picking up my coat and gun on the way to the door.

Graham was already standing at the door as excited as a puppy.

"You driving?" I asked.

"I brought the truck."

"Of course you did."

We stepped out into the morning light—cool and gray, with a thin cloud cover that made the world feel paused. No snow today. That was something. Living in Dayton lately was only slightly better than the North Pole, and I was getting sick of it.

I locked the door behind us and followed him toward the truck, the second donut in my hand and that dull pressure behind my eyes that only came from chasing specters.

We climbed into Graham's truck, a couple-year-old Silverado that somehow looked and smelled new. I couldn't figure that one out. Graham had the house full of kids, but it was my car that looked and smelled like I was living in it.

He turned the ignition and my ears were assaulted by screeching 80s metal.

"Sorry," Graham muttered, reaching for the volume knob. "Old habits."

I didn't even respond. I stared out the window, nibbling on my donut, letting the sugar seep into my system.

We'd been riding in silence for several minutes when Graham suddenly spoke—startling me out of my daze.

"You still seeing Daniella?" he asked as casually as if he were asking what I had for lunch.

I thought about ignoring him. If he hadn't been my brother, I probably would have.

"A little," I said. "It's nothing. Just hanging out."

Graham laughed out loud and looked over at me. "Hanging out? You in high school?"

That made me chuckle, thinking about how much younger Daniella really was.

"Daniella might be," I said with a grin.

"Well, anyway," Graham said. "You know Rachel's having my birthday party at The City Lights tonight. Bring her along. It'll be fun."

I shook my head. No commitment either way, just an I-don't-know. Bringing dates around family always felt juvenile, but maybe it could be fun.

We made our way across the city, finally passing by Dorsey's house around eight o'clock. The van was there, but it was backed in this time, which seemed off. Hiding the license plate? Maybe. The house was a dump—nothing new there—but something felt different. I couldn't quite put my finger on it.

The pit bulls were gone. That was odd, sure, but not what made me uneasy.

Then I saw it.

A large dent in the van's driver's-side grille and fender. Fresh. Crumpled metal, silver showing through the paint like exposed bone—and a shattered headlight.

"That definitely wasn't there yesterday," I said, pointing toward the damage.

Graham looked over but didn't seem too concerned. "Probably got drunk last night and hit a pole. He seems the type."

I wasn't so sure. I had a feeling this was something more. A hit-and-run, maybe? If so, we might have a reason to stop Dorsey the next time he moved. I made a mental note to check with Records for any recent broadcasts involving a purple van.

After driving by a couple of times, we started to worry we'd attract attention from the neighbors. So we looped around the block and pulled back into the same church lot as yesterday.

Once parked, I noticed something had changed. In the short time we were out of view, a ragged old pickup had arrived—and the dogs were back outside.

"Damn," Graham said. "We missed something."

"Hopefully it's a short visit," I replied. "We really need to know who that is."

"Yep," Graham said. "You stay here and take pictures. I'm going to walk by like I belong out here."

As Graham headed up the sidewalk, I snapped a few good photos of the pickup, the van, and the new damage. I wasn't expecting much else—but as he reached Dorsey's house, the front door opened, and two men stepped onto the porch.

One was clearly Dorsey—wearing the same militia-man camo from yesterday, and once again carrying that green duffel. The other guy was a mystery. Same outfit, same attitude, but his bag was black with the shape of a rifle case.

To my surprise, Graham stopped and started talking to them. Totally out of character. I couldn't hear what was said, but there was some pointing, a few animated gestures. Nothing confrontational, but definitely not casual, either.

Since they'd seen him, Graham couldn't double back to the truck. He kept walking around the block instead. I thought that might become a problem when both men got into the pickup, but then Dorsey climbed back out—holding the other guy's black bag in his hand.

While Graham was on his walk, I pulled out my phone and opened a new message.

Hey… Graham's birthday party is tonight. Rooftop bar downtown. You want to come?

I hesitated a second before hitting send. She didn't usually do crowds. But maybe...

Daniella: Sure. What time?

Me: 8. I'll pick you up.

Daniella: Looking forward to it.

I locked the screen and slipped the phone back into my jacket pocket. No smile. No expression. Just a quiet awareness that I'd crossed some invisible line. I hadn't told Graham. I hadn't told anyone.

And yet… I was picking her up tonight.

Graham made it back to the truck about fifteen minutes later.

"I got the plate from the truck!" he said, clearly proud of himself. "Also talked to those two assholes."

"I saw that," I said. "What was that all about?"

"I told them I lost my dog," he said with a grin. "They were super helpful. Told me they hadn't seen it and that I should keep moving."

We both laughed at the absurdity of the interaction, and I glanced at my watch.

"It's getting late," I said. "We'd better get home so you're not late to your own party."

Graham nodded, checking the time. "Yeah, you're right. But I think this was a productive morning. With the photos and that plate number, we should be able to ID this other guy. And if that van is tied to a hit-and-run, we might finally have a reason to stop Dorsey next week."

"Yeah," I said. "I'll get with Carol first thing Monday—see if anybody's looking for this van."

As we pulled out of the church lot, the pickup truck was already gone. Dorsey had gone back inside. The place sat silent—same as the other forgotten house on this block. The sagging porch, glassless windows, dented van, and two pit bulls patrolling the perimeter.

A few more clues, a few more questions. Another man with a gun-shaped bag. Another dead end waiting to happen—or maybe, perhaps, the thread that would unravel the whole thing.

I watched the house fade in the rearview, then leaned back against the headrest.

We weren't even supposed to be working today. It was Saturday. Graham's birthday. Tonight, we'd be clinking glasses and pretending not to carry the weight of a city waiting to catch fire.

But I couldn't shake the feeling that Dorsey was the match.

Chapter 15
High Enough to Hide

I'd been staring at the same spot on the wall for ten minutes. There was a nick in the drywall—maybe from moving furniture once, maybe older than that—but it was enough to catch the light at the wrong angle. I kept focusing on that tiny imperfection, wondering if I should've patched it, painted over it. Easier to focus on that than admit I was waiting like a stupid teenager for eight o'clock to get here.

I'd dressed up—well, for me anyway. Crisp, new jeans, white button-up shirt, dark sport jacket, and cowboy boots. I was glad I was bald—didn't have to worry about whether my hair looked right. But I was unsure. Daniella was young, beautiful, innocent. Bringing her around this crowd? Around Graham and Rachel? I would be handing over a secret I hadn't decided I wanted to share yet.

My living room smelled of aftershave. Not cologne—never that. It was enough to say I'd tried. I'd scrubbed my boots too, which probably said more about me than I meant it to. Shined leather instead of polished cufflinks—blue-collar pride dressed up enough to pass under the rooftop lights.

The TV was on in the background, volume low. Fox News anchor was ranting about politics as though he knew what the truth was. I walked into the kitchen, checking my watch on the way. Useless, but I checked it anyway. Waiting was brutal, and my nerves were going to kill me if I didn't get out of the house soon.

My eyes drifted to Penny's glitter-covered drawing propped on the end table. Crayon lines, clumps of glue, and sparkles that stuck to my fingers when I touched it. A reminder there were better things to be nervous about.

I started to text her to let her know I was on my way when my phone buzzed in my hand.

Daniella: *Sorry! I lost track of time. Caught up in a project. Can't make it back to change. I'll just meet you there. 8 sharp.*

I stared at the screen. A project? I wanted to ask what kind—but I didn't. Our relationship wasn't there yet. She didn't know what I did. I didn't know what she did. Maybe we'd get there someday. At least, I hoped.

Me: *See you there.*

I dropped the phone in my coat pocket, grabbed my keys, and headed downtown.

City Lights wasn't usually my kind of place—rooftop bars filled with rooftop people—but it was Graham's birthday, and you should always sacrifice for family. Plus, I knew there'd be guys from the job I hadn't seen in years. It might be nice to catch up.

I had to park a couple blocks from the restaurant—yet another reason to hate downtown. You couldn't go out for a nice meal without walking past a dozen homeless addicts looking for a handout. The usual gauntlet: piles of garbage, shopping carts full of God knows what, and that ever-present stench of urine and weed.

But when I stepped into the lobby, it seemed I'd crossed into another world. Gone were the tents and glassy-eyed stares. In their place—soft music, low lights, beautiful people. The air smelled of money and floral perfume. It felt more LA or New York than Dayton.

The hostess barely looked up from her podium. "Rooftop?" she asked.

"Yeah," I nodded.

There was something almost funny about the way she said it—rooftop was a whole different category of guest. We weren't just upstairs. We were elevated. Selected. Pretending to matter.

I'd never liked this part of town. Too polished. Too curated. The kind of place where hairline-cracked sidewalks were marketed as charm instead of seen for what they were. Where you paid fifteen bucks for parking and another twelve for a cocktail with too much citrus and not enough bourbon. What I really wanted was a mug of Devil's Tears Pitch Black—something strong enough to cut the nerves. But this wasn't that kind of place.

I took the elevator anyway. It was Graham's night. And because somewhere in the mess of liquor and cheap hors d'oeuvres, I thought I might figure out whether this thing with Daniella was real—or some passing illusion I wasn't ready to let go of yet.

The elevator rose quickly and opened directly into the heart of the party. A seamless continuation of the space below—same music, same curated mood. Strings of warm lights hung, crooked constellations over a patio filled with familiar faces. Half the department, a half-dozen propane heaters fighting off the chill, and three-quarters of Graham's extended family.

Rachel spotted me first.

"Angus! You made it!" Rachel beamed at me. She had a way of ribbing me about my dates, more a kid sister than Graham's wife. She gave me a quick hug, then stepped back to look behind me.

"Well, where is she?"

I smiled—mostly from awkward nervousness—and nodded toward the elevator. "She'll be here. She's running a little behind. Should be here any minute."

Rachel gave me that look of hers—half amused, half suspicious. The kind that let you know she didn't entirely believe you but wasn't going to call you out. Not yet.

She handed me a bourbon neat with the aggression of a relay baton. "I hope she gets here soon. I have a lot of things to tell her."

"Good to see you too, Rach."

She winked and wandered off toward a large group of women I didn't recognize, leaving me to fend for myself.

I did what I always did in these places—kept moving. I'd never been one to mingle, so I made a quiet stroll around the perimeter—sipping the drink, watching the crowd.

Graham was over by the bar, surrounded by a half-dozen old buddies. Jenkins was there too—laughing too loud at something that probably didn't warrant it. I'd never seen Sarge drunk, but he was well on his way tonight.

A couple guys from Vice were at a table near the bar, already retelling war stories as though they hadn't been at work together yesterday.

I exchanged a few handshakes. Heard about a promotion someone had finally landed. Caught sight of one of our former sergeants—retired, bitter, still talking like he ran the place.

I drifted toward the edge of the patio, letting the skyline pull my attention. It was a little past eight.

A plane blinked red in the distance, angling toward the airport. I tried to imagine where it had come from. Orlando? Chicago? Didn't matter. It reminded me how much of the world I'd never seen.

Then the elevator chimed.

I turned casually. One glance. That's all it took.

Daniella stepped out of the elevator with a couple of other arriving guests, moving with that calm confidence that only comes with knowing you're stunning. No heels, no dress—just dark jeans, a slate-gray sweater that fit her perfectly, and knee-high boots that made no sound at all on the concrete. Her hair was pulled back in a high ponytail, same as the day at the park. I hadn't realized how much I liked it that way until now.

She scanned the crowd, spotted me, and came straight over—no hesitation, no awkwardness. Daniella being Daniella.

When she reached me, she smiled and leaned in. A quick hug. Warm. Familiar. No pretense.

"You look great, MacLaren," she said.

"So do you," I replied. "I'm glad you made it. I wasn't sure your project would let you go."

"It almost didn't," she said with a grin. "But I didn't want to miss our date."

Date? I didn't know what to say to that—but I was damn glad she was here. I just nodded and offered her a drink.

She took something simple—red wine, no fuss—and we found a quiet spot near one of the outdoor heaters.

"So, this is the famous City Lights rooftop," she said, looking around. "It's a beautiful place, but terrible neighborhood."

I nodded in agreement. "Did you have to walk far from your car?"

She smiled and looked out over the city. "No, Uber dropped me off at the door," she said, shooting me a side glance. "But we passed some pretty rough-looking areas."

"Yeah," I said. "It looks bad, and the homeless can be annoying, but they're mostly harmless."

We both looked out across the city without speaking for several seconds before Daniella stepped back from the rail and looked at me.

"Do you not enjoy parties?"

I took the last drink of my bourbon, meeting her eyes. "No. Hate them, actually."

"Then why come?"

"It's Graham's birthday. He's family, and he puts up with my antics the other 364 days a year."

She nodded to say she understood. Maybe she did.

"I almost didn't come either," she said quietly.

"Why not?"

She took a long sip of her wine before answering. "I don't do well in crowds. Too many people trying to figure out where you fit—asking questions I don't want to answer."

I looked at her. "Hiding secrets?"

She shrugged. "No, but I'm not from here, and people are curious. It's fine, but it gets old. You know what I mean?"

I didn't. I'd never been anywhere else, but I nodded anyway. "Well, you fake it well. You seem 100% Dayton to me."

"I'm Dayton now," she said simply.

I blinked but didn't respond.

"That's the trick," she added, turning back toward the skyline. "You only have to appear to belong, even if you don't."

I wanted to say something. Something that matched that moment. But all I could manage was a quiet, "Yeah."

She changed the subject for me.

"Your brother looks happy."

"He is. Rachel's good for him, and so is this party."

"And you?" she asked, catching me off guard.

"What about me?"

"Are you happy?"

I didn't answer. Not because I didn't want to—but because I didn't know.

That kind of question sits with you longer than it should. Happiness. What does that even mean? A good day on the job? A case that ends with a conviction instead of a corpse? A weekend where I remember to call my daughter?

I glanced at Daniella as she looked away—calm, composed, but not guarded. Not really. She had a way of saying hard things without sounding hard. That was rare. Most people, they either buried it deep or wore it like armor. Daniella just let it be.

Daniella excused herself to find the restroom, and Rachel nearly fell over running to me.

"Angus. Angus."

"What?"

"Why didn't you introduce us?" She gestured wildly toward the direction Daniella had walked. "She is gorgeous. I mean stop-the-clock gorgeous. Are you kidding me?"

I rubbed the back of my neck.

"She's a little uncomfortable in crowds," I said. "I was letting her finish her wine before the gauntlet."

Rachel grabbed my arm. "Okay, but you better bring her to me soon! And Angus—you cannot screw this up."

"I'll try not to."

"I'm serious. She's beautiful, she's vibrant, she's not scared of you, she could certainly take someone apart if she had to."

That last part made me laugh harder than I should've. But Rachel wasn't wrong. There was something in Daniella—beneath the easy smile and perfect posture—that said she could handle herself. I'd seen it in the way she scanned the crowd when she arrived. The way her eyes lingered a second too long on exits and faces. She may have been trained for something, a world I didn't know.

But maybe that's what drew me in. Maybe I didn't want soft anymore. Maybe I wanted someone who didn't flinch.

"You're ridiculous," I said.

"Uh-huh. And you're lucky."

She wandered off again before I could argue.

The rest of the night passed in a blur of noise and warm light. I finally introduced Daniella to Rachel, and they disappeared into the crowd for a while.

"Girl talk," Rachel said. I didn't ask.

Graham made a toast. Someone brought out a cake in the shape of a squad car. When Daniella rejoined me, she stayed close, but never clingy. She didn't hover. She just... was.

"I just love Rachel," she said. "She wants to do lunch sometime."

I bobbed my head. That was absolutely something Rachel would do. When I was dating Lena all those years ago, I'm pretty sure they were together more than Lena and I were.

As the night wore on, I found myself watching Daniella more than I should've. Noticing the way she moved. How she only spoke when she had something worth saying, and how people leaned in when she did. She wasn't built for the spotlight, but somehow the spotlight bent toward her anyway.

She didn't seem to be a drinker. Nursed the same glass of wine all night—more for appearances than the alcohol. I liked that. Confidence without artificial support. I've never been a drunk, but I've dated some. They're always more trouble than they're worth.

Around ten, she touched my arm lightly.

"I should get going."

"Already?"

"I have an early morning. But I'm glad I came."

"Me too."

She leaned in and kissed my cheek. Not rushed. Not possessive. Just real.

"Let me drive you home," I said as she stepped back.

"It's okay, MacLaren," she said. "My Uber app says I'll have a ride in less than three minutes. Call me tomorrow, okay?"

I nodded silently.

Then she was gone.

I stood there a long while after she left. Graham wandered over at one point, drink in hand.

"She's something," he said.

"Yeah."

"You good?"

"I don't know," I admitted. "Maybe."

He clapped me on the back and walked away.

Chapter 16
This is Our Shooter

Graham's party turned out to be a good time. No surprise there—spending time with Daniella was perfect—but catching up with old friends was unexpectedly refreshing. Social events aren't usually my scene. I get a lot of crap for being the introverted detective.

How the hell does that even work?

Beats me. But somehow, it does.

Anyway, the weekend had come and gone. I'd talked to Daniella a bit on the phone yesterday—hopefully I'd see her for lunch this week—but now, reality was back.

Time to get back to the job—Monday again.

I walked through the kitchen, grabbed my gun off the table and a fresh cup of thick, black coffee, then headed out to my old Crown Vic.

Graham met me at the office early this morning. We wanted to get out to Dorsey's house before he went anywhere. From checking social media, we thought he was unemployed but couldn't be sure. That meant no set schedule. We had to go check.

I pulled into the lot around 7:15 a.m., and Graham was already waiting.

"Good morning!" he said, opening the door and sliding into the passenger seat, tossing a black leather gear bag into the back like he was unloading laundry—or something that didn't matter much. "You ready to solve the crime of the century today?"

"I'm ready for breakfast," I said with a chuckle.

We pulled out of the lot, and headed toward the east end—but I wasn't going to Dorsey's quite yet. He could wait. First stop was Oscar's Diner. Tiny little place on Valley St. with the best biscuits and gravy in the city. Exactly what a tired cop needed before a long stakeout.

"Smithville's the other way," Graham said once he realized I'd turned off Third St. "Where are we going?"

"Oscar's," I said. "Biscuits and gravy before surveillance—it's the rule."

"Still an old street cop. Always looking for the next meal."

I just grinned.

"Rachel says Daniella's the one person who might finally civilize you. If she drags you to brunch instead of this dump, I'm not complaining."

I snorted. "Yeah, she already warned Daniella about me. Probably over lunch."

Graham laughed.

Oscar's was old school—linoleum floors, Formica tables, clanking forks on cheap ceramic, and the smell of bacon grease that had probably soaked into the walls decades ago. We didn't plan to linger—just enough time for two plates of biscuits and gravy and a refill to go.

I spotted someone across the room—alone, hunched over a three-egg omelet, another Oscar's specialty. Heavyset guy with a scruffy beard, flannel shirt, filthy ball cap pulled low.

Graham noticed too.

"Is that the guy from the pickup? At Dorsey's Saturday afternoon?"

I nodded. "Looks him."

We didn't approach. We watched him for a second while the waitress poured our coffee, but he never glanced around. He ate like a man with nothing on his mind. But that was the thing, wasn't it? The worst ones always seemed to have nothing on their mind. I'd learned that back in my first year in Homicide—monsters didn't grow horns. They melted into flannel shirts and kept their heads down.

These guys could sit right across from you in a diner, the clink of forks and the hiss of old grease covering whatever thoughts they were chewing on between bites.

Seeing him here, again, two days later? That wasn't random. It seemed the universe was nudging us—quietly, insistently—toward a man who didn't want to be found. You learn to listen to those nudges.

And it was a funny kind of coincidence, seeing him again. We didn't even have a name for him yet. We were a little concerned he might recognize Graham, but he never looked up. We ate and got back to the car without giving ourselves away. Dorsey and his pals would figure out who we were soon enough—but later would be better.

As I drove, Graham called Records to follow up on the questions we'd been tossing around since Saturday. Any BOLOs out on a purple van? I sort of drifted off. Tuned Graham out as he talked, but perked up when I heard him say, "Thanks, Carol. I appreciate you. This is exactly what we needed."

"Well?" I asked as he tossed his phone on the dash.

"The van is wanted," Graham said. "Hit a parked car while fleeing a traffic stop in Miamisburg. Friday night."

"That's great," I said. "So… is there a broadcast for Dorsey too?"

Graham scratched the top of his head. "That's the thing. The Miamisburg officer didn't get a good look at the driver—all he said was beard and a ball cap."

I exhaled. "That doesn't help us much."

"We can stop the van, though. That helps us."

Graham nodded as I pulled into the church lot—our second home lately.

"Also," Graham added, "Pickup's registered to a Sam Thornton. Forty-five years old, six-one, two-twenty-five. He our guy?"

I nodded. "It's him."

Looking up toward Dorsey's house, we could see the van was there. Breakfast hadn't cost us anything. Technically, we could've gone in and taken it without knocking—but we needed Dorsey. What we really needed was for him to get in the van and drive out onto the street. And even then, we'd hang back. He might take us to something bigger.

We didn't need any over-eager rookies stumbling across the van and messing up our surveillance, so I grabbed my phone and called the dispatch sergeant.

"Dispatch, Sergeant Tally."

"Good morning, Sarge," I said. "This is Detective MacLaren from Homicide. We're hoping for a little assistance."

"I'll try, MacLaren," he replied. "What do you need?"

"We're sitting on a van out on Smithville. It's wanted by Miamisburg for hit-and-run, but we need the driver for something else. Can you let patrol officers in the area know to stay clear? We don't want to spook him."

"No problem," Sergeant Tally said. "I'll get it out now."

"Thanks, Sarge," I said. "We'll let you know if we need a car to stop him."

I hung up the phone, hopeful—but not convinced the cops would stay away.

We sat in silence, watching the paint on Dorsey's house peel in the wind. Time slipped by like a crooked cop walking his beat. Sweating. Waiting. Knowing the call from Internal Affairs was coming.

One hour. Two hours. Three.

I was starting to get hungry again, but then—I saw it.

The old pickup rolled into the yard. Thornton. Same guy from the diner. He pulled up alongside the van and climbed out.

I smacked Graham's shoulder. "Movement. Grab the camera."

He reached back for the black gear bag and pulled it open. I don't know a thing about cameras, but this one had a long lens and looked expensive. Good enough for me.

As Graham snapped off a series of shots, I lifted the binoculars and watched Thornton unload several bags from the truck bed. He carried them straight to the back of the van.

Even from a distance, they sure as hell looked like rifle bags.

A couple of minutes after Thornton arrived, Dorsey came out the side door of the house and walked to the back of the van. He must've startled Thornton—he dropped the bag he was loading inside.

The two camo-clad men talked for a minute or two, then climbed into the back of the van and pulled the doors shut behind them.

"That's weird," I mumbled.

"Yeah," Graham said. "Maybe the driver's door doesn't work now that Dorsey wrecked it. They must be leaving."

I nodded, but before the van moved, the passenger-side door suddenly popped open. Thornton climbed out and headed to his truck.

A moment later, Dorsey began backing the van out of the yard and onto Smithville—facing south. Right at us.

As the van passed the church, Graham and I ducked low, hoping he hadn't seen us. Once he was clear, we pulled slowly into traffic behind him.

Graham grabbed his radio. "417 to Dispatch."

"Go ahead, 417."

"Our suspect is on the move. We're following a purple, 1994 Ford Econoline—Ohio plate XZQ9812—southbound on Smithville at E. Third. Driver is a possible homicide suspect. We are not stopping, just following. No backup needed at this time."

"Okay 417," the dispatcher replied. "Let me know if anything changes."

We followed Dorsey on Smithville until he merged onto US-35 West. He stayed on 35 for miles, eventually leaving the city and driving deep into the sparsely populated backwoods of the county.

Finally, he turned onto a narrow gravel lane, marked by a barely visible, weathered wooden sign:
Patriot Shooting Grounds – Private

"Damn," I muttered as I eased onto the gravel behind him. "It's private. And there's a gate."
"I'd love to know what he's shooting," Graham said. "But it's not a huge problem. We've got the active broadcast on the van. We wait him out, then have a crew stop him when he gets back into the city."

I nodded. "Seems to be our only play."

We found a place to park and wait close to the gravel entrance, but I needed to know more. Grabbing my phone from the seat next to me, I opened Google Earth and entered our location.

The satellite images revealed nearly a quarter mile of trees between the road and the open area of the range. I was sure this range was specifically for long-distance shooting. I didn't see any indicators of handgun lanes.

I turned to Graham and showed him my phone.
"This is a rifle range," I said. "This is our shooter."

It settled in my gut, bitter as cold coffee grounds. A private range, a quarter mile from the road, surrounded by trees, with nothing but a weathered sign and a padlocked gate to keep out the curious. This wasn't where someone came to plink soda cans. This was where you fine-tuned precision. Where you learned to wait. Where the wind became your partner, and patience your religion. A person doesn't stumble into long-distance shooting. They choose it. Commit to it. Train until pulling the trigger feels as natural as breathing. And that person doesn't just shoot for sport.

The excitement was building, but we waited.

Dorsey wasn't a danger to anyone on the range and letting him get back to the city before arresting him kept things simple.

Patience—that was the real weapon.

Two hours passed before we heard the tires of that old van crunching on gravel and heading our way. As Dorsey turned off the gravel lane and headed back toward the city, we held back a couple hundred yards—close enough to see him, far enough not to be seen.

Graham picked up his radio once again.

"417 to Dispatch."

"Go ahead, 417."

"Our suspect is on the move again. We're heading back into the city and need to get this guy stopped. Can we get some crews to wait for us around Third and Liscum?"

"417, what's your ETA?"

"We're coming from the west—should be there in five minutes. He's driving the same purple van from this morning. Also, this is a violent felony suspect. Crews must approach accordingly."

"We're clear, 417. Cars are en route."

A couple minutes later, we were approaching the city limits. Up ahead, we could see the marked cruisers already in position. I dropped back a bit more to give them room to maneuver.

As Dorsey passed Liscum, two cruisers pulled out and fell in behind the van. Farther ahead, two more units waited at Third and Gettysburg. Dorsey was boxed in. Hopefully, he realized that and wouldn't do anything stupid.

The lead cruiser lit up its overheads—and Dorsey hit the brakes immediately. No hesitation. No panic. He seemed to know it was for him, even with a dozen other cars on the block.

He pulled quickly to the curb and stopped.

The cruisers behind him swung wide, blocking both eastbound lanes. The units at Gettysburg moved in fast, sealing the front.

Officers jumped out, patrol rifles up, staying behind their open doors. Every weapon was trained on the purple van.

The lead officer keyed his cruiser PA. "Driver of the van—exit the vehicle with your hands in the air! Down on the ground, now!"

I braced for resistance. For something to go sideways. But Dorsey stepped out calmly, hands high. He dropped to his knees, then onto his stomach, just as he was told. Not a word. Not a twitch. A man completely sure of his innocence.

I'd seen that same stillness before—in shooters who already made peace with what came next. It wasn't arrogance; it was belief. And belief is always more dangerous than fear.

That stillness… it unsettled me.

Most suspects panic. They curse, stall, run. Their bodies betray them long before their words do.

But not Dorsey. His behavior was that of a man who wasn't afraid of what came next.

It wasn't arrogance, exactly—it was confidence. And that was worse. I'm uneasy when a suspect is too calm. It means they know something I didn't.

Or thought they did.

Textbook felony stop—Dayton gets too much practice.

Once Dorsey was cuffed and the scene was secure, Graham and I pulled forward, finally stepping into the chaos to meet our shooter.

Chapter 17
The Man with the Rifle

The young officer stood near the rear of his cruiser, pale and jittery. Adrenaline was the only thing keeping him upright—dazed by the rush of what was probably his first felony stop. His hand rested near his holstered Glock, as though he thought Dorsey might explode out of the back seat, sudden as a snake striking from the brush.

He bounced nervously from foot to foot as Graham and I approached.

"Everything okay?" I asked, watching as he let out a breath—relieved, it seemed, that someone else was there.

"Yes, sir!" he replied—too quickly, and too loud. "He hasn't been any trouble. Threw his keys on the ground before we even got out of our cars. Real polite. Real weird."

Graham raised his eyebrows and glanced at me. "That's definitely not what we expected."

I nodded toward Graham but answered the officer. "We had him pegged as a sovereign citizen. That kills that idea."

"Yeah," Graham said with a laugh. "If he was one of those nuts, you'd still be out here arguing with him."

I checked my watch. It was pushing 3 o'clock. We needed to wrap this up.

"Officer, take him to the second floor and put him in one of the interview rooms. Just sit outside and wait. We won't be long."

"Yes, sir," he said. "I'll head up now."

As the officer drove away, Graham and I turned our attention to the van.

"Okay, Graham," I said. "Let's find that smoking gun."

Graham laughed out loud. "Literally."

I pulled open back door of the van, which the uniform guys had left ajar after checking for hidden passengers, and there it was—lying across the floor in a long black rifle case.

Our murder weapon.

I had absolutely no doubts, and I could barely contain my excitement.

Tomorrow was CompStat, and now we'd walk in with everything we needed to shut the brass up.

I carefully tugged the soft case toward the door, positioning it so I could reach the zipper. Slowly, I eased it open—around the end, then along the front—until Dorsey's tool of death lay exposed.

The rifle was a thing of beauty—and of purpose. Sleek. Black. Maintained with a reverence most men reserve for family heirlooms. It was clear Dorsey loved this weapon—took better care of it than his van, maybe even his house.

I pulled a pair of blue nitrile gloves from my jacket pocket and stretched them across my hands. I always grab a few extras from medics when I can.

With gloved hands, I gently lifted the rifle from the case and began to examine it—solid, heavy, purposeful.

And there it was, clear as day, engraved on the receiver: .338 Lapua Magnum.

"Graham!" I yelled, surprising even myself with the excitement in my voice as I pointed to the receiver. ".338!"

Graham dropped both hands to the floor of the old van and shook his head, grinning like a man crossing the finish line.

"I can't believe this is finally over."

I knew where he was coming from—and for a second, I wanted to believe it too. We had a rifle. A serious one. Right caliber, right vibe. It should've been enough.

But I'd worked too many cases to trust the feeling. Big breaks had a way of breaking you right back.

We searched the rifle case. Dug through every one of the bags Thornton had tossed in the back. Checked under the front seats. The glove box.

Nothing.

Just two unopened boxes of .338 Lapua ammunition. No notes. No targets. No maps or articles clipped from the paper. Nothing that connected Dorsey to anything but a love of precision shooting. And the clock was ticking. CompStat was coming fast, and if this didn't stick, we'd be walking in empty-handed.

No shell casings. No plan. No proof.

After we searched every inch of the van and came up empty, I finally waved over a couple of uniforms and handed them the rifle and ammo.

"Get this tagged into the property room right away," I said. "I want it there before they close—and let Sergeant Clarkson know it came from the sniper suspect. Lab needs it first thing tomorrow."

One of the officers took the rifle, his grip careful, as if it might fire on its own. The other glanced at the receiver and let out a low whistle.

".338 Lapua," he said. "Is that a Barrett? That'll punch through an engine block."

"It is," I muttered. "But yeah—let's hope it can punch through this case too."

"Better get going, guys," I said.

"Copy that, Detective. We're on it."

"Thanks, guys," I said. "I owe you a beer. Hell, I owe you both a case if this turns out to be the one."

As the officers drove away with our only clues, Graham and I stared at each other for a moment—letting the weight of the stop and our deep, burning need to make some progress ease off of our shoulders, if only for a second.

"We need to get back," I said to Graham as I removed the nitrile gloves and stuffed them into a back pocket. "There's a patrol officer here. He'll tow the van for us, so we can get to Dorsey."

Graham said nothing, but quickly walked to the remaining cruiser and spoke to the officer through the driver's window. I headed back to our car, finally taking a moment to look at my phone. Three missed calls—one from Sarge, a couple from unknown numbers, and a text from Daniella: "Hi." It didn't matter. Nothing did.

I sucked in the cold night air and let it out slow before sliding into the seat. The air scraped down my throat as rough as sandpaper. I felt stripped raw, like I'd left pieces of myself back in that van. The car door thudded shut behind me—the sound of a coffin lid closing on an old, forgotten truth.

I had just closed my eyes for a moment of reflection when the passenger door was ripped open and Graham slammed into the car with the force of a bomb. I must've dozed off, because I jumped. I was ready to fight.

"Let's roll, brother!" he yelled. "Time to get our confession!"

I couldn't help but laugh. I don't think I've ever had that much energy at work, but he was right. We needed a confession, and the clock was ticking. I drove around the van and lone cruiser, heading toward downtown. Dorsey was waiting to tell us everything. All we had to do was ask. I was sure of it—though somewhere under that certainty, a splinter of doubt stayed lodged, sharp and cold.

Arriving on the second floor, I was relieved to see our transport officer there, sitting uncomfortably in a hard folding chair outside Interview Room 3. Dorsey was locked away, waiting patiently to hang himself.

I paused briefly as I reached the officer.

"We've got a couple calls to make," I said. "Then we'll be right back. Hang tight for a minute."

The officer nodded and offered a whispered, "Yes, sir."

I really just needed to make one call. Sergeant Jenkins was heading into the hell of CompStat with us in the morning, and he needed to know what was going on. He didn't answer, but this wasn't something for voicemail. I left a message letting him know I'd call back.

Graham had slipped off to the restroom, so I grabbed a bottle of water and sat for a couple of minutes. It had been an adrenaline-filled day, and I was drained. Every muscle screamed, the weight of a bus and the drag of a marathon stacked on top of me.

When Graham made it back to the office, we walked down to the interview room. The rookie officer was glad to see us, but that was short-lived. We couldn't let him leave—not yet. One way or the other, Dorsey had to be transported. Hopefully, straight to the jailhouse.

"Hang in there," I said. "I know how it is, but you're part of a huge case so take it all in."

I handed him a bottle of water and looked at Graham.

"Graham," I said. "I've got this, but I want you in the other room. I want both of us hearing this confession."

Graham knew how I worked. Without a word, he started toward the observation room. I took another drink of my water, then set the bottle down on the table next to the door. For a second, I thought about the glitter-covered drawing sitting on my desk at home. Penny's stick-figure sun and her crooked little smile. A reminder of why this case had to break our way.

Then I walked into the room, closed the door, and greeted Dorsey with a grin straight out of grade school friendship. The room was standard issue—gray walls, one table, three chairs. No décor, nothing to distract or comfort.

"Mr. Dorsey," I said as I sat down in the chair next to him. "I am Detective MacLaren. Do you need anything? Water? Coffee?"

"No sir," he replied. "I'm good, but thank you."

I nodded, pretended to look at notes in my binder, then looked Dorsey in the eyes. "Mr. Dorsey, do you know why you're here?"

Dorsey lowered his head, and closed his eyes for a second. "I do, Detective," he began. "And I'm really embarrassed by it, but I really didn't think it was a huge deal."

That startled me a little. This guy is more cold-hearted than his pleasant demeanor says about him. I raised my eyebrows, paused for a moment, then said, "Not a huge deal?"

Dorsey shook his head side to side, then with a mild grimace, he replied, "Detective MacLaren, you have to believe me. I've never done anything like this before. I was with friends at that basement bar in Miamisburg, The King's Crypt or something. I had a few beers, and when I left, cops got behind me."

I continued listening to Dorsey, but I was shocked he believed this was about his traffic indiscretion.

"I did it," he continued. "I ran. I didn't want a DUI and I ran, and hit somebody's car."

I blinked. *Did he really think he was taken down by four cops with rifles over a hit-and-run?*

For a moment, I wasn't sitting across from a cold-eyed killer—I was listening to a guy in traffic court. Dorsey put both hands over his face and began sobbing—more baby than grown man.

"Mr. Dorsey!" I said, but there was no response. "Mr. Dorsey!" I said again. This time he looked up, but said nothing.

"Mr. Dorsey," I began. "You're right—your van was wanted for that hit-and-run, but we need to talk about something else. Something a lot more serious."

His eyes opened wide and he sat up a bit straighter.

"Tell me about the rifle we found in your van."

"My…my rifle?" Dorsey replied. "My rifle is legal. Why are you asking me about that?"

"What caliber is your rifle?" I asked, turning another page in my notebook, letting him wonder if I held the keys to every lie he'd told.

"It's a .338 Lapua," he said. "I love long-range shooting, and that round is amazing."

His fingers twitched slightly as he said it—barely a tremor, but enough to catch my eye.

I nodded my head and scribbled on my pad. "Is that why you were at the range this morning?"

"Yes, sir," he replied. "I've been a member there for years, go a couple times a week. It's expensive as hell to shoot .338, but it's my favorite thing in the world."

"Mr. Dorsey," I began, but paused as I looked him in the eyes. "Shooting at the range is a lot of fun, I get that. But what I need to know about is the other times you have fired this gun."

"I'm not following, detective." Dorsey said. "My rifle stays locked up unless I'm at the range. Did my neighbors say something? They're all assholes."

"No, of course not," I said. "What do you know about the two men killed over the last couple of weeks? One guy on Pruden Avenue – shot in the chest from long range, and another guy on Lexington Avenue – again, shot in the chest from long range."

Dorsey's eyes went as wide as quarters, and he slapped both hands down on his lap.

"Oh, shit!" he yelled. "You guys think I'm that sniper! Oh, hell no, Detective! I swear, I've never shot anything but a steel target at the range. My daddy was a cop. I grew up respecting the law and respecting people. Please, sir—believe me! It wasn't me!"

I wanted to believe him. Hell, part of me did. But something didn't fit. Not yet. And if it didn't fit now, it might tear wide open later.

The interview continued for about ninety minutes. Dorsey repeated the same claims again and again—his rifle was legal, only used at the range, and he had no connection to the shootings. There were no signs of hesitation or deception, no cracks in his story. Eventually, we knew we'd reached the end of the line.

I stepped out and called the Miamisburg PD.

"Evening. Detective Angus MacLaren, Dayton Homicide. I've got someone here who just confessed to a hit-and-run in your city. First name Keith, last name Dorsey. He admitted to leaving The King's Crypt bar a few nights ago and crashing into a parked car."

The detective on the other end sounded surprised but quickly interested.

"Hold him," he said. "We'll fax over the paperwork for a warrant. We've been looking for the owner of that van. If he's admitted it, we want him."

"Appreciate it," I replied. "He's yours—for tonight. We'll be wanting him back soon."

Chapter 18
Cracks in the System

Tuesday morning's CompStat hit with the force of waves crashing against a rocky shore—inevitable, unstoppable, and just as punishing. The first-floor conference room smelled old and moldy—cheap carpet and a dollar store air freshener failing at their best attempts to hide it. Graham and I sat shoulder to shoulder beside Sergeant Jenkins, *while the brass, all six of them, lined the far end of the table—buzzards circling overhead.* Nobody said much. We didn't have to. Everyone in that room knew the next body could drop any day.

Chief Robertson sat at the head of the table, trying to appear better than the rest of us—as usual. Next to him was Assistant Chief Carpenter, my old workout partner in the academy. He was drinking a cup of coffee and giving Graham a hard time about being a Browns fan. Major Trammell from Violent Crimes was there too. And as always, he sat there stone-faced, pretending to be the hard-ass he would never be. The other three majors—Simpson, Bradley, and Jameson—ran admin units and looked annoyed to be there.

Carpenter, tapping his pen with the beat of a metronome, was the first to speak. "We heard about the arrest. Walk us through it—is he our shooter?"

Jenkins looked at me, then at Graham, before turning back toward Carpenter. He cleared his throat. "Yes, sir. Yesterday, after a lengthy investigation and stakeout, my detectives stopped and arrested one Keith Dorsey. A single long-range rifle was recovered from his van—confirmed on scene as a .338. He was detained without incident. Dorsey is currently in the county jail on a detainer out of Miamisburg, pending ballistics."

Major Trammell looked over his glasses, "Detainer from Miamisburg? What the hell does that mean? Why isn't he locked up on our murder charges?"

Jenkins was clearly uncomfortable with the aggression from Trammell and was stumbling to reply.

I cut in—something usually frowned upon in these high-stakes meetings, but Jenkins didn't seem to mind losing the spotlight. He shot me a sideways glance, but he didn't stop me. We'd been through worse storms than this one together. He knew when to let the leash out—and when to yank it back.

"I won't be the guy pushing half a puzzle," I added. "Believe me, I'd love nothing more than to have walked in here this morning and set the case file on the table with a big-ass bow on it. But that's not where we're at."

"So no confession. No evidence."

"Major, we think he may be our guy, but we don't have the proof to pin it on him—yet," I said. "He's denying everything—he's offered plausible alibis—but his rifle matches the murder caliber, and he frequents a long-range shooting range. We're still waiting on the lab, and we'll be checking those alibis right after this meeting, but he looks good for this."

Major Trammell smiled with the arrogance he was known for. "So, just a hunch then?"

"No, sir. It's not a hunch—it's the pattern, the caliber, the timing, but we haven't nailed the proof down yet," I replied. "We don't have probable cause yet, but certainly more than reasonable suspicion. Everything about this guy screams shooter."

Robertson looked up from his binder and directly at me with the stare of an executioner. A moment later, he spoke. "Detective, I appreciate your belief that this guy is the shooter, but what if he's not? Are you going to continue investigating other leads until you know? Or are you so confident that you're going to Hawaii?"

"Sir, I packed swim trunks this morning," I said with a smirk before continuing, "But seriously, sir, I believe Dorsey is a strong suspect, but neither I, nor Graham or even Sergeant Jenkins, would ever end an investigation until we know. We'll keep digging until we all know. The last thing we want is to walk away now and read about another body tomorrow morning."

Robertson nodded as if he understood but said nothing else. Carpenter looked to the other commanders, asking if anyone else had any questions. With no response, he looked back to Jenkins.

"Sergeant," he began. "We appreciate the work your unit has been doing, and we all really hope you have our guy. Thank you all for attending this morning. The rest of the meeting is unrelated, so you are all free to go."

As we stood, Jenkins whispered, "Well, that could've gone worse."

Graham muttered, "Only because they haven't heard about the lab delay yet."

I raised my eyebrows at that comment, but Graham had already walked away.

After the CompStat meeting, we all went in different directions to take care of things that continued to pile up on us. I had lunch at the little deli on the corner—BLT with chips, while Graham went to an 11 a.m. meeting with the prosecutor. We met back at the car around 12:30 pm and went to follow up on a shooting over on Wayne Avenue. We talked to a couple witnesses. Checked a business camera that pointed straight up. Headed back with nothing but aching feet.

It was early afternoon by the time we were all back in the office. The Safety Building was usually quiet in the afternoon, making it a great time to get paperwork knocked out. I could hear a few phones ringing in the distance, and the occasional burst of cussing from the copier room bouncing through the halls, a loose round ricocheting without a target. The room felt muted, the building acting as a giant suppressor. Graham and I were sitting at our desks—not really working yet but working up to it. That post-CompStat hangover always hit harder than expected—adrenaline withdrawal with a side of caffeine crash.

Jenkins had slipped into his office, door and blinds shut, pretending to check emails. More likely, he was hiding from the drama. Jeffries and Koski were at their desks across the room. Doing the same as the rest of us—killing time. The glamor of being a detective.

I had just started typing up my supplemental report for the shooting when my phone rang.

"MacLaren."

"Angus, it's Chris from the lab." His voice sounded tired—frustrated after hours fighting a battle he knew he'd never win.

"What's up, Chris?"

He sighed. "I told Graham last night the firearms lab might be out of service. It's official now. Engineers found a crack running from ceiling to floor and ordered us out. We can't safely use the firing chamber."

"Shit," I muttered.

"They're going to try to stabilize the wall, but the crack is growing and the wall is starting to bulge. We will not be testing anything until at least the end of the week. Could be longer."

I stood up and walked toward the window overlooking the parking lot between our buildings. The sky had gone gray again, the kind that made the rooftops look tired and the alleys seem narrower. That rifle was our only thread. If it didn't match, fine—we'd move on. But if it did, it tied him to everything.

"What about outsourcing?" I asked. "Can we ship the rifle to another lab?"

"Columbus and Cincinnati have both offered to help, but they're buried right now. Much bigger cities, with significantly more crime. It could take two weeks, a month, maybe more to turn around. We're checking a private lab, but you know how slow procurement moves."

"Son of a bitch."

"I'm sorry, Angus. I know you need this one."

"Yeah," I said. "Yeah, we really do."

I didn't throw the phone. Didn't curse the ceiling. I stood there, letting the cold gray sky look back at me. I ended the call and stood there for a moment, watching as a garbage truck squeezed past an illegally parked panel van below. Graham glanced up from his desk.

"That sounded like bad news."

"A wall in the firearms lab is collapsing, they've been kicked out. We're not getting ballistics on Dorsey's rifle—at least not anytime soon," I said. "Could be a week, maybe more. Nobody's touching our rifle until the wall gets fixed."

He cursed under his breath.

Jeffries looked over and said, "Figures. First guy we get close to, and the damn building gives out before he does."

Jenkins' door creaked open just and he stepped out, holding a cup of coffee that I'm sure had been around since cops used call boxes.

"Everything alright?" he asked.

"Not even close," I said. "The firearms lab is out of service until who knows when, and the other large labs in the state can't help. We will not have confirmation on Dorsey's rifle anytime soon."

Jenkins rubbed his forehead. "Fantastic."

I turned back to my desk. Already planning how we'd break it to the majors if another body dropped while we were sitting on our hands. We needed something solid to hold Dorsey. Otherwise, we were going to lose him.

About an hour later, my phone buzzed again—this time a number I recognized: Miamisburg PD.

"MacLaren."

"Hey, Detective. This is Sergeant Fields from Miamisburg. Calling about your guy, Dorsey."

I closed my laptop and leaned forward. "Yeah, go ahead."

"We're dropping the detainer."

My heart dropped.

"What?"

"Our prosecutor wants him ordered in. The damage was minimal and no injuries, and it's obviously too late for a blood test, so, we have no choice."

"You're kidding me."

"Wish I was. If you've got something, put it on him now. Otherwise, we'll be processing his release within the hour."

I didn't respond right away. I wanted to scream. To throw the phone against the wall. Instead, I thanked him for the call, hung up, and looked over at Graham.

"He's getting out."

Graham blinked. "Already?"

"Unless we file something right now—and we can't. There's nothing. No confession, no murder warrant, and nothing in the van that could stick. Without ballistics, he was just a guy with a gun."

Jenkins came out of his office again. "What now?"

I filled him in, and for a moment, nobody said a word. The only noise was the hum of the overhead lights and the hollow tap of Koski's keyboard in the corner.

Then Jenkins cleared his throat, letting the silence hang long enough to make everyone shift in their seats.

"Fine," he said. "Let him walk. But keep him close—we're not done with him."

Not by a long shot.

Chapter 19
Dead Ends and Deli Sandwiches

My Thursday morning started off hectic. A trial was beginning on a three-year-old stabbing case, and I was scheduled to testify. I spent more than two hours in a courthouse conference room waiting for my turn when the judge finally recessed for lunch.

With a sigh of relief, I headed out for something to eat—maybe a hot dog from the cart over on Second Street. I checked my watch—11:30 a.m. Maybe Daniella was on lunch break too.

I pulled my phone from inside my jacket pocket and sent her a brief text.

Hey, I'm on break from court for lunch. Want to grab a bite?

Less than a second later, my phone vibrated.

Great timing, MacLaren. Heading across to the college cafeteria. Wanna go?

Yep. Where R U?

Meet me outside the Third St. entrance.

On my way!

Apparently, every judge in the courthouse recessed at the same time. I pushed through the crowd—it would have been easier to move through the pit at a rock concert—and made it to the security line to retrieve my gun.

I burst out the front door like a robber fleeing a heist. I didn't find a getaway car, but I did spot Daniella, waiting with an amused smirk on her face.

"Have a little trouble, MacLaren?"

"Nah, I love crowds," I said with a laugh.

Daniella grabbed my right hand. "Let's go. I'm starving."

That was new. We'd been hanging around a bit, but holding hands? That was an escalation—and I was all for it.

Her hand was soft. Warm. Firm. But there was assurance there—a calm certainty that said she'd done this a hundred times before. Daniella was in control.

I went along to see what happened next, and I couldn't be happier.

I didn't say anything. Just followed her down the street

***

The cafeteria was half full but buzzing with the low, constant murmur of students, staff, and a few stragglers in business clothes who'd wandered over from the government buildings across the street. We grabbed trays, sliding past the various options—stir fry, pizza, cheesesteaks, and a soup & sandwich bar. Daniella chose a bowl of tomato bisque and a grilled cheese. I went with the chicken wrap and a bottle of iced tea.

We paid, then moved past the crowd toward the far corner of the dining area, where a small table sat by the windows, mostly out of earshot.

She nodded toward the spot. "Looks quiet."

We sat. Daniella tucked one leg beneath her and pulled the soup close, dunking the corner of her sandwich with easy comfort. The smell of garlic drifted over from the pizza station. Somewhere nearby, a student-employee was gathering dirty dishes, the clatter of ceramic plates lost in the hum of cafeteria conversation. Across the table, Daniella blew gently across her soup, fascinated by the swirling red surface. I took a sip of my tea and leaned back slightly, watching her for a second. Calm, collected, seemingly unaffected by the chaos of downtown courtrooms and traffic.

"This your usual spot?" I asked.

"More or less," she said, glancing out the window. "I love to get out of the courthouse for lunch, and it's an easy walk. And nobody bothers me here. Food is good too!"

I nodded. Apparently the food was prepared by students studying to be chefs, so they did their best, showing off their skills.

We ate in awkward silence for a few minutes. I watched the way she dipped her sandwich with the same deliberate motion each time, even her lunch followed some kind of internal rhythm. It was oddly comforting.

Eventually, I broke the quiet. "I think I remember you mentioned once you moved here after getting married. Did I hear that correctly?"

She didn't answer right away. Just took another bite, chewed, swallowed. Then she leaned back and wiped her fingers on a napkin.

"Yeah. I was married," she said. "Divorced now."

I nodded slowly, not sure how much I should say. "Sorry to hear that."

She shrugged. "It was a long time coming. We stay close though."

"Close with your ex-husband?"

"Yeah, Ben Levine. He's a good man, but not the right one for me—not long term, anyway. But I owe him a lot. He's the reason I'm here. He brought me to Dayton."

I didn't know what I expected, maybe something simpler—a college sweetheart or a green card fling. But I didn't see this coming. She wasn't passing through Dayton. She'd made roots here, because of someone else.

I studied her face for a second. She didn't seem sad. No trace of bitterness. Just fond memories.

"He still in Dayton?" I asked.

She smiled faintly. "Yeah, he's here. Training to be an Orthodox rabbi."

I blinked. "Really? A rabbi?"

She laughed softly. "Yeah. Not what you expected?"

"Honestly? No. But hey, maybe I don't know you as well as I think I do."

Her eyes flicked up, sharp and unreadable for a moment. "Maybe you don't."

Something in her tone pinged faintly in the back of my mind—cop instinct, the kind that whispers *pay attention*. But before I could think on it, she softened again.

"Ben's at a synagogue here in Dayton. We don't talk all the time, but… sometimes. When it matters."

I nodded. "Sounds like one of those rare clean breaks."

"It wasn't clean," she said, tearing a napkin in half. "Took a long time to get it right. Weeks we didn't talk."

She paused briefly, dipping another piece of sandwich in her soup before adding quietly, "Then weeks we didn't stop. It's weird how grief and gratitude can sit at the same table and not argue. But it was honest. That's something, right?"

I didn't have a good answer for that, so I let the question hang.

A group of students laughed too loud at the next table, snapping the spell. Daniella glanced over her shoulder, then returned her gaze to me.

"You ever married?" she asked.

"Yeah. Once. Long time ago. Didn't stick."

"Kids?"

"Yeah. One. Penny. She's five."

She smiled at that. "You get to see her much?"

Her smile had changed—softer, with a trace of longing. I wasn't sure if it was about kids, or memories, or something else entirely. But it was honest. For the first time in that lunch, I wasn't sure who was holding whose hand.

"Not as much as I want," I said. "But that's on me and this damn job. Lena's great and lets me see Penny whenever I want, or can."

"Bet she's got you wrapped around her finger."

"She could ask for the moon and I'd start building a ladder."

Daniella laughed again—genuine this time. "Sounds about right."

We finished eating in silence, the kind that felt easy now rather than awkward. Outside, the clouds had started to shift, enough light cutting through to brighten the sidewalk. Daniella stood and picked up her tray.

"I've got to head back. You?"

"Yeah," I said, standing with her. "Back to the courtroom to wait."

We dropped off our trays and stepped back into the soft noise of the cafeteria.

As we reached the door, she slowed and looked at me.

"Thanks for lunch, MacLaren."

"Anytime," I said. And meant it.

She hesitated, just a breath, then leaned in and kissed me on the cheek—quick, firm, and confident. The kind of kiss that said: this wasn't the start of something… but maybe it was the middle.

Then she turned, grabbed my hand again, and began walking toward the courthouse. The breeze had picked up and was stirring the hem of her coat and sending flakes of snow dancing across the sidewalk: shattered dreams, haunting the edges of a new life.

I stood there a moment longer than I should've, the warmth of her kiss lingering on my cheek as an echo I couldn't quite name.

***

I got back to the office around 2:30, dropped my coat over the back of my chair, and poked my head into Jenkins' office to check in. Then I collapsed into my seat with a long, loud sigh.

I was glad to be out of court—but it was a temporary reprieve. The prosecutor had burned half the morning grandstanding with an expert, so I'd be back tomorrow.

I looked over at Graham's desk, buried in case files. Half a sub and a few chips teetered near the edge, threatening to join the unopened bottle of Coke Zero already rolling around on the floor.

"Hey Graham," I said. "You okay over there?"

He looked up, a bit startled. Then, shaking himself awake, he rubbed his eyes with the back of his hand.

"So, court done for the day?"

I grimaced and shook my head. "Yeah, but time management wasn't exactly a priority. I've got to go back in the morning. It's a long enough of a break to remind me what I'm missing here."

"That sucks," Graham said with a laugh. "Guess I'll catch this lunatic myself then."

"Yeah, whatever," I replied with a chuckle. "At least I had nice company for lunch today—maybe tomorrow too."

Jeffries spun around in his chair. "Daytime dating? Didn't think you had it in you, Angus."

Before I could answer, Koski looked up from the case file that had his attention. "If it was that Carol from Records again, I'm calling HR."

I smirked. "No, it wasn't Carol, although she is kinda cute. It was a sandwich and some small talk with a friend."

Graham snorted. "You only have one friend. Well, besides me. How is Daniella anyway?"

Jeffries raised a brow. "Daniella? The court reporter? A sandwich with a beautiful woman, I'm calling that a date." Pointing a pen in my direction, he continued, "Tell her she can do better—but also that we'll need her transcripts when this trial drags out another month."

I didn't answer. Just smiled to myself, the memory of her hand in mine fresh enough to feel.

The room quieted again, letting in the background noise from the hallway—phones ringing, the copier clunking, dying for the hundredth time, keys jingling on some patrol officer's overloaded belt. Why do cops always have so many damn keys?

Graham leaned back in his chair and cleared his throat.

"Since we're screwed on the rifle right now, why don't we check out Dorsey's alibis? We should be able to knock them out before quitting time."

I looked up at the clock. It was closing in on 3:00 p.m.

"Why not?" I said. "It's not like we're getting much done in here."

Graham grabbed a file from somewhere on his desk and started flipping through the documents.

Koski spun around in his chair. "What's the latest on the lab? You'd think a lab that important would've had that shit fixed by now, or at least a backup plan." He shook his head. "Apparently nobody is concerned this guy might be out there planning another one."

"You'd think," Graham said. "But they're not even guessing anymore—they're calling it indefinite."

Koski raised his eyebrows but said nothing. I pushed out of my chair and stepped toward the door.

"Come on, little brother. If we're gonna do this, let's get moving."

Every hour we wasted, the odds of a body showing up and getting us another ass-chewing went up. That's how it felt anyway.

Graham nodded, but didn't move.

We'd done our share of legwork on this guy already, but the edges hadn't sharpened. Now we were hoping his alibis would crack instead of hold.

"First one's that 24-hour pawn shop out on Valley. Says he was looking for reloading supplies—primers and brass. No receipt, no timestamp. Just says he talked to the owner."

"Turner's?" I asked.

"Yeah."

I rolled my eyes. "That guy barely remembers what he ate for breakfast."

"Right. He told me Dorsey's a regular. Was probably there if he said he was."

"A lot of damn good that does us then," I said with exasperation. "Cameras or something to help us out?"

"Apparently," Graham replied. "But he's kind of an ass. He said if we want to check for Dorsey, we gotta do it ourselves. So here we are, going to look at film."

I rubbed my forehead. "Okay. What about number two?"

"Second shooting—he says he was at his cousin Eli's house in Kettering, drinking beer and watching the game. Three people were there."

"They all vouch for him?"

"Haven't been able to reach Eli. His cousin Kyle says Dorsey showed up around dinner and hung out most of the night, playing cards. Of course, he also said he had been drinking a lot and it may have been their other cousin Terry that was there. The third cousin, Clarence, is in jail in Hamilton County. I'm not sure he was even there. He was arrested the next day, so I guess he could have been."

I leaned back and stared at the ceiling. "So we've got two maybe alibis, full of holes that we can't fill?"

"Yep."

I stood. "Grab your shovel, let's go see if we can fill them in."

Graham was already grabbing his coat. "Pawn shop first?"

I nodded. "Then Kettering. Let's hear it in their own words."

As we passed Jenkins' door, I knocked twice and cracked it open.

"We're heading out to check Dorsey's alibis," I said.

He looked up from behind a stack of reports. "You find something?"

"No," I replied. "And that's the problem."

He waved us off. "Keep me posted."

We stepped into the hallway. The antique fluorescent lights buzzed and flickered overhead like the set of a cheap horror film. Outside, snow fell again—big, lazy flakes that didn't know whether to land or vanish.

"I swear," I muttered, pulling my hat down closer to my ears, "if this guy walks and we get another body…"

Graham finished the sentence for me. "Then we'll be the ones getting roasted at the next CompStat."

We didn't speak again until we reached the car. That silence between us wasn't unusual—it was two detectives doing math in their heads, hoping the next stop wasn't a crime scene. The wind picked up just enough to remind us of the cold. Somewhere behind us, a siren wailed, low and distant. We kept walking.

We spent the next few hours working to break Dorsey's alibis—with little to show for it. The pawn shop cameras were working, technically—but the date and time stamps were frozen somewhere in 2018. We scrubbed through about an hour of footage and, sure enough, Dorsey showed up a few times. But without a reliable timestamp, it didn't prove a thing.

His cousin wasn't much help either. Eli answered the door glassy-eyed and reeking of weed. "Yeah, ol' Dorsey was here, man. He's here every day. In fact, you just missed him—he was here all night."

Which was interesting, considering Dorsey spent the night in the jailhouse.

Neither alibi held water—not enough to confirm, not enough to disprove.

Chapter 20
The Cost of Doing it Right

From here, the view up to the bus stop on Third—200 yards out, an easy shot for the Barrett MRAD—was flat, clear, and wide open. It was the perfect set-up for what had to happen when the 5:00 p.m. bus rolled in, bringing Travis Ledbetter the justice he'd earned.

Getting here had been a nightmare. They'd been trying to find him for weeks, but he didn't drive, didn't leave a trail, just drifted through the dirty side streets of Dayton like some long-forgotten ghost out of a deep Appalachian hollow—half-real, half-rumor.

They couldn't knock on doors and ask for him. Secrecy was crucial. So they patrolled the neighborhoods, scrolled endlessly through social media, and trailed old friends and girlfriends—waiting for something, anything, to spring loose.

And then it did.

They found his mother.

And she was sick.

Public records revealed her identity. Her own social media—a weakness he hadn't accounted for—announced the diagnosis: stage-four liver cancer.

He'd always been a momma's boy—and now his momma was dying.

The son would visit her—sure as taxes and sunrise. Finding her home meant finding him. A few keystrokes on a library computer, and there it was: 47 S. Horton Street.

Once they had the address, it took less than 48 hours. He walked right up to the house, another loving son—not the cartel's face of east Dayton meth.

The excitement and adrenaline rushed through their body—but precision demanded restraint.

Act without a plan, and you fail. They let him live that first day. And the second. And the third.

They learned everything they needed to get it right.

Every day at 5 p.m. sharp, he stepped off bus number 6, and walked half a block down S. Horton to his mother's house—same path, same timing. One hour later, he was back on Third Street, catching the next bus west.

Every single day.

After three days of watching and planning, Ledbetter's day of judgment had arrived.

It was early—a bit after 6:00 a.m.—when they turned onto N. Horton Street from E. Third. Arriving before sunrise added another layer of concealment. One more barrier against any curious eyes still awake.

The shooter watched the houses on N. Horton Street for nearly an hour before slipping into the back of the van, vanishing as the first light crept across the driver's seat. They settled in for the long wait. No reading. No phone. No distractions. Only silence, observation, and the occasional sip of lukewarm coffee to steady the edge.

Each visit over the past few days, they parked in this same spot, at the same time. Same routine. Arrive early. Avoid detection. Wait for hours. Watch Ledbetter exit the bus, walk to his mother's house, then return an hour later and vanish again.

***

Sleep. Food. Surveillance. The hours passed without incident.

At 4:30 p.m., the Barrett—essential to the mission, like a scalpel to a surgeon—was removed from its protective case and wiped down with a soft white cloth, as if it were a holy relic—something sacred and unforgiving.

Moving with the silence of a mountain predator, they climbed onto the shooting platform and eased open the roof hatch.

They lay prone on the van's built-up platform—steady and silent.

They placed a single .338 round into the chamber and slid the bolt home.

The rifle came into position.

They scanned the sidewalk—beyond the bus, all the way to Travis's mother's house. They noted every detail through the optics—the cracked sidewalk, a sagging porch swing, a dented Dodge Charger that hadn't moved in days. In this line of work, you noticed what others missed, and remembered everything.

The path was clear. Everything was aligned. It was just a matter of time.

Their watch ticked over to 5:00 p.m. As they watched the corner, bus number 6 appeared—right on time—hissing to a stop at the curb.

An odd mix of vagrants and clock-punchers moved on and off the bus…

And then—

There he was.

Travis Ledbetter, right on time.

But something was off.

He wasn't alone. Three times they had watched him visit his mother. Three times he arrived alone and left alone. But it wasn't that someone was with him—these weren't his crew. They weren't even adults.

Two children, no more than five or six, walked beside him. One held his left hand. The other, his right, dragging a stuffed dinosaur behind him. One may have been a girl, pink puffy coat, white hat with a big furry ball on top, and pink snow boots. The one with the dinosaur was probably a boy. Green-and-black puffy coat. Hood up. Black snow boots.

They were smiling. Skipping.

Ledbetter said something that made them laugh. Then stopped to help them with their mittens.

The sight of children caught them off guard.

They knew the man—at least, the version that lived in the files and surveillance footage. Thirty-four. Lean. Quick to laugh when it served him, quicker to anger when it didn't. A few arrests, a few trials, but no convictions. The research showed his friends and family—but no children.

Who were these damn kids? And why were they here? Was he just watching them until their mother got off the bus?

They swept the scope left and right, scanning for someone else. No one.

The kids were with Travis—and that was a problem.

They froze, unable to start what should've already been done.

Finger on the trigger. Their breath caught in their throat. Crosshairs steady on his back.

All the research. All the planning. All the waiting.

One simple squeeze—and it would be over. But they couldn't.

Not because they doubted the kill. Travis deserved it. But the children had no blame.

Unthinkable to let them see it.

They continued to watch as Ledbetter and the children walked the half-block to his mother's house. Were they her grandchildren? Would they stay behind, giving another opportunity to complete the mission as he left?

There was no way to know who the children were. All they could do was wait, watching for Travis to return to the bus—hopefully alone.

Five minutes passed. Then fifteen. Then thirty.

Finally, a figure appeared on E. Third—alone, it seemed.

The mission, nearly scrapped, was suddenly back on track.

They eased their finger onto the trigger, waiting for a family with a dog to cross the street. One more step, and it would be done.

Then—movement.

Both children stepped out from behind Travis and took his hands—playing follow-the-leader, or something like it.

A rare tightening gripped their gut.

If the family hadn't crossed his path, they would've taken the shot.

The round would've passed through Travis. One of the kids would be dead.

They laid the rifle down, slow and silent, and closed the window.

The mission was over.

Travis would see another morning.

Easing down from the shooting platform, they carefully unloaded the Barrett, lowering it gently into the Pelican case.

They moved slowly, the weight of what almost pressed heavily on their body. The image of the boy's dinosaur and the girl's pink coat lingered, cutting deeper than any missed shot. They peeled off their gloves, then reached for the thermos and the flask of bourbon.

Clear-minded before a mission. But sometimes, afterward—especially after this—a little bourbon helped.

There was no need to wait—police weren't coming. But they stayed in the lot for a while.

As the clock neared 6:00, they folded the blanket over the gear and moved to the front. Turning the ignition, the engine rumbled to life so quietly it might as well have been a sigh.

The van slipped up N. Horton quiet as a whisper, fading into traffic like they'd never been there at all. A few blocks away, in the yard where Ledbetter's mom lived, a rusted swing set rocked gently in the breeze, chains squealing with the same tired rhythm as the neighborhood itself.

No curse. No slamming the wheel. No muttering into the silence.

It wasn't emotionless. But it was controlled.

A simple, brutal fact: they wouldn't fire with the children there.

That line couldn't be crossed. Not ever. If a child was close, the shot didn't happen.

But not everyone walking beside a monster is an innocent child. Some are adults who knew. Some looked the other way. They sat at the same table, rode in the same car, stood beside that kind of man. And if they ended up in the way, it was a choice they made.

The list was long. The window was shrinking. Patrols were shifting. Patterns forming. Whispers starting to circle.

The next chance couldn't be missed. Not again.

Chapter 21
Justice Reassigned

The afternoon office was quiet except for the low hum of my floor fan and the tick, tick, tick of Graham's pen tapping on his desk. Most of the other detectives on the second floor were out on the street—making contacts, chasing leads, or pretending to—but not Graham and me. We didn't know who to talk to. We had no leads. We needed a break, and I didn't feel one was coming.

I'd been locked on my monitor so long I was half-asleep when Graham startled me, nearly knocking me out of my chair.

"You hear from Chris yet?" he asked. "We need those firearm results."

I didn't even look up. "Nope," I said. "Nothing since he first told us."

"Damn," Graham said. "The county's got one of the best labs in the country. If it was privately owned, that wall would have been fixed yesterday."

He wasn't wrong. The lab had racked up awards for excellence and pulled in millions in grant funding. But right now, the firearms unit was down because of that bulging wall—perhaps the building itself was tired of holding up under the weight of unanswered cases. When we'd dropped evidence off last week, the air down there had smelled like wet concrete, and a faint dusting of grit coated the floors from where the wall kept shedding itself. Structural engineers were "evaluating." Meanwhile, we were stuck.

"Yeah," I said. "I've got a friend over at the county admin building. Says they haven't even started figuring out a fix. I've got half a mind to test the damn gun in my backyard."

Graham shook his head. "I'd be glad to pick up the rifle and haul it to another lab, but you know the prosecutor would say the results wouldn't hold up in court."

I leaned back in my chair and rubbed my eyes. "Two recovered .338 bullets. One .338 rifle. We need to match them together, and the case is done, yet we can't even get that simple step completed."

Graham, who was walking toward the office door, chuckled bitterly and motioned toward the hallway. "We've got evidence carts parked in the corridor because the property room's full. That ought to be the city slogan."

I smiled, just barely. "Should put it on a T-shirt."

He gestured at the whiteboard on the back wall, scrawled with names of this year's victims and suspects. "You realize we've got more unsolveds than we've had in five years?"

I glanced at the board, then back to him. "Dorsey's our guy," I said. "We'll fill in the blanks soon." Even if I didn't quite believe it.

He laughed again and walked out. With his pen tapping gone, the room fell silent—but the calm wasn't comforting. It was the silence that made the walls feel closer, like the air had thickened with all the things we hadn't solved. The mood settled into that familiar weight—one part fatigue, two parts failure.

That's when my desk phone rang.

I turned toward the sound but didn't reach for the receiver right away.

I leaned forward and checked the screen. Calloway, Frank.

I frowned. What the hell does he want?

I stretched across the desk, picked up the receiver, and leaned back in my chair.

"Frankie Calloway," I said. "To what do I owe the pleasure?"

"Angus," he replied, his voice low and tight. "Thank God you answered."

I sat up straighter. The concern in his voice cut through my sarcasm. "What's going on?"

"Nothing—well, nothing today," he said. "But I found something I think you need to see."

That got my attention. "Go on."

"It's a blog. Local. And it's not just talking about the shootings—it's celebrating them. And pushing for more."

I leaned forward. "I'm listening."

"Looks to be run by a former sheriff's deputy. Female. Fired last year for lying to Internal Affairs. The blog's basically a running rant against the county, the MCSO, the city, DPD—pretty much anybody in uniform."

I grabbed a pen and notepad. "Name?"

"I don't have it yet. She's posting under the name The Court Whisperer. Pretty sure that's not on her birth certificate."

"No, probably not," I chuckled.

"It's mostly your standard bitter former employee nonsense—fired for no reason, everyone out to get her, you know the type. But there's a steady stream of court-bashing too," he continued. "Judges letting scumbags walk, defense attorneys playing games, cases tossed on technicalities. And here's where it gets frightening—she's got a list."

"A list?"

"Names. Eight of them. She calls them 'the forgotten injustices.' All local—county and city. Every one of them either beat the charge, walked on a technicality, or had the case tossed. It's detailed—case numbers, charges, dates, where it went wrong."

I felt a cold weight settle in my chest. "And?"

"She's got two of them marked with a big red banner across the top, 'Justice Served.'"

I didn't say anything.

"You following me, Angus?"

"Loud and clear. Who's marked?"

"Hassan Al-Khatib and Malik Walker."

I closed my eyes and exhaled through my nose. "You're sure?"

"Positive. Their names, their cases, the whole thing. The banners went up the day after each shooting."

I glanced toward the door as Graham and Jenkins walked in.

"What else is on the site?"

"Hard to say. It's a mess—black-and-red fonts from a teenager's manifesto. Rants about the sheriff, the courts, the city council. But this list... it's different."

"Does she make threats?"

"Not direct ones. But the tone's all about payback. Restoring balance. One of her headers says: Justice denied is justice reassigned."

"Subtle," I muttered.

"I'm not saying she's your shooter, Angus. But she's trained. She's angry. And she's got a goddamn hit list that's already two for two. Before I run with the story, please check her out."

I turned to Graham and Jenkins, nodded toward the phone, and lowered my voice. "We may have something."

"Frank," I said, "where'd you hear about this?"

"Old deputy I used to drink with. Said she was one of the best shots they had in SWAT before it all went off the rails. Called her unstable. Brilliant, but volatile. She went out ugly."

"No name yet?"

"I'm working on it."

I paused, eyeing the whiteboard behind Graham. "Thanks for bringing this to me, Frank."

"Of course. Look, I'm a reporter—and yeah, this story could win me an Emmy. But I'm not a sociopath. If she's the shooter and you can stop a third body from dropping, that's worth more than a byline. If she's harmless, no harm done."

"She's not."

Silence. Then—

"I sent you the link," he said. "But go straight to the list. That's where the fuse is burning."

He hung up.

I stared at the receiver for a second, then slowly set it down and looked at Graham.

"Get your browser open."

Graham glanced up as I walked over. He was leaning back in his chair, half-bored, mostly annoyed—the way he always looked when I disrupted his focus. "What?"

"Internet," I said. "We need to check out a website with a hit list—including the two already dead."

I gave him the URL and watched as his browser spun, one of those witches' cauldrons at a carnival. Sometimes the internet in this building was slower than dial-up AOL from the '90s. At least two of our printers were jammed with paper from Y2K.

After a few seconds that felt endless, the landing page finally appeared—and at first, it was more amusing than alarming. Clearly built by an amateur, the background colors clashed with the text and bled across the screen, bruises after a bar fight. Animated GIFs twitched in random corners, and a MIDI file looped in the background, clawing at our ears with every replay. Text boxes floated out of alignment, pop-ups stacked as high as mail on a dead neighbor's porch, and half the navigation buttons didn't work or led to unrelated pages.

Navigating this site felt the same as stumbling blindfolded through a hoarder's house. There were sidebar polls, half-coded, with questions such as "Should corrupt judges be disbarred or dismembered?"—the kind of thing you'd expect from an angry teenager, not a former law enforcement officer. Blog posts were titled in all caps or mismatched fonts, ransom notes screaming "THE SYSTEM BLEEDS US" and "JUSTICE ISN'T BLIND—SHE'S BOUGHT."

Each click dropped us down another rabbit hole. One page ranted about patrol shifts. Another accused MCSO brass of covering up internal harassment. There were court dockets, mugshots, and screenshots from internal emails—how she got those, I didn't know.

I was about to suggest we give up and knock on her door when Graham muttered, "Wait—got something."

After slogging through the hate and name-calling, we found the list.

And froze.

It wasn't hidden. No password. No warning. There was a bold heading and a scroll of names like it was someone's grocery list.

We'd been betting on Dorsey. But this blog—this angry little pocket of the internet—made a strong case for a new lead. The former deputy hadn't just named names. She'd written a manifesto. She wanted these people dead. There wasn't the same rage in her tone from her posts about the department. There was certainty. She marked them for death and was waiting for the bullets to catch up.

And she was thrilled that two already were.

This wasn't noise. This was a warning.

We needed to get ahead of it—fast.

Because if it was her—she wasn't planning the next name.

She was already watching them.

We needed to know more about this old deputy. We wouldn't get far with the county's HR, but I knew a guy.

Gary Stiles. Used to be here at DPD, but as many others had, he jumped ship for greener pastures. These days, he was enjoying the comfort of a desk job at the Sheriff's office complex, but he'd run their SWAT team for years.

If anyone had the info we needed, it was Stiles.

I grabbed my phone and punched in his number. I hadn't talked to him in over a year—not since his on-duty back injury relegated him to desk duty. Gary wasn't one who loved answering phones and typing reports, but he was sharp, dependable, and more importantly, he didn't blow smoke.

He picked up on the second ring. "Stiles."

"Gary. It's Angus MacLaren."

A pause. "Damn. You still alive?"

"Barely."

"What's going on?"

"I need the dirt on someone you might remember. Female deputy, fired last year for lying to IA. Used to be on SWAT. Might've been one of yours."

"That would have to be Ashbourne."

"If you say so," I said. "We've got a blog that's tearing into the MCSO—but more than that, it's calling out old cases where suspects walked. Two of the names on it are already dead—dropped by a sniper. Everything about the writing points to her."

Another pause. A longer one.

"She in jail?"

"Not yet," I replied. "Should she be?"

"Hell," he said. "That's a tough one, Angus. There's a lot going on with that girl."

"Talk to me."

He exhaled, as though pushing a weight from his chest. "Kyra Ashbourne was a darn good deputy—for a while. We pulled her onto SWAT because she was an ace with a rifle. Her dad was a big game hunter—safari animals and shit. Taught her how to take down elephants and lions, which transferred perfectly to being one of our long-gun operators."

He paused, running a hand over his jaw.

"She was kinda quiet. Detail freak. Got nicknamed Icehouse 'cause she never blinked. But she didn't trust authority. Always questioned orders—never outright refused—but you could feel the tension—a fuse always burning under the surface."

I leaned back in my chair. "She go out angry?"

"She went out like a fricken' bomb. A citizen complaint about a patrol call caught IA's attention—something about the number and descriptions of weapons she seized. It was just a he said/she said to me, but IA was convinced she was lying. Ashbourne said the citizen was. Might've been both—who the hell knows. Union tried to fight it, but they couldn't back up her version, and the brass wanted her gone. She turned in her badge and vest and walked out without a word. Didn't even clear out her locker."

"Any indication she might take that anger outside the department?"

"Back then? No. She was pissed, but not crazy. Lotta deputies get canned bitter. Doesn't mean they're putting together hit lists."

Stiles went quiet again, then added, "Off the record? She was the best marksman I ever worked with. Calm. Precise. If she wanted someone dead, it would be clean, quiet, and you'd never see it coming."

I nodded, though he couldn't see it. "Still think about her that way now?"

"Unless she lost an eye or joined PETA, yeah. She hasn't lost the touch."

"Appreciate it, Gary."

"Be careful, Angus," he said. "If it's her, you're not chasing a suspect. You're chasing a professional."

He hung up.

I set the phone down and looked at the list of names on Graham's screen. Two were already crossed off.

If Ashbourne was the shooter, she wasn't venting.

She was executing.

And if it's her instead of Dorsey—we're probably about to cross off a third.

The command staff isn't going to be happy.

Chapter 22
Man Down, Third and Monmouth

The alarm buzzed at 4:15 a.m., but the body in the bed had already been awake twenty minutes.

No need for coffee. The excitement and adrenaline of the day's mission were all the stimulant required.

Preparation moved quickly, each motion carried out with the same cold precision that would, before long, leave Miguel Rojas dead in the street.

By 4:45, the van rolled toward the same alley as last week's rehearsal—off E. Fourth, between a boarded-up church and a decaying storage facility. Both buildings, along with nearly everything else in the neighborhood, were coated in graffiti. One symbol dominated the layers: a sharp-edged "V" inside a jagged crystal shard.

L.V.C. territory.

El Cuchillo sat at the other end of the block, its flickering neon sign casting a faint green haze through the filthy window of the rusted steel front door. Nothing about it looked inviting—the bullet holes in the door and the tattered strip of police tape clinging to a nearby light pole made sure of that. El Cuchillo was no stranger to violence.

Nevertheless, the locals thought it was a tropical cantina—some kind of sanctuary carved from Dayton rot. People gave El Cuchillo a wide berth for a reason. It was the kind of place you only entered if you were invited—or suicidal.

That's where Rojas always went.

He'd crossed the border in the belly of an avocado truck, muscle for La Voz del Cristal, the dominant force behind the Midwest's meth trade. Once in Dayton, he carved out a reputation fast—ruthless, loyal to no one, and feared on sight.

After weeks of surveillance, the patterns were clear. Rojas was unpredictable—where he went, who he met, when he vanished. Trying to guess his next move was a waste of time.

Except when it came to drinking.

He drank every afternoon like it was his job, usually stumbling back out onto the sidewalk around 4:00 p.m. Rojas wanted his Tecate cold and his Hornitos straight from the bottle. And he drank a lot of it. His drunkenness would be the death of him; he just didn't know it yet.

But he never touched the meth. Too many years in the trade had shown him what it did to the body. Strength was a tool, and he maintained it with the same devotion others gave to prayer.

He'd been arrested once—two brothers on Drummer Ave. tried cooking their own meth and paid for it within hours. L.V.C. found out fast. Their bodies were left in the ashes of their own lab, a warning to every other backyard chemist in the city.

Two witnesses had escaped as Rojas stormed in. They were the key to the indictment—until they vanished. Most figured the L.V.C. shipped the bodies to Mexico.

They're still missing.

Rojas was L.V.C.'s star enforcer—the guy terror cartels used to keep their people scared and their rivals buried. The organization didn't mind sloppy, as long as it worked. Rojas delivered both. That would be his downfall.

Rojas left El Cuchillo the same way every time: alone, on foot, too drunk to walk straight. He wouldn't see it coming if the shot came from across the street—or straight to his face.

The decision to take out Rojas had been made days ago—but the mess with Ledbetter threw the whole schedule off. If the mission was going to stay on track—and ahead of the cops—Rojas had to die today.

The van arrived before sunrise and settled into place by 5:15 a.m.—same alley, same shadows. The city was asleep. Porch lights flickered on timers, but there were no kids, no parents, no traffic. Just silence and the filth of the streets.

As perfected in the weeks before, once the van was parked, it was time to wait. Time to watch. The streets looked quiet, but caution came first. No movement unless it was certain there were no eyes or ears nearby.

Everything looked clean.

A few minutes before first light, it was time. A quiet shift to the back of the van—for eleven hours of stillness, tucked out of sight, hidden in plain view.

The hours passed in silence—reviewing the case notes, replaying routines, and mentally cycling through the remaining targets.

Closing the notebook, the verse stood strong—waiting, commanding. They let their eyes rest on it before sliding the notebook away, focus narrowing to the mission ahead.

The Ledbetter mission failed. That was not going to happen today.

A light breakfast. Brief rest. Then came the wait.

Traffic thickened, school buses groaned past, and the corner store across the block shrieked open its steel grate. At 3:15, the distant bell of dismissal echoed off the bricks. A few kids walked past, heads down, fast. Nobody lingered. Not here.

By 3:30, the street was quiet again.

The silent alarm, set to vibrate, buzzed at 3:45 p.m., a reminder to prepare. Just enough time for a final observation sweep and weapon prep.

By 4:15, the Barrett MRAD was loaded and laid out at the edge of the perch. The shooter climbed into position, slow and controlled, and eased the rifle into place.

Daylight increased the risk tenfold. Every movement had to be deliberate. Every sound avoided. Even the faintest noise or tiniest movement of the van could jeopardize concealment.

Looking through the optics at exactly 4:30 p.m., they studied the door of El Cuchillo with the patience of Job.

4:35.

4:40.

Rojas was late, but there was no panic. Time was on their side. Darkness was rapidly approaching.

At 4:48, the front door opened, and a visibly intoxicated Rojas staggered out onto the sidewalk, jerking, off-balance, and dead on his feet. He turned right out of the bar, away from the van, but after only a few steps, pivoted back around, nearly falling into the street as he stumbled toward the entrance again.

Pausing briefly, Rojas pulled a cigarette from his shirt pocket and fumbled to light his Zippo.

With the cigarette lit, he swayed and took three uneven steps—directly toward the shooter's position. Unknowing. Exposed. Perfectly framed.

The suppressed shot broke like a hammer dropped on stone—loud enough to hear, soft enough to leave doubt.

Rojas collapsed into the street. No one would check. He ended up there most weeks anyway.

No scream. No panic. One dead man and a city too used to gunfire and drunks to look twice.

***

Graham and I were sitting in the office around 5:00 p.m., tying up some paperwork before heading home, when east side crews were sent to Fourth and Monmouth on a shots fired call. Usually, there's nothing to these calls—crews get there and find nothing.

But we knew this area. This was gangland. Mexicans. And El Cuchillo was at the other end of the block. With that place's cartel clientele, if they were involved, there'd probably be a body.

We decided to hold off on going home until we knew for sure.

A minute later, the call was upgraded to a man down at Third and Monmouth – El Cuchillo. The caller had looked out their window and saw a man lying in the street. It was sounding more ominous—but it could still be a drunk from the bar. They always seemed to have trouble cutting people off when they'd had too much.

I was at my desk, thinking about calling Lena to see if they'd be home later, when the radio crackled:

"135 Dispatch, we need a medic and a supervisor to the front of El Cuchillo. One male down—appears to be shot in the chest."

Graham looked up from a sandwich he wasn't really eating.

"El Cuchillo?" he said. "That place should've been shut down years ago."

I dialed the dispatch sergeant to let him know we were on our way, and we were out the door in seconds. The location didn't scream sniper. This felt local—but it was still our job to sweep it up.

By the time we arrived, the scene was already taped off. A couple of uniforms were standing by the front door of the bar, and the sergeant and field lieutenant were with the coroner's investigator, standing over the body. There were no other people around.

Fear clung like damp smoke—seeping into brick, bone, and memory. Nobody wanted to cross L.V.C.—and it was clear everyone assumed this was their work.

Slipping under the tape, I approached the body and froze when I saw the face. I knew this guy.

Miguel, or more commonly Mico, Rojas.

His face looked the same as always—cold, swollen from too much tequila, mean. But now it was the expression of a statue after the sculptor walks away. Finished. Empty.

Who the hell had the balls to take out L.V.C.'s most feared enforcer?

A hit this efficient could only mean one thing—as dangerous as Rojas had been, someone out there was worse.

The way this story was moving was unsettling. A slow, cold knot was forming in my stomach—not fear exactly, but something close. An instinct that wakes you up before the bad news comes.

Rojas was lying face-up in the gutter, arms slack, legs twisted mid-turn, as if he'd tried to pivot and never made it. There was a smear of blood on his jacket—high, center mass. The coroner's investigator was poking his gloved hand around inside the coat, pulling it out when he saw me approach.

Pointing his bloodied index finger toward Rojas's chest, he looked up and said, "One shot. Dead center—right there. This guy was dead before he hit the ground."

I nodded and knelt down for a closer look. "Is the round in the body?"

The investigator chuckled and rolled Rojas toward him. "Not this time, Angus," he said. "This fella's got a hell of a hole in his back. Wasn't no .22 that took him down."

"Damn," I muttered. "Nobody's going to talk around here. We need that round. It's probably the only evidence we'll get."

The investigator, now back to poking around the body, said, "E-crew's looking, Angus. Hopefully it hit something close."

Before I could walk away, one of the uniforms called me over to the edge of the tape. He pointed toward a pile of busted pallets stacked against the side of the barber's shop two doors down. Wedged between the boards was a short length of black PVC pipe with duct tape wrapped around one end.

"Could be nothing," he said. "But it's kinda weird, maybe a homemade silencer or something."

I crouched, looked it over without touching it. The tape was frayed, and there was a faint smell of gasoline. It didn't match what I knew about a sniper's setup, but it was enough to muddy the waters.

"Bag it," I told him.

If it was connected, it could point to a street-level job, not a professional. And if it wasn't, well… false leads had a way of wasting more hours than the truth ever did.

Graham walked up and crouched beside us. He gave the body a once-over.

"Damn. That's Mico Rojas," he said. "Cartel must've been pissed at him for something. Nobody else in this town would've had the guts to take a run at him."

Sergeant Pendleton shook his head. "Yeah," he said. "Rojas was a terror in this neighborhood for years. People were scared to even look at him. Some of my own guys were."

"Someone finally had enough," I muttered.

We canvassed the scene, knocked on doors, walked through El Cuchillo—but it was the usual wall of silence. One drunk guy claimed he'd heard a car backfire. Another swore there was no sound at all. One woman just stared at the sky like she hadn't noticed the body on the sidewalk.

Up the street, I saw the E-crew digging something out of a large oak tree standing near the curb. Please let that be our bullet, I thought, not really believing we could be that lucky.

I jogged over just as he extracted a mangled piece of lead from the bark, gloved fingers holding it up to the beam of a nearby streetlight. A faint metallic tang hung in the air.

"Anything?" I asked.

"Definitely a bullet," he said. "No way to know right now if it's the one you're looking for, but it's warm and sticky with blood and tissue. The lab will figure it out."

"How about caliber?"

"Same deal," he replied. "Can't really tell out here with the damage. Gonna need a microscope—or whatever magic the lab guys use. But it's a big one. Definitely not a handgun round."

I thanked him for the find and headed back toward Graham.

"Anything?" he asked.

"Yeah. He found a round, but all he'll say is it's large caliber," I said. "Graham—no shell casing, no witnesses, one shot, center mass. Was this our guy again?"

Graham nodded. "I was waiting for you to say something. But yeah—I'm afraid it was."

Chapter 23
Harmony in the Bones

We had spent nearly two hours at El Cuchillo, but hadn't really gotten anywhere. There were witnesses—there had to be—but nobody was ever going to talk. There wasn't much else we could do until the lab came back with something, so I dropped Graham off at the office to get his car and called Lena.

"Hi, Angus!"

Caller ID had ruined the art of surprise. No such thing as an unexpected call anymore.

"Hey Lena," I said. "I'm leaving work. Thought I'd stop by and see you guys for a bit."

"You know you're always welcome, but Penny's a bit tired tonight. She may not be much fun."

"That's okay," I said. "I love seeing her, but I want to talk with you a bit too."

"Okay. See you soon!"

I pulled into my old neighborhood around 7:15 p.m., and even on a dark, cold winter night, people were out—walking dogs, jogging, being suburban. I missed this street more than I would admit. It was a place that looked unchanged by the world—sealed in amber sometime back in 1998.

Lena and Penny were waiting by the front door when I pulled into the driveway. They both came running—Lena with a smile and a hello, and Penny, as always, straight into my arms, shouting

"Daddy!" my favorite word in the world, hitting me as hard as a freight train wrapped in sunlight.

Wouldn't have it any other way.

"Hey guys," I said, holding Penny in a bear hug. "Let's get inside—I've been out in the cold all evening."

As we headed toward the door, Lena turned and smiled again. She paused for a second, then said, "It's really good to see you, Angus," before turning back ahead.

Inside, I set Penny down and slipped out of my coat, tossing it across the couch.

"You said you just left work?" Lena asked. "Why so late?"

"We caught a body around five," I said. "We thought it'd be simple, but we're thinking it's tied to the others."

"The others?" she asked. "You mean the sniper?"

"Looks that way."

"Wow," she said, shaking her head as she moved toward the kitchen.

"Did you get to eat?" she asked over her shoulder.

I told her I hadn't had time. We cleared the scene, and I came straight here.

"Go play with Penny," she said. "I got you."

It felt like a couple minutes, but closer to thirty passed before Lena called me into the kitchen. She'd put together a perfect cheeseburger—crisp green lettuce, thick slice of tomato, and a generous pile of golden crinkle-cut fries. She knew my weakness.

I was about halfway through the meal when Penny came in and climbed onto my lap.

"Daddy," she said. "I have to go to bed now. Can you tuck me in and read me a story?"

"Of course, baby," I replied. "Let Daddy finish eating and we'll head up."

Lena was leaning against the counter, arms crossed, as we watched Penny run back out of the kitchen. When I turned back to my dinner, her soft smile carried the same warmth as the stove.

"I love how much she loves you."

"What's not to love?" I asked, taking another bite of the burger.

Lena's smile faded a little. "You know, she still asks me at least once a week why you don't live with us. I never know what to tell her."

I didn't know what to say either, so I just nodded and finished the last few bites of my burger. I grabbed a couple more fries and stood up.

"I'd better get upstairs before she calls to report me missing."

"Go on," Lena said, picking up my plate. "You take care of her, and I'll take care of this. I'll see you in the living room when you get back down."

After reading to her for about twenty minutes, Penny finally drifted off. I headed back down to the living room. Lena was already on the couch when I walked in, and she handed me a full glass of red wine as I sat down next to her.

"You know how my day went," I said, giving her a tired smile. "What about you two?"

She took a sip of her wine and leaned her head back. "Honestly? We've only been together the last couple hours. Penny was at the sitter all day. I picked up an extra shift at work—didn't get off until a little after five. Swung by to grab her and stopped for take-out. We didn't get home until about 5:45."

I nodded, filing it away with the rest of the background noise. "Long day for everyone, it seems."

"Yeah. But then you called," she said, smiling.

She paused, swirling her wine slowly. "So… was it the sniper?"

I raised an eyebrow.

"The shooting," she clarified. "At El Cuchillo. I caught something in a news alert, but they're saying almost nothing."

I nodded. "Yeah—well, maybe. We found a bullet in a tree, but no lab results yet. We won't know for sure until they run some tests. We don't even know if it's the right bullet. In front of El Cuchillo, it could be anything."

Her eyes lit up. "So it definitely could be them?"

I hesitated for a heartbeat. Something in the way she'd asked it—calm, confident—brushed a nerve. Lena wasn't guessing; she was weighing what she already knew. I filed that away, the way you mentally tag a detail without knowing yet if it's important.

"It's early, but yeah. It's looking that way."

Lena shook her head slowly. "I know I shouldn't say this, but... I'm jealous."

"Jealous?"

"That you're on this case. I've been following every article, every podcast, every comment thread like a maniac. I know it's horrible, but I'm just... fascinated by it. I'd love to see a scene before the news even gets there."

I laughed softly. "Lena, I've told you before—you've got better instincts than half the guys I work with. Your degree's not just for show. If anything, you're already involved. Now, I'm not saying you're getting a badge," I said, tipping my wine toward her, "but yeah. You don't see things the way other folks do. You remind me of an old, seasoned detective."

Lena smiled at the praise, so I continued.

"Guy we found today was bad news," I said. "Rojas. Mico Rojas."

Lena's eyebrows lifted. She didn't have to fake recognition—everyone in Dayton knew his name.

"The enforcer?" she asked. "L.V.C., right?"

"Yeah. Nasty, stone-cold killer. Torched a meth lab with two guys still inside a couple years back. Case went nowhere—witnesses vanished before trial. No one's seen them since."

"So you're thinking cartel retaliation?"

"We did," I said. "But now, we just don't know… I'm thinking it could be the sniper."

She paused, lowering her glass. "Why the change?"

"Everything's the same. Single shot, center mass. No casing, no witnesses, nothing to work with. And the round we dug out of the tree? Big caliber."

"So that matches the others?"

I looked over. "You asking—or telling me?"

She shrugged, not quite hiding her smile. "I've read a lot. And I listen. But the news doesn't say everything. I'm guessing because you don't tell them."

I smirked. "I knew you were smart."

She tucked one leg beneath her. "So Rojas makes three, right?"

I nodded. "Yeah. All three were known criminals, but nothing ever stuck. First guy was a trafficker out on bond. Second was a gang boss—walked on robbery and gun charges. Now Rojas."

"That's not random," she said. "It's a list."

The word lingered, brittle and electric, a spark looking for dry kindling.

She smiled, but something flickered behind it—a glint of hunger polished smooth. Like she'd glimpsed a secret and couldn't wait to turn it over in her hands.

"Funny you mention that," I said. "We found a blog this week—ThinBlueLie.com. Mugshots, rap sheets. The first two victims were already crossed out. Rojas probably is now too."

"You said Rojas was shot in the chest?"

"Same as the others. Whoever this is, they're consistent."

A pause stretched between us.

"You ever wonder if they think they're helping?" she asked, her voice softer now.

The question hung in the room like gun smoke after a shot—thin, sharp, and impossible to ignore.

Lena tapped her nails against the glass, her mind racing ahead. She'd never worn the badge herself, but she'd been raised by two who had. She had a degree in criminal justice, and she'd been devouring true crime podcasts for years, especially cold case work. She knew how criminals thought. More importantly, how detectives worked.

"Let me ask you something," she said, leaning forward. "The first three victims—what's the one thing they all had in common?"

"Criminal records a mile long, but they all walked," I said.

"And if they hadn't walked?"

I frowned. "Then they'd be in prison right now."

She nodded slowly, letting that settle. "And if they were in prison… what would your shooter be doing instead?"

"Nothing. They wouldn't have a reason to pull the trigger."

Lena didn't smile, but her eyes told me she'd led me where she wanted. "So maybe," she said carefully, "you're not chasing revenge. Maybe you're chasing someone who thinks they're correcting mistakes—closing gaps in the system, one name at a time."

Her words hit me with the power of a heavyweight's punch—unexpected, but dead on.

And if she was right, then this list—whatever its length—wasn't just a tally. It was a clock, ticking toward an end I couldn't yet see.

Taking the last sip of wine, I stood up from the couch and stretched—a lion after a kill, slow and deliberate, bones creaking as old floorboards do.

"Lena," I said. "Thank you for feeding me, for the wine, and—of course—for the eye-opening insight. But I guess I need to get going."

Setting her glass on the end table, Lena stood too, then wrapped both arms around my back—warm, familiar, grounding.

Normally I'd have stepped away. But the day's weight—Rojas's body, the chief's warning, the fear we were losing ground—sat heavy. Going home to a cold, empty house felt unbearable in that moment.

"Angus," she said gently. "I know there's something building with Daniella—Rachel told me. I don't want to interfere with that."

I leaned back in her grasp, staring into her eyes, looking for the answers that might be hiding in the deep blue.

"I hate to admit it, but tonight… I don't want to be alone."

Her eyes softened. "Then don't be."

She kissed me. It was comfortable, familiar. An old song that knew the harmony in your bones. I don't remember even answering her. She took my hand and led me upstairs to our old room.

The bedroom was dark, warm, and quiet.

Afterward, we lay side by side in the hush. Silence you don't dare fill—not because it's awkward, but because it feels balanced.

I stared at the slow-turning shadow of the ceiling fan slicing across the wall.

"You okay?" she asked into the dark.

"Yeah," I said. "Yeah, I am."

***

I wasn't sure when I fell asleep, but I knew it was deep. I dreamed of cold alleys and sharp L.V.C.s painted on brick. Of tree bark cracked around hot lead. Rojas, swaying. The drop. The quiet. Always the quiet.

Then—light. The harsh chirp of my phone alarm. I had to get home or I'd be late for work.

I managed to dress quietly, moving slow, carefully, not to wake Lena. But as I stepped into the kitchen, I realized I wasn't as quiet as I thought.

"Daddy?"

I nearly dropped the glass I'd just filled with water. Penny stood in the doorway in her unicorn pajamas, her hair a tangled halo of sleep.

"Hey, baby girl," I said, forcing a smile. "Daddy's heading out for work."

"Oh." She blinked. "Why were you in Mommy's bed?"

I looked up—and saw Lena coming down the stairs, her sweater pulled on halfway, barefoot and brushing her hair back with her fingers.

"Yeah, Daddy," she said with a laugh. "Why were you in Mommy's bed?"

I rubbed my face. "Well… Daddy was really tired last night. Mommy didn't want me driving home, so she let me sleep over."

Penny tilted her head, squinting. "Are you sleeping here now?"

Lena knelt beside her and ran her fingers gently through her hair. "Just for the night, honey. Daddy was very tired after work. That okay with you?"

Penny nodded slowly, but not before pausing—her eyes full of questions her mouth wasn't quite old enough to form.

"It's early," Lena said. "Why don't you go watch some cartoons?"

"Okay, Mommy." Penny turned and bounded down the hall, her little feet tapping on the floor so fast it sounded like three kids at once.

Lena looked at me, eyes soft, but her mouth twisted into a crooked grin. "Well, that could've gone worse."

"She's going to tell Rachel."

"She's a kid," Lena said, walking over to me. "She's allowed to narrate her world."

I filled the coffee pot and poured the water into the machine. The scent of morning felt sharp after the night before—too real, too fast.

"Yeah," I said quietly. "But her world has become a little more complicated."

Chapter 24
Old Habits Don't Retire

I got to the office early—too late to go home and change, and with nowhere else to go. So I sat at my desk, replaying the last twelve hours at Lena's over and over in my head.

I'd stopped by innocently enough, same as I have for years. But somehow, things took a weird turn. We slept together. And now I had no idea what it meant.

Was it a one-time thing? Did Lena want to get back together? What about Penny? And Daniella?

I needed to figure it out before our next visit.

The furnace kicked on with a metallic groan, blowing out air that somehow managed to be both stale and not nearly as warm as it should have been. The place had an odor of old paper, cheap coffee, and the lingering ghost of yesterday's lunch. I stared at my monitor without even seeing it—watching the cursor blink like a malfunctioning traffic light.

The office was quiet—only the soft hum of my desk fan and the click of the old wall clock near the break room disrupted the peace. My coffee was cold before I remembered I'd poured it. I must've been daydreaming when Graham arrived. I didn't realize he'd come in until he shoved my right shoulder.

"What the heck, Angus?" he said, smirking. "You sleeping in your clothes now?"

I looked down, not sure what he was talking about.

"No, why?" I asked. "Are they wrinkled?"

"Nope, but they're the same ones you had on yesterday," Graham laughed.

I gave him a side-eye. "You're the guy who noticed when I wore the same hoodie twice in high school."

"Yeah, because you'd 'borrow' mine and spill chili on it," he said.

"And you've clearly forgiven me."

"Not a chance." He grinned, but there was that familiar brother's satisfaction in being right.

Typical Graham—always picking up details most people missed.

"I was with Lena and Penny last night. Had a little too much wine and crashed on the couch."

"The couch, huh?" He raised his eyebrows and grinned—that look that meant *You're lying, but I'm not gonna call you out.*

I smiled but didn't respond. I didn't care if Graham knew what happened, but he'd tell Rachel—and I wasn't ready for that conversation. She loved Lena, but she was also pretty fond of Daniella. I was already hearing the lecture. Since the divorce, she'd become my self-appointed sister and made it her mission to keep me in line.

I'd seen Rachel destroy Graham with nothing but a raised eyebrow. If she found out I'd spent the night at Lena's, she'd have that lecture chambered and ready to fire before I even walked in the door.

"Good morning, Sarge!" I said as Jenkins walked in, carrying a large coffee and a white box dotted with grease stains.

"Hey, guys," he replied, setting the box on top of the printer. "I've got donuts here for you. Help yourselves."

I stood to check out what he brought, but before I could say thank you, my phone rang.

"Dammit," I muttered. "It's too early to be talking to folks."

I reached for the receiver and placed it against my ear as I flipped open the donut box—glazed, chocolate, and one jelly already bleeding out in the corner.

"Homicide, MacLaren."

"Angus," the voice said. "Jack Turner. How you been, brother?"

I turned and sat back down in my chair. I hadn't heard from Jack in years. We met at the academy, closed a lot of bars together, and even rode side by side until our assignments split—he made sergeant, I went to detectives. He'd retired a few years back, and I wasn't exactly sure what he was up to these days. Rumor was he was teaching at an elementary school.

"Jack," I said, leaning back in my chair. "Been a while. To what do I owe the pleasure?"

His voice crackled over the line like it was coming through an old cruiser radio.

"I was watching the news last night—top story was a homicide at El Cuchillo."

"There was," I replied. "Cartel enforcer. Taken out with a single shot. You do it?"

"Not this time," he laughed. "Angus. Might be nothing," he began. "But yesterday morning, I noticed a dark delivery-type van—no windows, high-top roof. You know the type. It was parked across from the school when I got to work. Seemed odd, so I kept an eye on it from my classroom. Figured it was probably stolen. There was never anyone near it, and it was still sitting there when I left yesterday afternoon. But it's gone this morning."

"Never seen it before?"

"Nope," Jack replied. "That's why it caught my attention. Old habits, and all that," he added with a laugh.

I chuckled with him for a second, then leaned forward, my tone shifting. "I'll be honest with you, Jack. We're spinning our wheels here. This case has become so damn frustrating. We've got virtually nothing to go on. A couple suspects—each with flaws—but this van? That might be critical. One of our suspects drives a van. It's a deep, dark purple, but it could definitely appear black from a distance."

"Yeah," Jack said. "I didn't get closer than a couple hundred yards, so it may have been purple."

"Jack, you're a lifesaver. I'll let you know if this pans out. Now, tell me about this school. You teaching now?"

"I am," he replied. "Third grade at East Side Elementary. This is my fifth year. Can you believe I've been gone from the PD that long?"

"Time flies. But that's fantastic, Jack. I'm sure those kids benefit greatly from your time on the streets."

"I like to think so."

"East Side Elementary—is that the one on Fourth Street?" I asked.

"It is. Corner of Fourth and Monmouth. The van was on Monmouth, facing Third."

"Thanks again for the info, brother. I'll let you know if anything comes of it."

We shared our pleasantries and goodbyes, and I hung up the phone.

Graham heard the receiver click and looked over.

"Who the hell was that?"

"That was the clue we've been waiting on."

I filled him in—told him about Jack, about the van and where it had been parked. Then I told him I wanted to head back out to the scene. If this was our suspect's van, it might be our first shot at understanding the distance they were working from.

We brought Jenkins up to speed, grabbed our coats, and headed for the car. Jenkins peeled off toward a separate tip—he'd follow up with a CI and would meet us later if it panned out.

Monmouth was quiet when we pulled up. A working-class neighborhood—most everyone was already up and gone for the day. Mid-morning sunlight cut between bare trees, glinting off windshields and trash can lids. The corner of Fourth and Monmouth looked no better than any other patch of the east side—chain-link fences, cracked sidewalks, old houses with too many satellite dishes, and East Side Elementary.

Before I looked at the curb, my eyes went up. Windows, rooftops, trees—anywhere I'd put a rifle if I wanted to see without being seen.

Nothing screamed shooter's perch. But the van had been parked here. Hopefully, we could tie it to the shooting.

A squirrel darted across the cracked sidewalk, tail flicking in the air. The neighborhood was quiet—not peaceful, just waiting for something. The stillness that collects in places where trouble happens fast and no one wants to remember it.

I parked in the school lot and looked across to Monmouth. From here, it would be tough to tell the difference between black and dark purple.

Graham and I got out of the car, crossed Fourth Street, and walked about fifty feet up S. Monmouth. The cold air bit at my ears as I zipped my jacket higher. Graham stood beside me, hands in his coat pockets, eyes scanning down the street.

"Jesus," Graham said. "If they took the shot from here…"

I followed his gaze. From Monmouth, you could barely catch a glimpse of the edge of El Cuchillo up on Third. It was a straight line, but not an unobstructed one—trees and utility poles cut the view, and parked cars didn't help—but if someone was skilled. And patient. The shot was there.

I'd seen shots like this in the Marines—long-distance shots through wind, glass, trees. You don't make that kind of shot with anger in your hands. Whoever pulled that trigger had ice in their veins.

"That's got to be at least 250 yards," Graham said. "Close to 300."

I nodded. "And not a clear shot, either. That's threading a needle."

We walked the sidewalk, checking the spot where Jack said the van had been—and anywhere a marksman might've set up without being seen. We also checked for shell casings, out of habit. Nothing.

"With that distance, you'd need height," I muttered. "Rooftop, tree... inside the van."

Graham nodded, still scanning. "And they were parked long enough for a retired cop to notice. That's not a coincidence."

We needed witnesses, so we moved on to the houses. There were eight total on the east side of the block—four with a direct view of where we thought the van had been parked. We started with the closest.

The first three were dead ends. No one home, or no one willing to talk.

At the fourth, an older man answered the door wearing sweatpants and a thermal undershirt. He studied our badges as though they were toys from the mall.

"Did you call the police about the gunshot the other day?" I asked.

"Yep." The man continued, saying he and his wife had been watching Wheel of Fortune when they heard a loud bang that scared the hell out of them. He didn't see a vehicle, just assumed it was a drive-by.

"Anything else unusual? A parked van?"

He shook his head. "Nah, that's it."

I gave him a card and thanked him. "If anything else comes to mind, give me a call."

The fifth house was another bust. Number six had a woman home with a baby on her hip who said there was a van that morning, but she didn't think anything of it.

"It was dark-colored," she said, shifting the baby. "Not a regular one that parks on the street, but it's not unusual for vans to be here. Didn't think to look twice."

"When did it leave?" Graham asked.

She shook her head. "Not sure. It was gone when I came back from the grocery. That's all I know."

The seventh house was empty. The eighth house had a man in his twenties who said he was working on his car the morning in question and thought he saw a dark van, "maybe black, maybe purple."

"Wasn't parked long," he said. "Didn't see anybody get in or out. It was there, and later it wasn't."

"Anything else stand out? License plates maybe?"

He shrugged. "Didn't have plates. Or at least, none I could see."

No one had cameras. A few had Ring doorbells, but none were working—or hooked up to Wi-Fi, or in one case, even installed. Cameras everywhere, but no one's watching. The whole block had eyes, but they were painted on—just for show. The shooter hadn't only picked the right angle. They'd picked a street full of blind spots.

After the last door, we headed back toward the car.

"Well," Graham said, exhaling hard. "That was a bust."

I didn't answer right away. Cold bit at my collar, and the silence felt personal—like the city itself was holding its breath.

"Not a bust. We've got at least two other folks saying the van was here. That's more than we had yesterday."

He gave me a skeptical stare. "Yeah, but nobody knew if anyone was in it. No plates. No direction of travel. No casing. No camera. We keep chasing shadows."

Chapter 25
Shooter, Saboteur, Crusader

"You're out of your damn mind," Koski said, a half-eaten sandwich in his left hand. "Dorsey's got the background, the training, the right rifle. He's got serial killer written all over him." His tone carried that street cop edge—half gut feeling, half brag—the sound of a guy who trusted the whispers in back alleys more than a lab report. A fleck of bread clung to the corner of his mouth, but he didn't bother to wipe it away.

I sat at my desk, leaning back in my chair, letting them run their mouths. Koski's voice bounced off the concrete-block walls, sharp and fast, more noise than persuasion. This was how it had been all afternoon—arguing our views without hearing anyone else's, and we were nowhere near a consensus.

Jeffries had rolled his chair over next to mine, arms folded, watching the argument with as much interest as a tennis match. He wasn't moving much, but his eyes tracked every line as if keeping score. Jeffries had that quiet, almost academic patience—the kind of guy who double-checked a warrant before signing it and didn't open his mouth without evidence backing it up. He could let you talk yourself in circles for twenty minutes just to get to the one question that knocked your whole theory over.

Koski was sitting on the edge of Graham's desk, legs swinging idly, jaw tight. Graham stood over by the coffee maker, refilling his cup, believing another sip might help him come up with a better theory. The pot was almost empty, burnt down to that thick, bitter sludge that tasted more tar than coffee. He drank it anyway, face tightening at the bitterness.

The room carried that stale mix of old paper, mildew and the faint tang of dust from the heating vents—air that had been circulating too long. Somewhere down the hall, a copier clunked as though losing a fight, and a phone rang twice before someone picked it up.

Jenkins leaned in the doorway of his office, sipping from a bottle of water—supervising, as he called it. He looked on as a man might watch a slow-motion train wreck—disgusted, but not enough to step out of the way.

"It can't be Dorsey," Graham said, turning around. "Guy's walked on so many charges, he belongs on the list, not crossing it off. And his temper? The sniper's ice-cold. Doesn't fit."

"That makes no sense," Koski fired back. "Sometimes what seems obvious, is. Half of us are hotheads. Doesn't mean we can't wait for the right shot. Dorsey's the guy. You don't need a chess master to squeeze a trigger."

They were on their third round of this, circling the same suspects, shooting holes in each other's theories—blind to the holes in their own. Everyone was tired, and it was starting to show—not just in the bickering, but in the way nobody had shaved, the way the trash hadn't been taken out, the way we all stared at the same corkboard waiting for it to start talking back.

I'd let it roll because, as much as I hated to admit it, we needed this. The lab hadn't given us much, CompStat was coming up fast, and we were all starting to think we were chasing shadows with flashlights that wouldn't turn on. And no matter how heated the arguing got, it was flushing out what each man really believed.

That meeting was going to be bloodsport, and we were the ones walking in without shields. The brass wasn't going to care that we had three victims and no clear suspect. They'd want a name. A story. A scalp. And we had zero to offer them except maybe a few more educated guesses than last time.

Jenkins got a call and stepped back into his office. I caught the faint murmur of his voice through the thin wall, then the scrape of his chair as he stood. He returned a few moments later, his face unreadable—his usual irritated appearance. Jenkins had a face carved from stone and a tone that could sand paint. If he was bringing good news, I almost didn't want to hear it.

"Finally, some good news," he said, leaning against the doorframe once again. "I don't have the official report yet, but... lab results came back on the Rojas shooting. The round pulled from the tree was the right one. DNA matched Rojas—same blood type, same STR profile."

We all turned toward him. Jenkins had everyone's full attention now—like a man who'd walked in from the edge of the woods and said he found a footprint. It wasn't a breakthrough, but it was proof something had passed this way.

"They also confirmed what we all knew. Rifling marks are a match to the first two scenes. Same weapon, three kills."

Graham let out a low whistle. "How'd they move that fast?"

Jenkins shrugged. "Apparently they're catching hell for not being able to test fire anything. Not just from us—brass all over the county's been complaining. They fast-tracked the DNA and comparison work to make up for it. Three, maybe four days, start to finish."

I didn't care why they did it—only that they did. For once, the lab had thrown us a rope before we sank all the way under.

Koski leaned back too far, nearly sliding off Graham's desk. "So that's it, then. We've got a legit pattern—three shots, same rifle, same shooter."

"And still no name," I muttered, running my hands across the top of my head. "A spook with a scope. The kind of ghost that didn't rattle chains—this one locked in, squeezed the trigger, and vanished."

Koski nodded toward the board. "If it's not Dorsey, then who? Callahan?"

I looked up at the board again. Three names, one motive, zero hard evidence. We were trying to solve a puzzle after someone's thrown away half the pieces and lit the rest on fire.

Jeffries exhaled through his nose. "I don't like thinking it's him. But he's got motive. And if the facts start pointing that way, I'll go where they lead."

"Yeah," Graham said. "He definitely has more motive than either of the others. His daughter gets trafficked, the system gives him nothing, so he gets his own justice. He liked the feel of correcting the system's failures. Now, three dead bodies later, he's become obsessed with rectifying."

"Is he ex-military?" Koski asked. "It seems half this damn city's long-gun-qualified these days."

"Not that we know of. But we haven't looked too deep," Jeffries said. "I've met the guy. He's direct. Blunt, yeah, but not shady. I don't see him slipping through neighborhoods with a rifle and vanishing into thin air."

"He's not unstable," I added. "Angry, sure. Bitter. But not chaotic. If anything, Callahan's focused. Calculated. I'll be honest—I dismissed him as a suspect the day I met him. He didn't seem to fit. Now, I'm not so sure."

"And maybe that's what makes him dangerous," Jenkins said. "He's the kind of guy who stews in it. Quiet for years, doesn't draw attention—then something triggers him, and he turns into a ruthless vigilante."

Jeffries looked over. "Any holes in his alibi?"

I shook my head. "He's got verified whereabouts for the first killing. Not so much for the others. Says he was home alone—same as half the city."

"So we can't dismiss him," Jenkins said. "Doesn't fit perfectly. But fits enough."

Koski stood from the edge of Graham's desk. "Better than Ashbourne."

The room shifted. That name always did it, a spark too close to a gas can.

Graham raised an eyebrow. "You sure about that?"

Koski didn't answer.

Graham tossed his stir stick in the trash and turned to face the room. "I'm telling you— Ashbourne is the one that keeps me up at night."

Jeffries frowned. "You still think she's the shooter?"

"I think she's connected," Graham said. "Have you seen her site lately? She's logging every dropped charge, every dismissed case, every mistrial in the county. Then she's posting it all for everyone to see. Have you seen her kill list?"

"That doesn't make her the killer," Koski said. "It makes her a pissed-off blogger with too much time and too many grudges. But that doesn't pull a trigger."

"It's more than that," Jenkins added. "She's not just listing cases. She's editorializing—calling out judges by name, ripping into defense attorneys, and absolutely unloading on law enforcement. Especially MCSO."

"She hates the Sheriff's Office," Jeffries said. "Every other post is about corruption, incompetence, cover-ups."

And she wasn't wrong about any of it. That's what made her dangerous—not the anger, but the accuracy.

"Yeah," Graham said. "And she's not subtle about it. 'The system protects the guilty. The badge protects the predator.' That's a direct quote from her last post."

"She's five-four and a hundred and twenty pounds," Koski said. "You think she's the one climbing rooftops with a .338?"

"Maybe," Jenkins said. "Or she's not pulling the trigger. She could be giving someone else a reason to."

I'd read her stuff too. At first, it had come off like watchdog journalism—aggressive, yeah, but sharp. Then something changed. The whole blog became personal. The tone had shifted—from a call for reform to a demand for revenge. She didn't want the system exposed. She wanted it embarrassed.

"She's not releasing crime scene photos or leaking inside info," I said. "But she's tracking every failure, every crack in the system—and making damn sure her readers know who's to blame."

She didn't need bullets. She had followers, and the kind of audience that wasn't simply reading—they were waiting. The worst part? She was good. Smart, precise, inflammatory enough to bait a following without tipping into full conspiracy. And if she was connected to the shooter, that made her even more dangerous—because it meant the message was more than noise.

Sighing, Graham took another drink of his coffee. "It takes only one juror to set them free, and she only needs one reader to send them back—forever, this time."

It was the same calculus the shooter was using, whether he knew it or not: justice, by the ounce. One life for another. Simple math, until it's your name in the ledger.

Jenkins folded his arms. "Callahan's got motive and skills. Dorsey's got background and rage. Ashbourne has reach. And an agenda."

"Great," Koski muttered. "So we've got a shooter, a saboteur, and a crusader, and any one of them—or none of them—could be guilty."

Graham nodded toward the board. "We've pulled everything we can from her blog. But we've not laid eyes on her."

"I made a call to Stiles over at MCSO," I said. "Said she was one of their best. Former deputy. Expert marksman. Got cut loose after IA thought she lied during a missing weapons investigation. Never proved anything, but they fired her anyway."

And now she was out in the cold—smart, bitter, and skilled with a rifle. That's not a loose end. That's a fuse. And if she was half as careful as her blog suggested, she wasn't going to slip up just because we knocked on her door.

Jenkins leaned against the doorframe. "Then it's time we talk to her. Track her down. Let's see if she thinks she's got all the answers when she's the one in the hot seat."

Jeffries gave a slow shake of his head. "Assuming she even agrees to talk to us."

I wasn't so sure she would. But I knew one thing: if she did, it wouldn't be small talk.

Jenkins' words hung in the air for a second before anyone moved. Graham set down his empty coffee cup and grabbed his coat from the back of his chair.

"I'll drive," he said.

I stood and stretched, my lower back popping like a log cracking in a fire. My body's reminder that I was too old for this nonsense.

Jeffries was already typing something at his desk—probably digging for an address. Koski was perched on Graham's desk, clearly in no hurry to move. Jenkins hadn't left the doorway, arms crossed, eyes following us, anxious to see what we'd find.

"She's probably gonna slam the door in your face," he called after us.

Graham didn't look back. "Then we'll knock harder."

Chapter 26
Pressure Mounts

Graham and I got to Ashbourne's neighborhood around 6:00 p.m. She lived in Kettering, so Graham called the local PD to let them know we'd be in the area—part courtesy, part insurance in case of trouble. We didn't know Ashbourne, but we knew what she could do. If she was our shooter, things could turn bad fast.

Our destination was her house at 310 Glenridge Road. Our digging into her past had turned up nothing else. If she wasn't there, we were out of luck. As we pulled up in front, I turned to Graham.

"You sure this is the place?"

"That's what it says—310 Glenridge."

I shook my head at the sprawling Tudor—steep roof, stone trim, probably had a wine cellar she didn't use. The kind of place where people liked the *idea* of justice but didn't want it tracked through their white carpet.

"How the hell does a fired civil servant afford this place?"

This was the kind of neighborhood where the streets were narrow on purpose—a trick of the privileged to keep the curious from slowing down long enough to gawk. There was nowhere to park, so against every instinct burned into us from years on the job; we pulled into the driveway and walked up to the door.

The polished oak double doors were massive—less an entrance and more a statement. Someone on the other side wanted you to feel small before you even knocked. Graham rapped his knuckles against the wood, but the sound vanished—dead and muffled by the weight of the oak, like the house didn't want to be bothered.

In the city, I'd have banged on the door with my flashlight without thinking twice. But out here, where the front doors probably cost more than my yearly salary, restraint was the smartest move.

We waited a few seconds, but no one came.

I tried again—one sharp knock, then two more. Still nothing. No movement inside. No lights, no footsteps, not even a shadow behind the blinds. I looked for a doorbell, but I guessed that was too middle class. Might've disrupted the beauty of the entry.

Graham gave me a look. "Walk the perimeter?"

I nodded.

We stepped off the porch and made our way around the house. The side yard was manicured better than a five-star resort—perfect grass, mulched flower beds, and a garden gnome positioned perfectly. The back of the house was all glass and quite elegant. Inside, the kitchen could have been staged for a magazine shoot. Spotless. Empty. Soulless.

"No car in the drive, no lights, no signs of life," Graham said. "You think she's in the wind?"

I didn't answer right away. Something about it didn't sit right. If she was on the run, she'd leave a mess—a half-packed bag, a back door ajar. This felt too clean, too controlled. Too controlled. There was a staged feel to it. Whoever left here had planned it weeks in advance. That kind of quiet always worried me more than a broken door or blood on the floor.

"I don't buy it," I said. "That kind of quiet doesn't come from a last-minute flight. She's here, but doesn't want to be found."

We were circling back to the front when we heard the scrape of rubber soles on concrete.

"Hey! You there! This is private property!"

We turned to see a hunched woman in a quilted jacket and orthopedic shoes coming up the driveway, jabbing her cane at us, the self-appointed captain of the Neighborhood Watch.

"I live next door," she snapped. "What do you think you're doing?"

"We're police, ma'am," I said, holding up my badge.

She squinted. "Don't call me ma'am. My name is Mrs. Branson. Now, let me see that. Up close."

I stepped forward. She peered at it, apparently inspecting every inch for smudges.

After a long pause, she straightened just enough to stop poking me with her cane. “You don’t look like police. I guess you don’t look like burglars either. But you can’t be too careful—people will steal anything these days. Even gutters.”

“We’re not after gutters,” Graham said.

She grunted, clearly unimpressed.

“Do you know if anyone is home?” I asked.

“They’re away.”

“Where?”

She hesitated, deciding whether or not to trust us. “Africa. Safari, I think. Gone a couple weeks now.”

“Anyone else live with them?”

She paused again. “Their daughter.”

“She around?”

“I haven’t seen her today,” she said. “But that’s not unusual. She keeps odd hours.”

“What’s the daughter’s name?”

“I’m sure you already know it if you’re real police.”

Graham gave me a look. I smiled politely. “Yes, ma’am.”

The woman narrowed her eyes but said nothing more.

“Anything unusual lately? Suspicious visitors? Arguments, deliveries?”

She shook her head, then hesitated. “No… well, my dog went crazy barking at their back fence a few nights ago. Real late—midnight, maybe later. I don’t usually see much back there, but something had him riled. Could’ve been a raccoon. Could’ve been someone moving around.” She shrugged, it wasn’t her problem. “Not that I was watching. I mind my own business.”

I grinned at the contradiction, filing it away. If her dog had a reason to bark, I wanted to know what it saw. “Appreciate your time.”

She didn’t reply—just turned and hobbled off. She disappeared around the corner, muttering about badge numbers and pensions. I stared at the house a moment longer. If Ashbourne was gone, she hadn’t gone far. And if she was hiding… she was doing a damn good job of it.

***

Walking into CompStat carried the weight of a death sentence. Every seat was taken by someone with more authority than we'd ever have—and even more were lining the walls. The FBI was there. The mayor. The whole damn city council.

Jenkins, Graham, and I wouldn't be sitting today—we were expected to stand at the front of the room.

This wasn't going to be a friendly chat with old friends. We were here to be crucified.

We hadn't even reached the podium when Chief Robertson exploded. This was odd—Assistant Chief Carpenter usually led the meetings. Robertson was probably grandstanding for his bosses.

"Sergeant Jenkins! Were we not explicitly clear at the last meeting that these shootings had to stop?"

Jenkins gave a tight nod. "Yes, sir."

"Then explain to this room how another citizen ended up dead—on your watch!"

Jenkins was a hell of a sergeant, but he didn't do well under pressure from above. He muffled a sneeze and shuffled through the stack of papers he'd brought with him.

"Yes, sir," he began. "Our unit has been working nonstop on this case. We've developed three viable suspects, but the shooter is smart. Other than the spent round, not a single piece of evidence is being left behind. No clues. No witnesses. Chief, we're chasing a phantom."

"I understand the difficulties, Sergeant. But your job—what all of you are paid to do—is to catch this guy. Tell me about your viable suspects."

Jenkins shuffled through his papers again, pulling the list I had written up for him—the one with the key details on all three possibles.

"The first is a guy named Joseph Callahan. Callahan is the father of Erin Callahan, one of the trafficking victims linked to Hassan Al-Khatib. He was in court the day Al-Khatib was released and made verbal threats—directly stated he wanted to kill him."

Robertson nodded, jotting notes. "Anything else linking Callahan?"

"Not much, Chief. His alibi's shaky, but he has a military background. He's the weakest of our suspects, but we're monitoring him."

"Okay, Jenkins," Robertson said. "You're telling me your first suspect is probably not the guy. You're not off to a great start. We need something solid. Who's next?"

I was much more comfortable dealing with these arrogant pricks, but Jenkins needed to appear in charge. I watched with empathy as he wiped sweat from his forehead and adjusted his tie.

"The second guy is Keith Dorsey. We were put onto Dorsey on a tip that he was buying a lot of .338 ammunition—the same used in the shootings. My guys watched him for a couple days, eventually following him to a long-distance range where he was firing a sniper rifle."

Jenkins paused, glancing my way for support.

"Go on, Sergeant," Robertson said. "We've all got other places to be this morning."

"Of course, Chief. My guys followed Dorsey as he left the range and had patrol officers stop him. Inside his van, they recovered a .338 rifle and several boxes of ammo. There was nothing specific that tied him to the shootings, so we had to let him go—pending ballistics testing on his rifle."

Robertson stopped writing and looked up from his notes. "And?"

"We thought we had the rifle; however, the round recovered from the Rojas scene was fired from the same gun as the other two. Dorsey's rifle is still in the property room—it is not the murder weapon."

"The rifle he turned over was clean," Jenkins added, "but we've got a source saying Dorsey's a collector. Odds are, he's got another one stashed somewhere—something he didn't hand us."

Robertson dropped his pen, spreading both hands in front of him.

"You know Dorsey's rifle isn't the murder weapon, yet you're trying to convince me—convince this room—that he's good for it. Sergeant, I'm not sure I'm following."

Jenkins took a long sip from his water bottle, then cleared his throat.

"Dorsey is a known precision shooter. He openly told us he practices weekly. We strongly believe he's hiding another rifle—the one used in the killings. But without probable cause we're boxed in."

Before Robertson could respond, Councilman Marcus Whitaker leaned forward. Dressed as if he were heading to Easter services in a tailored pastel suit and gleaming gold chains, his voice dripping with disrespect.

"Excuse me, Sergeant Jenkins," he said, his tone dripping with condescension. "But it seems to me that if Mr. Dorsey is purchasing large quantities of .338 ammunition and is known to frequent long-range shooting ranges, that should be more than enough to justify a search of his premises. What exactly are we waiting for?"

Jenkins straightened, his eyes narrowing slightly. "Councilman Whitaker, while your concern is understandable, the law requires us to establish probable cause before obtaining a search warrant. Suspicion alone, even if it's strong, doesn't meet that threshold."

Whitaker scoffed, shaking his head. "So you're telling me that despite all this, your hands are tied? That seems like a convenient excuse for inaction."

Robertson interjected, his voice firm. "Councilman, our officers are bound by the Fourth Amendment and state laws. We cannot and will not violate constitutional rights, regardless of public pressure."

Whitaker leaned back, crossing his arms. "Well, perhaps it's time we re-evaluate this commitment that's hindering our ability to protect the public."

I bit my tongue. To the Whitakers of the world, the Fourth Amendment didn't matter until it defended someone they despised. But when the boot pressed on their necks, they'd be the loudest to scream.

The room fell into a tense silence.

I was stunned by Whitaker's comments. To suggest the police department operate outside of constitutional restraints should be an immediate disqualifier from public office.

After a long pause, Robertson brought the room back to order.

"Sergeant Jenkins, you said there were three suspects. Please. Continue."

"Of course, Chief. Late last week, a Kyra Ashbourne was brought to our attention. She is a former MCSO deputy. She was fired last year for lying to Internal Affairs. She also has an extensive history with long-range shooting—she was a long-gun operator with the County SWAT team. But the most compelling information is her blog: ThinBlueLie.com.

It's full of rants—not just about the sheriff's office, but our department, the courts… it seems anyone remotely connected to law enforcement. But that's not the most troubling part. Ashbourne has also published a list of people she believes have escaped justice. Names, photos, addresses, case histories—eight in all. And that list includes all three of our victims.

She's placed large red banners across their photos that say: Justice Served."

"And where is your investigation into this person?"

"We've been unable to locate her. My detectives went to her home in Kettering, but she wasn't there—or at least wouldn't open the door."

Robertson let the silence linger. Then he leaned forward, hands clasped on the table.

"Find her. Today. I don't care how quiet she's been or how clever you think she is. If she's out there posting kill lists with banners celebrating death, then she's either behind this or knows who is."

He looked around the room, eyes landing on each of us like a warning shot.

"You've got seventy-two hours," he said. "Seventy-two hours to bring me something solid—or I pull this case from your hands. I'll bring in BCI, and they won't care whose toes they step on to close it."

His gaze moved from Jenkins to Graham, then landed on me.

"If we're still standing here empty-handed by Friday morning, don't expect me to defend you in front of the mayor or the cameras."

Nobody spoke. Nobody needed to. The clock had started ticking.

The meeting ended without another word. Nobody moved until he was gone. Robertson had dumped gasoline across the floor and flicked the match.

Chapter 27
Just a Blogger?

As we walked out of the war room, the hallway was electric from the heat we caught in CompStat. The chief's last words rang louder than a 12-gauge at the range. Message received.

He gave us seventy-two hours to make something happen. After that, the investigation would be gift-wrapped and handed to BCI—them doing us a favor he said.

No pressure.

All we had were a name, a website, and an address we'd already checked. Not much—but it was something. The kind of "something" that barely qualifies as a lead, but it keeps you moving because stopping means you're admitting you've got nothing.

I pointed toward the car, "Let's head back to her place."

***

The sun was glaring overhead as I turned onto Ashbourne's street, easing to a stop one house short of her driveway. The heat shimmered off the asphalt in faint waves, distorting the edges of the curbs and mailboxes. Mrs. Branson—the old lady neighbor we spoke to yesterday—stood at her mailbox, a stack of letters in one hand and a pair of leather gloves and her cane in the other.

While we sat in the car for a moment—watching the house, she stared us down with unsettling focus, steady and unblinking. But as we stepped onto her clipped and ruler-straight front lawn, her stare softened. She must've remembered us. I might've even seen a smile.

"Good morning, Mrs. Branson," I said as I walked toward her. "Do you remember us from yesterday?"

"I remember. Still looking for that girl, huh?"

"We are. Have you seen her?"

Mrs. Branson looked toward the Ashbourne house, then back at Graham and me. "No, but somebody's there now. Could be her. That big black behemoth showed up about twenty minutes ago. I was out here feeding the squirrels and had to go in for more peanuts. When I came back out, that thing was there."

"You didn't see who was driving?" Graham asked.

She looked at him like he'd just started speaking Martian, then turned to me and smiled. "Is he stupid? I'm sure you heard me say it showed up while I was inside."

I chuckled at the scowl Graham was trying to conceal. "Thank you for your help, Mrs. Branson. We'll go on over and see who's home."

We crossed her yard and walked up the driveway to the stunning, blacked-out Chevy Suburban. The windows were too dark to see if anyone was inside, but the hood was cold—whoever had driven it had been inside awhile.

We kept walking toward the house.

"You take the side door over there," I said, pointing, as I headed for the front walk. "I'll knock and see what happens."

Graham gave a nod and jogged down the side of the house, and I moved toward the front, eyes scanning the doors and windows. No movement in the curtains. No dogs barking. No shadow at the door. Just the quiet of a place that could either be empty or holding its breath.

I stepped onto the porch. But unlike yesterday, I wasn't playing polite. I was pissed about the chief's arbitrary deadline, so I pounded the door with my flashlight—the same way I knock on every busted-up flop house from here to Belmont.

BANG, BANG, BANG.

"DAYTON POLICE!"

I hadn't even finished shouting "POLICE" when the front door swung open—smooth and silent. Not like the creaky hinges I live with. I guess that's what money buys.

Standing in the doorway was a woman who had to be Kyra Ashbourne. I guessed mid-thirties, jeans and a soft-worn hoodie, barefoot on the hardwood floor. Her brown hair pulled into a tight ponytail—the same way Daniella wears hers when she's trying to get under my skin. I've always had a weakness for women with ponytails—don't know why. Maybe it's the last remnants of my first girlfriend.

Kyra was sharp-featured, confident—the kind of pretty that didn't need makeup to get noticed. Her gaze was steady, almost challenging.

I stared—less than a second, but too long. She spoke first.

"I was wondering when you guys would be back."

That told me two things right away—she knew we had already been there once, and she didn't care. Not the usual reception when someone thinks they might be arrested.

I blinked. "Excuse me?"

"I'm Kyra Ashbourne. I run ThinBlueLie.com, and I'm guessing you're here because of my list."

I wasn't sure how to respond, so I keyed my radio. "Graham, come around to the front."

Ashbourne didn't wait for my response. "I know how it looks, but I've got nothing to hide. You want to talk? Fine. But I had nothing to do with the killings." She stepped back from the door. "Come in if you want."

***

I followed Ashbourne through the door as Graham stepped up onto the porch. The inside of the house felt as pretentious as you'd expect from someone who vacations on safari on the Serengeti. Twenty-foot ceilings, polished hardwood floors so shiny they could double as mirrors, and furniture that looked imported and expensive—likely European, with five-digit price tags to match. The air was faintly scented with something floral, but odd, probably from a store shelf instead of a garden.

It didn't feel like a home—more a museum meant to inflate egos and impress, not comfort. The mounted heads of African animals reflected the darkness, pressing heavier with every step into the room. In a mirror the size of a garage door, I caught my reflection and felt as inadequate as a grease stain in a linen showroom.

With a wave of her manicured index finger, Ashbourne pointed us to the couch, where I saw a small laptop open on the coffee table next to a stack of public court records printed on cheap paper.

"Can I get you anything? Coffee? Water?"

"We're good, thank you," I replied.

I remained calm on the outside, but I could feel my pulse quicken beneath the surface.

"Ms. Ashbourne, you have to know this looks bad."

She dropped into the armchair across from Graham and me, tucking both legs under her, settling in for a night of binge TV and wine instead of being questioned about possibly being a serial killer. "So. You think I killed those men."

"We think it's possible," I said. "You've got the skills, and the list on your site shows some serious planning. We don't see a motive."

She tilted her head. "You read the list?"

"We did. All eight names. Three are dead. Even if you're not the one pulling the trigger, we believe you're inspiring—or guiding—whoever is."

"I'm not surprised. I knew this was going to attract attention." She tapped her chest. "But I'm not behind the trigger."

Graham leaned in. "So what's the point of the site, then?"

"To tell the truth. MCSO doesn't. Your department doesn't. The courts sure as hell don't. Somebody's got to let the people know how many dirtbags are walking free after skating on serious charges. It makes me sick. There has to be some type of accountability."

"And why is that your responsibility?" I asked.

"Because I've lived it," she said.

"In what way?"

"I was one of you. Road deputy. SWAT marksman. A dozen commendations. But it was all taken away by a bunch of self-righteous bureaucrats over a bullshit policy violation. I'm sure you've heard the story."

She sat up, eyes on mine, unblinking, voice rising with an unexpected anger. "Now, I see all of these assholes—actual criminals—walking without even a slap on the wrist. So yeah, I'm pissed. Really pissed. And if somebody kills them because I called them out, I'm not losing a second of sleep over it. In fact, maybe they deserved worse."

A faint breeze from the HVAC stirred the edge of a court document on the table, flipping a couple pages. Seeing her spiral into that angry rant left me more convinced than ever she was capable of being our killer.

"You mentioned you were a sniper with MCSO—do you still do any shooting?"

Ashbourne nodded. "Yeah, I keep my skills sharp. Even if I don't get my job back, I'm a hunter." Her tone shifted—defensive, the question seemed to rub raw skin. "It's not illegal to practice at the range. Not a crime to stay proficient."

I raised my eyebrows and glanced at Graham. "You're trying to get your job back?"

"Damn right I am. Those jackasses railroaded me." She said it like she'd rehearsed it a thousand times.

"Hmm. Maybe you should rethink what you post about MCSO, then."

She rolled her eyes. "Whatever. I've got nothing left to lose."

"Okay, Ms. Ashbourne, a couple more questions," I said. "Do you own a .338 rifle?"

"I did. Sold it. My dad has a couple at his lodge though."

"Where's his lodge?" Graham asked.

"Montana."

"Any long-range rifles here in the house?" I asked.

"No. Just a handgun. Everything else is at the lodge or locked in Dad's safe at the gun club."

"Do you have access to the safe?"

"No." Her answer came fast—a little too fast.

"Okay," I said, pointing toward the laptop and papers on the coffee table. "Let's talk a little about your blog."

"What about it? I told you what it is. It's nothing more than public records. Anybody can look this stuff up. I have no job, no friends, and no money. I blog to stay sane."

I raised my eyebrows and glanced around the room at the mention of money.

"Daddy's house, Daddy's money," she said, catching my look. "I don't have a dime of my own." She shrugged, but there was bitterness in it. "Anyway, what I'm trying to say is—I've got time, I'm furious, and I'm doing something about it."

"But you've created a hit list. A literal guidebook on who to kill."

"It's not a hit list," she snapped. Sharper now. "It's documentation. Public records. Court transcripts. I don't tell anyone to pull a trigger."

"But you don't exactly discourage it either," Graham said.

Ashbourne crossed her arms and stared him down, her voice dropping to a near growl. "Look, I'm sharing the data. What people do with it—that's on them. If someone out there is using my list as a playbook, I'm not going to cry over guys like Hassan Al-Khatib or Rojas. Tell me something—did any of those people get convicted of what they were accused of?"

"No," I said.

"Exactly." She sat back, keeping her arms folded, eyes hard. "That's the problem. If the system won't deal with them, why shouldn't the people know who they are?"

"You realize that because of what you're sharing, you've become part of an active homicide investigation," Graham said.

She stood. "Then do your job. Check my prints. Check your ballistics. But you're not going to find a murderer here. I'm a woman who used to believe in the badge—and got shredded for it."

I nodded as I scanned through my notes. "We are going to need to know your whereabouts the night of each shooting. I really hope you have solid alibis."

She shook her head in disgust. "I really don't know what to tell you, Detective. As I said before, I have no friends. Everything I do is just me. I could tell you what I was doing, but you couldn't prove it either way—so what's the point?"

"I'm sorry to hear that. I was really hoping to take care of this today."

She smirked and spread both palms out in front of her, thumbs up as if to say, *Oh well.* The gesture felt jarring in a house lined with polished floors and mounted heads.

"Detective, unless you're going to arrest me, I think we're done here. I'd like for you to leave now."

I looked at Graham in frustration. We had nothing to hold her on, and we both knew it.

"No, we aren't arresting you. Yet. But please understand, this isn't over. Please reconsider sharing your alibis."

She shook her head and pointed to the door.

Graham and I stood and walked toward the exit. As I began to step out, I turned back to Ashbourne. "We'll be in touch," I said. "Soon."

As we stepped out into the sunlight and closed the massive door behind us, I looked at Graham and shook my head. He didn't say anything at first. Then he stopped and turned toward me.

"She's not our shooter."

"Really?" I asked. "Because I think she's good for it. She's got the skills, the tools, the anger—we need to dig deeper on this one."

Nothing else was said as we made our way back to the car, both of us replaying everything we'd learned, realizing we were running out of hours—and still stalled.

Chapter 28
Pull the Thread

It had been a couple days since we talked to Kyra Ashbourne. I continued to believe she was good for the shootings, but we had nothing. Nothing tying her to anything—and nothing for the chief. By his clock, we had less than twenty-four hours to solve this case. I didn't see that happening, so I figured I might as well get some breakfast and trade war stories with an old friend.

I glanced at the dash clock as I pulled up to Doog's Brunch Hut—8:15 a.m. Damn. Late again. Ray was going to have fun with this.

Doog's was one of those joints that looked horrible from the street and only barely improved inside—linoleum floors yellowed from decades of spills, booths patched with duct tape, and the same two burnt-out neon letters since 1997. But the scent of bacon grease, maple syrup, and fresh diner coffee hit you the second the door opened, and just like that, none of it mattered.

I swung open the old metal-framed diner door, the glass bearing the scars of more than one drive-by shooting and spotted my old pal Ray. He was waving from the same corner booth he's been holding down for the last thirty years, flashing his annoying smart-ass grin. The same one I first saw years ago when I missed a turn and drove my cruiser straight into the river—right before he snapped a Polaroid. Then asked if I was okay.

Ray Collier was probably my best friend—a genuinely decent guy, and one hell of a cop. He'd been my sergeant when I was a rookie beat cop, and later, I worked for him again when I first made detective. He molded me into the cop I am today, and I still bend his ear on tough cases. He eats it up—loves it as much as it helps me.

I waved to let him know I saw him but made a stop for coffee before heading to the table.

"Hey, Wanda," I said, leaning on the gleaming stainless-steel counter—the only thing, or person, in this place not showing its age.

"Morning, honey. It's good to see you again. Here's your coffee. Ray said you were on your way, so your breakfast is almost ready."

"Thank you," I replied, smiling as I walked away.

Maybe I came here too often. I never had to order anymore, which was probably a little weird—but I liked it.

Ray stood up and shook my hand as I reached the table.

"Angus, so glad you decided to show up," he said with a smirk.

"Yeah, yeah, Ray. Good to see you too, brother."

I settled into the booth across from Ray and took a drink of my coffee. I don't get why younger folks spend seven bucks on some trendy latte or *capochino*, or whatever they're calling it now—there's no way any of it beats fresh, hot diner coffee.

As Wanda brought over several plates overflowing with pancakes, bacon, eggs, and biscuits & gravy, I thanked her, then turned to Ray.

"How's that retirement agreeing with you? Ready to come back yet?"

There was that damn grin again.

"Angus, brother, if I was any happier, the neighbors would start placing bets on whether my wife left—or if the FBI would be out back digging her up."

I shook my head. Ray's humor hadn't changed a bit. He was always cracking wife jokes, but everyone knew—nobody was a more devoted husband than Ray Collier. And to be fair, Carla was as much a smartass as he was.

"Seriously though, retirement's been fantastic. Carla and I have been traveling. Europe mostly—she loved Paris. It's not bad if you can ignore the part where every street smells like piss. For me, I'd move to Scotland today."

He paused, lifting his mug to his lips. "How 'bout you? How are things down at the old PD?"

I swallowed the oversized bite of eggs I'd shoveled in and chased it with a big swig of lukewarm coffee.

"Same old, same old. You know how it is—when things start working great, they change crap for no reason. The new chief's a prick, and he's messing with everything. I think he gets off on hearing us bitch."

Ray sat quietly for a second as he poured half a bottle of maple syrup over his pancakes and eggs, then looked up at me as he picked up his fork.

"I heard morale's at an all-time low. Of course, guys have been saying that for years, so who really knows. I hate you guys are having to deal with that shit. I survived three chief changes in my career, and it's always the same. The cops push through, and pretty soon, this jerk'll be gone. Just hang in there, brother."

I nodded as Ray continued.

"How's Lena and Penny? You see them much?"

I smiled at the mention of their names. Lena and I might've been divorced, but we were still family—and I loved those girls.

"I do," I said. "At least once a week for dinner. They're both doing great. Can you believe Penny's five?"

"What? Five? Damn, where do the years go? Please send them my love—and tell them to come see me sometime."

He paused long enough to swallow another bite.

"Now, Angus… how about you? You taking care of yourself? Seeing anyone?"

Ray being Ray. He cared about his cops as much as he did his own kids. Maybe that's why we made such a strong connection all those years ago. I was a kid trying to survive the midnight shift and Ray always took the time to make sure I was okay.

"You know, Ray, I'm not sure how I'm doing. I'm trying to see someone—Daniella, a much-too-young court reporter—and I find I'm too damn tired sometimes."

"Not sleeping again? I seem to recall that was your default stress response. Something bothering you?"

"It's this damn sniper case Graham and I are working. We've got three people dead and nothing else. No shell casings. No witnesses. No fingerprints or DNA. We have nothing. We are living in a maze with no exits—countless dead ends stacked on top of dead ends."

I paused and rubbed my eyes.

"The pressure from the chief's office is crushing us. We're working seventy, eighty hours a week and aren't any closer to finding the assailant. Bodies keep dropping, and the chief's a few hours away from yanking the case and handing it to BCI."

"Do you have eyes on anyone?"

I shook my head. "I mean, yeah, there are three or four people who could be involved, and I even told Graham I believed the last one we talked to was our shooter. But I don't know if I believe that or not. Every one of them has compelling pieces that make them likely, but just as many pieces that clear them. I keep telling myself there's something there, but damned if I can find it. I don't know, Ray."

Ray set his fork down next to his plate and wiped his mouth with his napkin. He leaned back in the booth and lifted his coffee cup—stopping short of taking a drink. He seemed to be thinking about what to say, as if he knew the answer but didn't know if I was ready.

"Listen, Angus, I've worked some multiple homicides—although nothing like this. Had five bodies in one weekend once, but nothing with the precision and discipline you're dealing with. Even so, killers are killers. They all have things in common, so does how you investigate them."

He paused, watching me.

"I learned a long time ago that when cases stall, there's always one common denominator. Do you know what that is, Angus?"

I shook my head, never taking my eyes off Ray.

"Some poor, overworked detective got tunnel vision and missed what was right in front of him. You can't outwork that kind of mistake. So before you grind yourself into powder trying to beat the clock, take a second and zoom out."

He pointed a syrup-covered fork in my direction.

"You and Graham—stop chasing shadows and look for patterns. Vehicle movement. Purchase histories. Online maps. Even far-fetched tips. Somewhere in all that junk is your thread."

He leaned back again, tapping the edge of his plate.

"Pull the thread."

"Pull the thread," I mumbled to myself as I nibbled on my last piece of bacon.

Ray took a sip of his coffee, then set the heavy ceramic cup down with a thud.

"You know, Angus… I once chased a guy for three weeks straight. Triple homicide out in Greenwich Village. Guy checked all the boxes—violent record, bad attitude, lived two blocks from the scene, known to have argued with at least one of the victims. We blew his alibi up in five minutes. I was sure we had him. But every interview, every lead, every search warrant—nothin'."

He shook his head, smiling at the humor now—even though it clearly hadn't been then.

"Turned out the real guy was the victim's cousin. Quiet type. No priors. Worked in a body shop. He was in the damn yard while we worked the scene. Even gave me a witness statement. You know how we caught him?"

I raised an eyebrow.

"Dumb luck, really," Ray said. "I was frustrated, so I went back to the scene—just walking the yard. Behind a dilapidated garage, I spotted a trash can that looked like it hadn't been emptied in years. Maybe the gun was in there. I crawled through the weeds and took a look. No gun—but inside the third plastic bag I pulled out, there it was. The female victim's purse. Bloody, empty… and stamped with a smeared but full thumbprint."

He drained the last of his coffee and flagged down Wanda for a refill, then leaned in.

"Lab pulled eight matching points—victim's cousin—we couldn't believe it. Not enough to charge, not even close—but it gave us a direction. We brought him in, laid it out, and he folded like a cheap tent. Full confession in under an hour."

Ray leaned back in the booth and smiled.

"We pulled the thread."

I nodded slowly, letting Ray's words sink in. I knew he was right. The answer was there—but we'd been looking in the wrong place. We'd been chasing shadows, hoping for a break, but Ray confirmed what we already knew deep down.

This wasn't going to be solved by waiting for the perfect clue. No—we'd have to crawl through the weeds and find the bloody thumbprint ourselves.

Ray watched me, waiting on a response I didn't have. He stretched and let out a satisfied sigh, patting his stomach—a toddler who had devoured an entire stick of Irish butter.

"Damn good food," he said. "Cholesterol be damned. Carla's been hiding the bacon since my last bloodwork, but what she don't know, as they say."

I stabbed another piece of pancake and popped it into my mouth. "Must suck to be old."

Wanda strolled by with the coffee pot at just the right time, eyes sharp enough to catch our empty cups from the kitchen.

"Refill, boys?" she asked, already pouring.

"Only if it comes with a defibrillator," Ray said.

Wanda rolled her eyes. "You've been threatening to keel over in that booth for thirty years, Ray Collier. I'm still waiting."

"You'll miss me when I'm gone," he muttered.

"Maybe," she said, patting his shoulder before moving on.

Ray watched her walk away and shook his head, smiling. "You know, you oughta think about retirement someday. Might even enjoy it."

"I'll retire the day someone handcuffs me to a beach chair," I said.

Ray laughed. "That could be arranged."

As Ray and Wanda traded jabs like the old friends they were, my thoughts slid back to the scenes. I'd been circling them for days, but Ray's crack about the thread snapped me toward them again.

It echoed louder the second time around.

We'd tossed a half-dozen tips over the last week—stuff that didn't fit the profile, leads that went nowhere. One of them was an unfamiliar van near the last shooting. An old cop passed it along, but it was so vague we let it die. Maybe too soon.

My coffee sat untouched, cooling fast. A small thread began to appear—not a lightbulb moment, nothing that sharp—but something. A flicker.

I didn't say anything to Ray. Not yet. I didn't want to jinx it.

Instead, I finished the last bite of biscuit, washed it down with a swig of cold diner coffee that had officially passed the point of no return, and pulled out my wallet. Habit, mostly. We never paid for a meal at Doog's—not because we asked for freebies, but because Wanda would throw a fit if we even tried to tip.

I needed to get out of there. As soon as I was back in the car, I was calling Graham.

I stood, thanked Wanda for the meal, and shook Ray's hand.

"It was great seeing you, Ray. Send Carla my love—and I'll see you here next month."

"Same, brother. And I won't tell Carla where I saw you, just that I saw you," he said with a laugh. "Be sure to keep me posted on your case, Angus. I'm invested now."

"I will," I said. "Take care now."

I walked toward the door, pulling out my phone as I stepped onto the sidewalk.

Dead-end tips.

Maybe one of them wasn't so dead after all.

Chapter 29
Collateral

I picked Graham up for work this morning. He called as I was leaving the house, begging for a ride. His truck was in the shop again—something about the front-end alignment this time. Graham's truck was always in the shop—lift kit this, suspension that. It had more appointments than a crooked city councilman. I think he spent more time at the garage than with his family. Still, he was my brother, and he always had my back, so I didn't mind the detour.

The unexpected stop made us a little late, and Jenkins was already texting:

Where the hell are you guys? Soon as you get in, see me in the LT's office.

That didn't sound good. Lieutenant Branson's office was down the hall from ours, and the door was open when we walked up. Jenkins stood near the window, arms crossed, watching two men in dark blue suits seated in the LT's chairs, their folders lined up with the precision of a White House briefing. Everything about them was crisp and perfect—from their identical haircuts to their Brooks Brothers suits and the shine on their Allen Edmonds wingtips.

You could smell the Fed ego before they even opened their mouths.

Jenkins looked up with a bit of relief when we walked in—like a guy who'd just been handed a live grenade and we brought the pin.

"Detectives," he said. "Special Agents Vaughn and Ramirez from the FBI's Dayton office."

Vaughn stood first—tall, crisp, eyes cold as the snow outside. As I expected—they sent the SAC. FBI brass, here to take the credit and bury the rest. I knew him from a case years back. Surprisingly, he recognized me too.

"Angus," he said. "It's been a while. Good to see you again. We've been tracking your recent homicides."

"Tracking, huh?" Graham muttered, arms crossed and leaning back slightly. It was his suspect face—silent, unimpressed, daring you to lie again.

Ramirez stood too. Younger, with the lean build of a runner. He gave a nod but said nothing. He and Vaughn stood stiff and expressionless—telling us we weren't even worthy of sharing the same room. These guys didn't bend—they creaked, old floorboards in a trap house. Everything about them—from tone to posture—said:

We're here to clean up your mess.

Vaughn didn't waste time. "We're concerned about your three related homicides, which may fall under federal jurisdiction. The consistent caliber and shooter behavior suggest a sniper, of course, but the possible terrorist connection we were advised of recently appears to be the most likely motive.

"As you know, your first victim, Hassan Al-Khatib," Vaughn added, "was also known as Tariq Al-Mansour. He was wanted in three countries. We've intercepted encrypted chatter overseas that mentions a cleansing operation in the States to eliminate problems before they can be arrested. If your shooter's tied to that, this isn't just your city's problem."

"It's happening on our streets. Why the hell would we think it's our problem?" I said, my voice dripping with sarcasm.

Jenkins gave a grimace and a slow blink.

Vaughn said, "We recognize you're good detectives, but with our resources and expertise, we're better positioned to bring this to an arrest."

He paused for a response that didn't come. "This isn't about turf. It's about who's best equipped to find the shooter. We're offering to take over coordination and responsibility. That means full access—case files, evidence logs, witness statements—and that you defer to us on every move."

The silence lasted maybe two seconds. I could feel Jenkins' stare, waiting to see if I'd fire the first shot—or if he'd have to.

I leaned against the table, gave them both a look, and said, "So, not here to assist. Here to hijack."

Ramirez finally spoke. "The mayor's office called us directly. Public pressure's mounting."

"That so?" Jenkins' voice dropped half an octave. "Mayor's not police."

Vaughn gave a diplomatic smile. "You've done solid work. But these killings may fall under federal statutes. If the shooter has crossed state lines, or if a civil rights violation is identified—"

"There's no federal jurisdiction yet," Graham cut in. "No ransom. No extortion. No federal facilities. No out-of-state travel. These murders happened on Dayton streets—our streets."

Vaughn turned to Branson. "I know it's hard to hand something over once you're deep in it. But you're sitting on a serial case. You need the Bureau's tools more than your instincts."

The LT exhaled through his nose. "You've got good tools. So do we. My detectives know this city—the neighborhoods, the bad guys—and they're already deep in it. We're not handing it off."

He didn't raise his voice. He didn't need to. Every word landed like a brick on the table.

A long pause. Vaughn's expression didn't change, but Ramirez's pen stopped moving.

"Fine," Vaughn said. "But understand—at the first sign of federal jurisdiction, we step in. No request next time."

"Do what you gotta do, Vaughn," Jenkins said. "But this is a homicide case. It needs real homicide detectives—not white-collar pencil pushers with guns."

The agents stood. Vaughn gathered his folder, buttoned his jacket, and turned to Branson.

"We'll be seeing you boys soon. I just hope no one else dies while you're protecting your turf."

They walked out with the kind of in-your-face arrogance you only see in an under-qualified, over-confident fed.

The door clicked shut behind them. Silence hung for a moment, the kind that settles after a threat leaves the room but doesn't actually go away.

Jenkins turned to Graham as the door closed, letting out a breath of relief and frustration.

Graham grinned, amused by the rare snark from Jenkins. "White-collar pencil pushers with guns? Well done, Sarge."

Jenkins only smiled sheepishly.

"I hope you're right about this thing being local," he said as he walked toward his office. "You know as well as I do—they'll be back with a fury if another body falls."

I nodded, but I wasn't sure if we were right or not.

"I've been looking over what we have on Ashbourne," Graham said, leaning against the doorframe. "I can't directly connect her to any of the shootings. If she's involved, she's hiding her tracks."

"She wore the badge. She knows how we work," I said. "If anyone could throw us off their track, it'd be her."

He shook his head. "I don't know, man. I think she's clean."

I didn't respond. Because the truth was, I could still see her across that coffee table—calm, steady, like she was waiting for the right moment to pull the trigger.

***

They arrived on Wayne Avenue in a dark blue rented Kia. Their own car was at home—the van in storage. Nobody would notice a common Kia at that hour—and if they did, they'd probably assume it was stolen, not being used to plan a murder. It wasn't that their personal car would stand out, but they knew that if they ever became a suspect, the car's GPS data would be a problem.

According to the clock on the Kia's dash, it was just past 1 A.M. as they drove past the diner.

Christopher Redmond should be arriving soon. They'd been watching him for a couple weeks. Every night, same routine. Always surrounded by several large, gym-built enforcers—bodyguards, maybe? And it was this way wherever he went, he seemed to know he was being watched.

But then he came to the diner. Redmond always sat on the inside of the booth, apparently believing that with his bodyguard on one side and the glass on the other, he was safe.

Naïve.

Wanting to be hidden before Redmond arrived, they found an abandoned pharmacy across the street from the diner and backed up next to the building under the canopy of some overgrown trees. In the unlit lot, they would be hard to spot, even in the van, but they were much closer than they wanted to be.

The diner was perfect. The neighborhood was the obstacle—tight blocks stitched together with sagging porches and chain-link fences, the kind of streets where every shadow had a set of eyes behind it. Houses, storefronts, fences, cars—and of course, a big hill right behind the pharmacy. Nowhere they looked gave them more than 100 yards of clear sightline. Ninety-three, to be exact.

Far too close.

Less time to aim, less time to run. Less time for anything if something went wrong. But it was this or nothing—and it scared the hell out of them.

From the front seat of the Kia, they had a clear line of sight to the diner's glass front. Fluorescents buzzed overhead—far too many. The place was lit up as if afraid of what lurked outside. Five old booths lined up along the windows as ducks in a row—greasy red vinyl, seams splitting like busted lips. The target's booth—the last one to the right—offered none of the protection Redmond hoped for. It would be clean. Too clean.

But tonight wasn't about the shot. Not yet. Tonight was about timing. Predictability. Escape routes.

They sat and watched—silent, dark—the tablet's glow the only light inside. Outside, a neon sign flickered, pulsing with the heartbeat of a deserted street. They logged notes on foot traffic, vehicle flow, and passing patrols. Pedestrians were sparse: three in the last hour. A man walked a dog. A woman cut through from the bus stop. The third was a teenager on a bike who didn't even glance at the diner. Vehicle traffic stayed light—mostly locals and a bus or two. One cruiser had passed twenty minutes ago but didn't stop.

This setup wasn't good. There was a side street, but it was one-way onto Wayne. Technically usable in an emergency—but people who live on one-way streets always notice when someone goes the wrong way. And they love calling the cops. Getting pinched for a traffic violation screamed amateur. The risk was too high. Only two routes made sense: north or south on Wayne, assuming the lot entrance wasn't blocked.

They noted the number of people already in the diner. It was nearly at capacity, which wasn't ideal. They preferred fewer witnesses, of course—but more people also meant a greater chance of an unintended casualty. It didn't matter. For this mission, that couldn't be a deciding factor. It was here or nowhere.

As they waited for Redmond to arrive, they took a few photos of the diner from the driver's seat—frame, angle, glass clarity, sightlines. The interior lights helped identify where people were seated, but at this range, through a scope and a window, the glare would make confirming Redmond's identity difficult. That would have to happen outside—on the sidewalk, before he went in. After that, it was just a matter of following him to his booth.

The minutes dragged, one painful click at a time. They'd been waiting about forty-five minutes, and doubt was starting to creep in. The questions piled up. Had they misread Redmond's pattern? Had he realized he was being watched? Were the police already on the way?

Their legs bounced. Fingers tapped. Face pressed in the palms of both hands like they were fighting off a migraine. A restless rhythm of nerves.

This was a bad location. They might be burned. Every instinct screamed to get the hell out.

But every name on the list mattered.

Redmond would not walk away.

Then they heard it—loud voices, the kind that bounce everywhere when a group of drunks is staggering home.

They glanced at the diner. The neon sign flickered, casting a slow pulse of red across the sidewalk.

And there he was. Late, but there.

Same jeans. Same ball cap. Same crew of bodyguards shielding him from threats—or so they thought.

It was easy to follow Redmond as he entered and sat down. Booth five. Next to the glass. Same as always.

Everything was in place. As long as Redmond showed again tomorrow, his penalty would be applied. The light on the sidewalk was perfect for identification. The diner lights allowed him to be tracked to his seat. The line of sight was clear.

There was only one unexpected problem.

Redmond wasn't sitting alone. One of his bodyguards was right next to him. If the shot was taken with him there, he'd die too.

The plan was to see Redmond arrive and take his seat before heading home for the night, but they decided to wait until Redmond left, hoping for a lapse in security—some chance to take the shot without killing anyone else.

The mission had rules, and breaking them meant losing control. They'd passed on shots before, and they would again if the risk outweighed the gain. But the pressure was building by the day. To finish the mission, some risks would have to be ignored.

A little over an hour after he walked in, Redmond rose from his booth and moved toward the door. It looked like he'd exit alone, but just before stepping outside, he stopped. His security detail moved first, spilling out onto the sidewalk. Redmond followed, and the group disappeared down the block.

They'd run the angles, mapped the timing, studied the light. The shot was too close. The risk too high. The margin for error was nonexistent.

But it was happening anyway.

One way or another, Christopher Redmond would die in that booth. And if someone else died with him?

Then so be it. Collateral damage was part of the cleanse. Somebody always gets caught in the splash when you drain the swamp.

Chapter 30
One Shot, Two Down

Last night had been for planning. Tonight was for killing.

The neon OPEN sign above the door of the Wayne Avenue diner buzzed and flickered in the dark as the shooter adjusted the rifle's scope, eyes fixed on Christopher Redmond as he walked toward his booth. As he flirted with all of the waitresses and made his way to the last booth, the shooter replayed what brought them here.

Christopher Redmond was a problem—always shadowed by multiple bodyguards, even after days of surveillance. He was careful, yet he had a weakness: he couldn't resist the pull of a late-night burger and fries. His penchant for early A.M. grease was why the shooter was now lying in the shooting perch of the van, scope to the eye, watching. Waiting.

Their jaw tightened as they recalled the previous missions. They had been simple and safe—shots taken from nearly 250 yards out, where detection was nearly impossible, all aimed at center mass. Any rookie with a long-gun could make those shots. But this was different: a headshot from a fairly exposed position less than 100 yards away.

Tonight, the risks were high, but another failure to act would end the mission for good. There would be no reset tonight.

The planning had been meticulous—clean shots, rigid timelines, no mistakes. But the delays, the close calls, the children—those had already stolen too much time. Every missed chance meant another week of exposure, another week for the police to close the gap.

Opportunities didn't arrive gift-wrapped. They came in fleeting alignments—targets in the open, angles that worked, a few seconds where distance and cover meant control. Those seconds didn't care who else happened to be standing nearby.

Their finger hovered outside the trigger guard. Uncertainty lingered. What about the man sitting next to Redmond? The .338 was designed for long distances—over 1,000 yards. At this range, even through the glass, the round might over-penetrate and hit the other man.

Collateral damage was the cost they'd accepted—a debt that would never be paid off, a ghost that would never stop trailing them.

They could already see the face of the second man in their dreams—one more soul to join the others. One more name they'd never learn, one more face they'd never forget. They took a deep breath, held it in, forced their mind to focus, and slipped the finger onto the trigger. One shot. One chance.

A silent squeeze. The crack of the suppressed Barrett—loud enough to be heard if someone was near, but to most, it would be lost among the late-night noise of the city. The clanging metal from garbage trucks emptying dumpsters, the sirens from passing emergency vehicles, and the echoes of sporadic gunshots absorbed the noise of the rifle like a roaring river swallowing a pebble's splash.

They watched Redmond's head snap to his right shoulder, the round striking just above his ear. A spray of blood, brain, and bone spattered across the man beside him before the same bullet tore through and dropped him too. Within a second, both men were slumped over the small table, chaos erupting around their bodies.

They shut the roof hatch and climbed down from the perch. Their routine was to never watch the aftermath. Maybe it made it too human, or maybe it bored them—they weren't sure—but it was better that way.

***

A sudden, sickening thud—an axe splitting oak—cut through the laughter and loud banter of the after-hours club crowd. For a moment—silence. Staff and patrons were frozen in shock at what they had seen. A waitress, who moments before had greeted

Redmond as he came in, stood motionless, tray in hand, eyes wide as she took in the scene. Then—chaos.

Screams filled the air. Someone shouted, *Get down!*—maybe they didn't care. Everyone surged at once—scrambling to escape, knocking over chairs, tables, and each other in their panic to reach the back door. Dishes crashed to the floor, shattering into pieces, as they all surged toward the path through the narrow galley-style kitchen. The floor, slick with spilled drinks and food, became dangerous as patrons scrambled for the exits.

An elderly man, knocked to the ground when his cane was kicked away, clutched his chest, gasping for breath, as he crawled toward the back door. No one saw the shooter. Just the hole in the glass and two dead men. Everyone had the same goal—getting out the back door.

Amidst the pandemonium, one of Redmond's associates, face spattered with blood and visibly shaken, dropped to the floor next to his dead friends. His hands trembled as he fumbled for his phone, finally managing to dial 911.

"911, what's your emergency?"

"Their heads just… exploded! Oh God—what the hell is happening?"

"Sir, I need you to stay calm. Where are you?"

"Wayne Avenue Diner," he stammered. "They dead... I don't know where it came from. Just—please, send help!"

The dispatcher assured him that units were on the way. Around him, the diner's once-cozy atmosphere had transformed into a scene of horror. The air was thick with the smell of blood and spilled food, and the panicked screams of those too terrified to run. The wail of approaching sirens provided a small amount of comfort to those inside, but not the shooter.

The chaos. The screams. The sirens. They knew they were too close, and tonight was not the night to get caught. They slipped into the driver's seat of the van and started the engine. A pair of headlights flashed across the windshield—just a passing car. They froze anyway, heart pounding, until the taillights faded. Without turning on the headlights, they eased the van out onto Wayne Avenue and disappeared into the night seconds before the first police arrived.

***

Within three minutes of the 911 call, the first crews arrived and rushed into the diner, sidearms held at low-ready. The caller, hiding beneath the table, looked up at the approaching officers with extended hands.

"I called…my friends…somebody shot my friends."

An officer motioned the caller to come out from under the table and move toward the second officer walking in. The place stank of grease, blood, and fear. Booths were overturned. A tray of food lay scattered across the floor like it had been dropped mid-step. The first officer stepped closer to the booth, took one look at the mess, and keyed his shoulder mic.

"212, dispatch."

"Go ahead, 212."

"We've got two down. Get a medic and a supervisor rolling. And send more units for crowd control."

***

I was sleeping good when the phone rang—first decent sleep I'd had in weeks. But I was wide awake now. Two more bodies, same signature as the last ones. Our sniper had struck again, and this time, it was escalating fast.

We were in crisis mode. I didn't even stop for coffee. I threw on some clothes and ran out the door. We had to get to the scene and get ahead of the story—before the brass got wind and made it worse.

When I walked into the diner, I was stunned by the disarray. I had eaten in here many times when I worked nights, and it was always clean, bright and energetic. Tonight, it looked worse than a haunted house, the horror lingering long after October ended.

I stepped around puddles of coffee and pancake syrup, and over shattered plates and broken mugs, until I reached the last booth. The coroner hadn't arrived yet, and the medics were already gone—but I didn't need anyone to explain what happened here. The damage to their heads was catastrophic. And final.

The escalation was troubling. It had only been a week since Rojas was killed, and now we had a double homicide. Why the change in pattern? Was one or both of these men targets? And if it was one—then which one?

I turned to the patrol officer standing to my left.

"Do we know who these guys are?"

"Yeah. The caller was with them," he said. "Guy by the window's Chris Redmond. Other one's Billy Pritchard. Couple of local thugs."

He hesitated a beat, then added, "I knew Redmond. A pimp—well, was. Mostly local girls. Kept 'em doped up and working out of the pay-by-the-hour spots."

I scribbled the names in my notebook and turned to head outside, nearly bumping into Jenkins.

"Hey, Sarge. Glad you're here. Downtown's going to explode when they hear about this. You can talk to them if any show up."

"Maybe it's somebody else."

"I sure as hell hope not. The thought of somebody else killing with this kind of precision terrifies the shit out of me. You seen Graham?"

Jenkins nodded. "Yeah. I sent him to the back of the diner to get statements from the witnesses."

I filled Jenkins in on what we knew so far, then stepped out onto the front sidewalk. I wasn't sure what I was looking for, but I needed to figure out where the shot came from.

The window was shattered, but based on the injuries to the victims, the round could've only come from straight out front.

I pulled out my phone and called Graham.

"Go ahead," he answered.

"Anybody see the shooter? Or at least the direction the shot came from?"

"Nope. Nobody saw a thing. One second people were laughing, clinking glasses—the next, the window blew apart like it had been hit with a brick of ice. Shards everywhere. Folks dove under tables, and when they came up, two people were down, and the whole place was slick with glass and blood."

I hung up and looked across the four lanes of Wayne Avenue. An abandoned drugstore with a wide, empty parking lot sat directly across from the diner. Behind it, a steep hill climbed toward a cluster of apartments.

No one saw the shooter or heard the shot, which meant it came from a distance—somewhere across the street. Maybe the sidewalk, but more likely the empty lot behind it. The angle was right.

The area was quiet now. Whoever fired the shot was long gone—slipped away before we even got close.

As I walked back toward the door, I noticed a gray Ford Explorer pull up in front. I checked my watch—I'd been there over thirty minutes. Finally, the coroner. I walked toward the SUV. "Hey Jerry, did we wake you up from your nap?"

"Screw you, Angus," he said with a laugh. "I'm working my ass off tonight. This is my fourth death scene since dinner."

I laughed and shook his hand.

"Better late than never. We've got a hell of a mess in here."

We walked back to the bodies. Jerry looked them over, made a few notes, then opened his camera case. After documenting the scene, he pulled on a pair of black nitrile gloves and started examining the wounds—first Redmond, then Pritchard.

"A single shot." He pointed above Redmond's left ear. "Entered here, exited the right side—where the rest of his head had been. Then it hit Pritchard, right through his left ear. No exit wound. Bullet's in his brain somewhere."

"Damn," I muttered. "I've never seen shit like this before."

"Not much surprises me, Angus, but I'm with you. This is some next-level stuff—something straight out of a Fallujah memoir, not a diner in Dayton."

I left Jerry to finish up and went to find Graham and Jenkins. I told them about the likely trajectory—the shot coming from across the street—and the extent of the injuries.

"We'll get the bullet after the autopsy," I said, "but I'm already convinced it's going to match."

"And fellas, I'm a little concerned. I think the shooter's getting bolder. Whether the shot came from the sidewalk or the lot, both positions were wide open. And taking out two? I don't know if that was planned or accidental, but either way, it spells trouble. An open-lot shot isn't just bold—it's loud, risky, and messy. Either they feel untouchable, or they're on the clock."

Jenkins shook his head as his phone started to ring.

"Damn. It's the lieutenant. How the hell does he already know about this?"

Graham and I looked at each other, patted Jenkins on the back, and headed toward our cars. Tomorrow morning was going to be brutal for everyone. This had all the makings of a political storm, and storms roll downhill.

Chapter 31
Before Another Body Drops

Graham and I got to the office early, knowing the chief's office would be calling about the shooting last night. We needed a plan—something that showed we were making progress. The pressure was coiling tighter by the hour. A little more time. That's all we needed.

The radiator knocked in the corner, stubborn against the morning chill.

While Graham poured the coffee, I pulled up ThinBlueLie.com on my desktop and scrolled through the hit list, eyes scanning the names as though I were checking off a death pool—one box away from a full blackout. I was looking for either of the victims from the diner. If we found one, I figured we could buy ourselves a little breathing room before the brass started talking about pulling the case.

First name in my notes: Billy Pritchard, who'd been sitting on the outside of the booth—on the aisle, opposite the window. At first, we weren't sure if he was a target or collateral damage.

His name wasn't on the list.

Which told me our shooter was getting sloppy—or that Pritchard was in the wrong place at the wrong time.

Redmond, though: he was there.

That hit like a hammer to the chest, knocking the wind out of me. Five shootings now, and four of the five victims from the list.

Ashbourne was more likely to be a mermaid than innocent.

And I don't believe in mermaids.

We didn't have enough to lock her up—not yet—but this had to be enough to convince the chief to back off. At least for a little while.

"Graham!" I called out—louder than I meant to, especially in our broom-closet-sized office. "Redmond's on the list."

He looked up from his coffee. "Pritchard?"

"Nope. Just Redmond."

Graham frowned.

"Doesn't matter," I said. "Pritchard could've been bad luck. But Redmond? That makes four of five."

I made a note beside Pritchard's name anyway. Not being on the list didn't mean he was clean. If there was one thing this case had taught me, it was that assumptions had a nasty way of blowing up in your face.

I spun the monitor toward him. "This is as close to a smoking gun as we're going to get. It keeps the list in play and gives us a fighting chance at stopping the next one."

"So we work the rest of the list?"

"Hard. Let's dig up everything we can on all four of them. Somebody is next—we just need to find them."

Graham slid his chair over beside me, coffee in hand, squinting at the screen.

"Let's see what we've got left, maybe we can build an argument for a stakeout."

I scrolled down. The list wasn't long to begin with—eight names total, four of them already dead. That left us four possibles to get ahead of before the shooter did.

"First one's Julian Ortega," I said. "That name ring a bell?"

Graham shook his head. "Nope."

I opened a browser tab and punched it in. Didn't take long. Local news had a few hits. A headline from three years back jumped out: CHARGES DROPPED IN GANG RAPE CASE.

I read aloud. "Seventeen-year-old girl, assaulted behind a party house in the UD Ghetto. Ortega was one of three arrested. DNA inconclusive. Witnesses flaked. Victim refused to testify after the preliminary hearing."

Graham let out a low breath. "Jesus."

"He walked without a trial," I said. "Other two took pleas. Ortega? Clean record now."

"Fits the profile," Graham said. "Brutal crime, no conviction. Plenty of outrage to go around. Do we have a last known?"

"Yep, Lamar Street."

"Checks all the boxes then."

I nodded and typed it into a separate file: Ortega – Strong candidate.

"Next up—Kenny Voss." I clicked the next file and frowned. "He's older. Fifty-eight. Arrested six years ago for possession of child pornography. Got off on a bad search warrant. Judge tossed the whole case."

"Was that the guy they found filming little girls in the locker room at the Y?" Graham asked.

I blinked. "Yeah. Damn, good catch."

"I remember the DA was furious. Defense tore up the chain of custody."

"Not just the DA," I said. "Public outcry was huge. Parents at his school lost their minds, even though he was a custodian and not a teacher. He got fired but never charged again."

Graham tilted his head. "Guy's gotta know he's hated. Any signs he's gone off-grid?"

I checked the most recent address. "He's living with his sister out in Riverside, but he works night shift at a printing company on N. Main."

"Living outside the city makes it tougher, but we can watch his job for a bit," Graham muttered.

"Yeah, I'm not sure how the shooter is picking them, but they've all had some tie to the city. Let's put him on the list, at least till we've checked them all."

I typed his name beside Ortega. Voss – Possible candidate.

"Next up is Zhao Wang – con man. This asshole runs scams targeting old ladies. He was charged for the death of some poor old widow who overdosed after he took her for two hundred and fifty K. Charges were dropped when they couldn't tie him to more than a casual night on the town."

"Damn," Graham said. "Easy to hate, but would he really be worth the shooter's time?"

"Seems a weak choice, but he's on the list for some reason." I frowned. *"Someone thought he deserved a bullet."*

Graham nodded in agreement,

I scrolled again. "Alright, last one on the maybe pile—Travis Ledbetter."

"Ledbetter," Graham repeated. "Sounds familiar."

"It should," I said. "He's the white face running meth for L.V.C. East side's his turf. He's stacked more ODs and ruined lives than anyone can count."

Graham grimaced. "Another one that skated."

"Yeah, but he's different. The whole city knows, but we've never caught him holding. And his victims? They'd rather keep their dope than testify."

"I get that. People hate rapists and predators. But the guy who sells them a buzz? Doesn't piss folks off the same way."

"Still makes the list, though," I said. "Our shooter's definition of justice isn't exactly nuanced."

Graham tapped the desk. "He's a notch below Ortega and Voss. But I wouldn't rule him out."

I added him to the file. Ledbetter – Possible.

We sat there a minute. Somewhere in the ceiling, the ductwork popped and settled, a hollow, metallic heartbeat keeping time with the silence. Outside, traffic passed by in slow intervals, muffled through the thick windows and weak insulation.

Graham broke the silence. "We do anything with this today?"

I shrugged. "We can't sit on all three. Even with Jenkins on board, we'd need six bodies just to run a proper rotation."

"So we talk to them?"

"Maybe. Ortega and Voss are solid enough for surveillance, but a knock at the door might scare off the shooter—or worse, tip off the target, and suddenly we're dealing with the press. Suddenly we've got a panic and a grandstanding mayor."

Graham gave a dry snort. "So that's a no on the door knock."

"For those two, yeah." I rubbed my jaw, "Ledbetter, though—he's close, and if we tip the shooter, it might work in our favor; send him toward one of the guys we're watching. We could swing by casual. Say it's a follow-up on an old DV case."

"You really want to bluff that guy?"

I shrugged. "I don't like sitting on my hands."

He didn't answer right away. "I say we pitch surveillance. Ortega and Voss. Quiet, long-range, unmarked."

"Okay then, we won't knock yet. We'll see how the stakeouts go first. I'll draft something for Jenkins," I said. "Toss in the list analysis and make the case. Worst he can say is no."

"Worse he can say is the chief already called BCI."

I glanced at the clock. Not even lunch time yet. The whole day ahead of us.

I had a feeling it was going to be a long one.

***

We ate lunch at our desks—cold sandwiches from the corner deli, barely noticed between browser tabs and PDF files. I had Voss's old search warrant up on one screen and Ortega's probation hearing on the other. Graham was digging through property records, zoning maps, anything we could use for eyes-on without blowing our cover.

"Voss works nights at Century Printing up near Forest and Main," Graham said, pointing at the screen. "Rear lot, no gates. Surveillance might work from that used tire shop across the alley."

I nodded. "Wide view. Fewer people passing by at night, too."

"What about Ortega?"

I dragged up a satellite image of Lamar Street. "Not much to work with. Maybe this building at the end of the block, but we'll have to see it in person to know.

Graham leaned closer. "That's our spot, if it hasn't been posted."

"I'll send someone by to check it before we burn it." I switched over to Word and started typing up the pitch for Jenkins. "We'll request surveillance on both—one car per location. I'm thinking 2100 to 0300—that covers the time window on all four shootings."

"So Voss and Ortega?" Graham asked.

"Yeah. I think they're our best shot."

Graham nodded, then tapped the desk with the edge of his phone. "You really think Jenkins'll sign off?"

"I think he'll fight for it if he believes it'll keep BCI out of the way."

"If they're not already in," Graham said.

I didn't answer. That possibility had been there all morning—cold, quiet, and growing louder.

The chief wasn't patient. If he'd already made the call, we'd find out soon enough.

I stared at the screen for a second, then kept typing. The report read like a defense brief:

Pattern of confirmed victims matching the list

Redmond made it four out of five.

Risk level for Ortega and Voss based on prior cases, public sentiment, and timing

Surveillance recommendations by location, shift, and expected needs

By the time I was done, it read tight—and just desperate enough to be honest.

"Want me to take it to him?" Graham offered.

"Sarge is gone for the day," I said. "I'll hit him first thing tomorrow."

Assuming the chief hasn't already cut us off at the knees.

He nodded. "I'll start pulling plate data for Voss and Ortega, see what else we've got on their vehicles."

I printed a copy, saved the file, and attached it to an email.

Subject line: Request for Surveillance — Ortega / Voss — Priority Review.

***

The rest of the day passed in a blur of small tasks—calls that went nowhere, files that confirmed what we already knew, dead ends dressed up as leads.

By 5:30, the office was quiet. There were a couple patrol officers hanging around, but me and Graham were the last detective holdouts. We would need to leave soon too—Graham's coffee had gone cold again. Outside, the sun dipped low behind the courthouse, throwing a hard amber light through the blinds.

Thinking about the list, I stared at the wall hoping it might offer up the next answer.

Four names left. Two of them ticking louder than the rest.

We shut down for the night without saying much. The questions would be there in the morning.

***

I got in early, but Graham was already there—tie askew, sleeves rolled, hands wrapped around a fresh coffee, the cure for a long night. He turned as I stepped in.

"Heard from anybody yet?"

I shook my head. "Not yet. But we will."

We didn't have to wait long. Five minutes later, the phone rang.

Jenkins barked before I even finished saying hello. "Lieutenant wants you both upstairs. Now."

We didn't speak on the walk. No need.

The conference room was dim, quiet, and stale—like an attic someone had just remembered existed. It smelled faintly of old paper, dust, and political pressure. The blinds were drawn halfway, slanting pale light across the long table.

Jenkins was already seated at the far end, eyes on a manila folder he wasn't reading. Branson stood with his arms folded. Chief Robertson was at the window, hands behind his back, staring out at downtown.

He didn't turn when he spoke. "Where are we?"

It wasn't a question. It was a challenge.

I stepped forward. "Our primary suspect is a retired deputy, Kyra Ashbourne. She's posted a sort of hit list on her blog. Four of the five confirmed victims are on it. We believe with near certainty the next target is too. We've identified two names—Julian Ortega and Kenny Voss—as likely targets. Both have criminal histories similar to the previous victims, and we'd like to set up surveillance. We've submitted the request to Sergeant Jenkins. I brought a copy as well."

Facing the window, the chief asked, "How long have you had this list?"

"A few days. We only confirmed Redmond yesterday."

"And you waited until now to act on it?"

"We've been vetting the names," I said. "Prioritizing based on risk level, public exposure, and logistics."

Robertson turned then. His face was calm, but his eyes were loaded.

"Why aren't you watching Ashbourne?"

"We considered that, Chief," I replied. "But she isn't our only possible suspect. We don't have the manpower to tail everyone *and* watch the likely targets. She's a trained former officer—she'd spot us before we got within half a block. But if we're right about the list, the best chance we've got is covering the people in danger."

Robertson stood silently for a moment, then nodded. "That sounds reasonable. But you must understand—I've already spoken to

BCI. They're standing by, but since you were right about the list, I'm inclined to hold them off a bit longer."

Graham shifted beside me but said nothing.

Jenkins cleared his throat. "Chief, we appreciate any extra time. We're close. This isn't just a list—it's a pattern. A plan."

I followed up. "If we can get eyes on Ortega and Voss, we've got a real shot at stopping the next one. We're not guessing anymore—we're reacting."

Robertson crossed to the table and placed both palms flat against the wood. "The press already smells blood. City Manager's breathing down my neck, and I've got the Attorney General's office asking why we haven't handed this off. I want to trust your team, but it's getting hard. Is the list all you have?"

"We believe the shooter is using this list and likely traveling in a black van," I said, keeping my voice even. "We received a tip after the Rojas shooting—Jack Turner, retired DPD sergeant, saw it. And if he's suspicious, so am I."

"Why didn't I hear about this earlier?"

"It's one tip among many, Chief," I said. "It's in our supplemental Report."

"Okay, what do you need for the surveillance?"

"Four detectives to watch the targets, and a SWAT apprehension team staged to respond if the shooter appears. We're dealing with an extremely high-powered rifle, so their expertise—and their armored truck—will be critical."

Branson cut in, his voice calmer. "Chief, we can make this happen. But I want a SWAT long-gun with each detective team. Angus, will three hours be enough?"

"I think six," I replied. "In our request, you'll see we want to be on post from 2100 to 0300."

He nodded. "Okay, Angus. Six hours. One night. If it doesn't work, we'll re-evaluate."

Robertson didn't speak right away. He looked at each of us, measuring something behind his eyes.

Then he nodded once.

He didn't pound the table this time. Just rested his hands on the folder. "Every move we make tonight gets judged in real time—by the mayor, the media, half the damn internet. If this goes wrong, It's my badge, and maybe yours."

He paused, his tone hardening.

"And if we miss, I'm done protecting you. I'll hand this over to BCI and tell the press we're out of leads. Your names will be in it."

The words landed like a gut punch. It wasn't a deadline—this was a warning that if we failed, we'd fail in public.

I knew "no choice" didn't just mean BCI. If this spun any further out, the Bureau could roll back in under the counterterrorism mandate and take the whole thing over. We'd seen it happen before—local case gutted, dropped into a black hole of federal jurisdiction.

He left without waiting for a response. The door clicked shut behind him.

Jenkins exhaled and looked up at the ceiling. "Well. I guess that's a yes."

A yes wrapped in a threat. Forty-eight hours to catch a ghost with a rifle before the state—or worse—pulled the plug. The kind of clock you could hear ticking even after you walked out the door.

Chapter 32
Site 1, Site 2

We chose Sunday night. Three of the four shootings had landed on a Sunday, and if the pattern meant anything, this was our best shot.

Four names left on the list. Two teams available. A fifty-fifty chance—better odds than we'd had all week. But we'd chosen our targets carefully. I had no doubt we'd get our shooter.

Jeffries and Koski had mostly been on the sidelines for this case, and they were eager to be involved. The six hours of OT didn't hurt. With everyone in the office, I closed the door and asked if they had any questions or concerns.

Jeffries leaned forward first. "This about the list?"

I nodded. "We've got approval for surveillance on two of the four remaining names—Julian Ortega and Kenny Voss. Both match the profile, and based on timeline and proximity, we think they're high risk."

Koski folded his arms. "We watching the houses or the guys?"

"The guys," I began. "Well, technically, just the area where they should be. You two will sit outside Ortega's place. Intel says he rarely leaves after dark, except to walk his dog. We'll take Voss. He works nights at a printing company over on N. Main. Chances are we won't see either one, so I want you to watch the street. The only thing we've got is a the van. That's our focus tonight."

Graham added, "You won't be alone. Each team will be paired with a SWAT officer with a long-gun. They'll be in direct contact with the apprehension team, which will be staged at D1."

Jeffries raised an eyebrow. "Sniper?"

"Yes," I said. "We're dealing with a .338 Lapua. We want an immediate, long-range response if this turns hot."

Koski gave a low whistle. "Jesus. Alright."

"You'll stay in place all six hours," Graham continued. "You know the drill—bring food, coffee. No lights, radio silence. We're dealing with a skilled operator—they're probably monitoring our channels, and they'll spot you if you slip up."

"What about the apprehension team?" Jeffries asked.

"SWAT's BearCat will be staged at D1," I said. "Close enough to roll fast, but tucked away on police property to keep things quiet. You see something, call it in—they'll move."

"And if it's nothing?" Koski asked.

"Then it's nothing. We wave them off—and yeah, we're probably burned," I said. "But it's your call. No shame in playing it safe. I'd rather call and be wrong than not call and be wrong."

They both nodded.

I paused before continuing. "This could be our only shot. We're pretty sure the shooter's using a black van and working off this list, but we don't know how much time we've got. If we're lucky, we spot the van, make the stop, and bring this to an end."

"And if we're not?" Jeffries asked.

I met his eyes. "Then we're in the chief's office Monday morning begging for another week."

Graham handed out the printed packets—maps, notes, names, photos.

"We meet with SWAT at D1 on Sunday—1700 hours sharp for the final briefing. You'll pair with SWAT member and roll out from there. Any questions?"

Jeffries stood and cracked his knuckles. "Nope."

"Alright then," I said. "See you Sunday."

Koski gave a tight smile. "We'll be there."

***

It was early afternoon after briefing Koski and Jeffries, so Graham and I headed out to get another look at the two locations. We didn't want to scream cop, so we ditched the Crown Vic and took his truck, ball caps low.

We already had a decent idea where the shooter might set up, but we needed to find the best spot for our own eyes.

First stop: Ortega's place at 1415 Lamar. We parked a block over on Troy and walked the rest on foot—plain clothes, nothing flashy. Just two guys from the neighborhood, or close enough.

Ortega's house sat off the intersection of Lamar and Troy. From the layout, it made sense the shooter would stage a couple blocks east, probably near Deeds. That stretch offered good cover and long lines of sight.

We found the abandoned warehouse on the corner. It would work. From the roof, we'd have a full view of the street. The façade extended above the flat top, like a parapet—enough cover no matter which direction the shooter came in from.

"We'll need a lightweight ladder to pull up behind us once we're on the roof," Graham said as we walked through the overgrown weeds behind the building.

"Yeah. SWAT should have something. I'll give them a call when we leave here."

I scanned the alley behind the warehouse in both directions. The area was fairly concealed from the street, but if the shooter drove through before setting up, our vehicle would definitely stand out. We also couldn't walk in carrying a ladder and weapons. We'd have to be dropped off.

"I think we're going to have to pull Jenkins in on this."

"Why?"

"I think he's going to have to drop us off."

Graham nodded. "Yeah. I see your point."

I took a few photos, then we made our way back up the alley toward the truck.

On to the next stop: Century Printing.

Century Printing was a small company in an old building at 1317 N. Main St. that sat right on the sidewalk, like a storefront from some vintage downtown. The only entrances were the front door and a single dock door at the rear. The lot was barely big enough for deliveries—employees had to park in the neighborhood. Depending on what was open, that could mean anywhere within several blocks. We had no idea where Voss liked to park, which created some problems. Multiple approach routes meant multiple angles of risk.

We figured the front door was the most likely kill zone. That narrowed it to two directions.

North of the building, N. Main ran straight and flat for blocks, but decent cover would be hard to come by. To the south, the layout looked similar—except for a parking lot at the corner of N. Main and Helena. It offered a good view of the entrance and an easy escape in any direction. If I were the shooter, that's where I'd be.

For our surveillance, there weren't a lot of options.

"I don't know, Graham," I said. "That location is ideal—but where the hell are we going to set up? I think we might be screwed on this one."

Graham scanned the area, then pointed across the street to a large church on the opposite corner.

"There," he said, loud enough to startle me. "That church has a flat roof. We can hide up there—but it's in direct line of sight from the lot. We'll have to stay low to avoid being seen."

I shook my head. "Graham, they're not going to let us up there. That pastor's made it pretty clear he doesn't want the police around."

Graham chuckled. "Let me handle Reverend Albers. We go way back."

I watched in confusion as he opened his phone, scrolled through his contacts, and hit send—then speaker.

"Hello?"

"Reverend Albers, this is Graham MacLaren. How you been, brother?"

"Detective MacLaren, so good to hear from you. You know I always pray for you and your brother."

"Thank you, Reverend. We do appreciate that. Listen, I'm here with my brother now, and we really need your help."

"Of course, Graham," the Reverend said. "You know I'll help if I can."

"Well… this request might offend some of your parishioners, so if you can't help, we understand."

"What is it, Graham?"

"We're trying to catch a serial shooter and need to do a stakeout on your block Sunday night. We really need to use your roof."

There was a pause on the line. Some shuffling. A door closed in the background.

"That's a significant ask, Graham. A lot of our people could see that as a serious betrayal."

"I know, Reverend. I really do. But we're in a bind. We need to catch this guy before he kills again—and we believe his next target might be someone who works nearby. We're absolutely not targeting anyone who belongs in your neighborhood. We're trying to save one."

Another pause.

"Okay, Graham," the Reverend said at last. "I've been following this on the news, and a lot of our members are worried. I think they'll understand—given the circumstances. You're welcome to use the roof as long as you need."

"Thank you, Reverend. You don't know how much we appreciate it. I owe you big time."

"Come back to church, Graham. That's all the thanks I need."

"We'll see, Reverend. We'll see."

He hung up, and I stared at him—bug-eyed and slack-jawed—like he'd told me he dug up Jimmy Hoffa.

Graham noticed my look and smiled. "Don't ask. It's a long story."

I shook my head as he pulled the truck out onto Main St. and headed toward the office.

***

Graham and I arrived at First District just before 5 o'clock Sunday. We wanted to double-check every detail—gear, positioning, radio channels, vehicle placement. If the shooter showed up, we'd only get one chance. Everything had to be tight.

We were printing the final op packets when Sergeant Jenkins walked in with SWAT commander Lieutenant Morales. Koski and Jeffries showed up ten minutes later, followed by the rest of the SWAT detail.

I stepped to the front of the room and cleared my throat.

"Alright, looks like we're all here. I'll keep this short. Each of you has a packet with maps, notes on the surveillance target, staging assignments, and a description of what we believe the shooter's driving. Be advised: this suspect is highly skilled, heavily armed, and won't hesitate. Stick to the plan. Stay sharp."

I watched as they flipped through the files.

"Jeffries, Koski—you'll be with Officer Lester on the warehouse roof at 1201 Lamar. It's a single-story structure, so stay low. Ortega's place is at 1415 Lamar, and we believe the shooter's most likely setup point is in the 1200 block; right where you'll be. From your position, you'll have perfect sightlines if they show.

"Now this is important. There's nowhere to hide a vehicle, and we don't want you walking in with a ladder and weapons. Sergeant Jenkins will drop you off in the alley behind the building.

"You're designated Site 1. If anything comes up, that's your call sign."

They both nodded.

"Graham and I will be on the roof of the Methodist church at Main and Helena with a second SWAT operator. We're Site 2. Same rules apply."

I looked over to Morales who added, "SWAT will be staged at D1 in the BearCat—doors closed, engines off. Close enough to roll quick but discreet on police property. We'll respond fast if called. If we need to flush a barricade, we've got forty-millimeter CS and a tri-chamber canister in the kit. Standard issue."

"Your radios stay on TAC-1," Graham added. "No chatter. No open mics. You'll only hear two words if something goes down—Site 1 or Site 2. That's your cue."

Koski raised a hand. "If we see something but we're not sure…?"

I nodded. "Yes. As we discussed Friday, the van is our only clue. It's your decision to make the call, but if you see a dark, full-size van pull in and nobody gets out, I urge you to make the call. But please remember, even though you'll get no grief from me if you're wrong, our cover is blown as soon as the BearCat rolls in, and the op is done."

A few quiet nods around the room.

"This is our best chance to stop this guy," I said. "The pattern points to tonight. If we're right, we get one shot to intercept. If we're wrong, you already know."

A few of the SWAT guys cracked faint grins.

I stepped back and looked around. "Any questions?"

Nobody spoke.

"Good. Grab your gear. Let's get this done!"

Koski cracked his knuckles. "Let's do it."

***

Graham and I, along with Officer Connor from SWAT, arrived at the church a few minutes before 2100 hours. Reverend Albers was waiting at the back door and led us through the building to the roof access. Outside, the air was heavy—gray, humid. It felt like snow, but it wasn't quite cold enough.

We crawled over to the south side of the roof and looked out across the empty parking lot where we hoped our shooter would appear.

The roof gave us exactly what we needed. A flat surface, clear line of sight to Century Printing, and—if we stayed low—plenty of concealment. The SWAT shooter set up behind an HVAC unit while Graham and I positioned ourselves along the wall, binoculars and radios in hand.

Once settled, I called Jenkins and confirmed Koski and Jeffries were in place. By 2115, we were locked in.

Now we just had to wait.

Nothing happened.

Main St. was unusually quiet, not the hectic drug and hooker market I remembered from my days in a cruiser. An occasional car passed. A few kids rode by on bikes. Voss stepped outside twice to smoke—once around 2230, again a little after 0200. He stood alone under the yellow light, hunched and fidgety, oblivious to how close he might be to dying.

No van.

No movement.

No shooter.

Just the empty street watching us back.

Koski and Jeffries checked in around midnight—quiet and bored but alert—and again at 0130. Still no sign of Ortega. And no van.

We waited.

And waited.

By 2:15 a.m., my legs were numb and my eyes burned from staring through binoculars. I checked my watch. "Thirty more minutes," I said. "Then we call it."

Graham nodded, barely moving.

That's when the radio came alive—crackling, static, then a voice I didn't recognize.

"Attention all crews, shots fired downtown. Cargo van fleeing north on Patterson, high rate of speed."

The voice was clipped, urgent—the kind that meant we were already too late.

I looked at Graham.

He looked at me.

"Son of a bitch!" we screamed at the same time.

We'd wasted a night stalking the wrong guys. Somewhere else in the city, the shooter wasn't wasting a minute.

Chapter 33
Fifth Shot, First Fear

Stepping out of the club at the corner of First and Ludlow, Zhao "Johnny" Wang checked his phone. It was nearly 3:00 a.m. The Uber he'd scheduled to take him to the Cincinnati Airport had canceled, and now he'd have to walk home to make other arrangements.

He knew he was going to miss his flight, but Wang felt no urgency. The past few weeks—since he walked out of court free of all charges, he was working harder than ever before. Clients had come crawling back and the money was flowing again. Business was up and he was looking forward to getting to Miami to look for a new condo, but mostly he was looking forward to the sun—warm on his face, the breeze easy on his neck—the kind of breeze he remembered from the beaches back in Xiamen, before suits and cell phones.

It was several blocks to his place on Patterson, and Wang intended to make the most of it. He put in his earbuds, queued up a Mandopop playlist, and strolled toward Third Street—completely unaware that someone had been following him all night.

As Wang turned onto Third, the van rolled past, the driver assuming he was headed home. They continued on and parked on W. Third, east of Patterson—a perfect vantage point to watch him approach without a care.

Wang didn't carry a gun. Didn't run drugs. But he left just as much wreckage behind. Romance scams. Phony sweepstakes. Medicare fraud targeting the elderly. One woman in Kettering lost everything—savings, dignity, will to live. Two weeks later, she swallowed a bottle of pills. She left a long note revealing everything Wang had taken from her. Kettering police tried to make a case, but couldn't get an indictment. Wang walked away—and vanished.

And now—for the first time in weeks, they knew where he was. Knew where he was going.

He was unpredictable. Not careful—erratic. Random turns. No routine. No warning.

It was maddening. They couldn't plan around chaos.

And now—now—he was walking straight down Third Street. They couldn't miss this chance.

Ten minutes. Maybe less. Enough time to load the Barrett and get into the perch.

They could take the shot. Clean hit.

But downtown was a risk. Even at this hour, the streets were full of activity.

Pedestrians. Bikes. Cameras everywhere.

Somebody would hear. Somebody would see.

They'd ID the van. Maybe even get a plate.

They might not get away this time.

But Wang had to die.

The cops were closing in—just a matter of time.

There were more names. More work to do.

But if this was the last one...

If this was it—then it had to count.

Through the night vision: Wang, crossing Jefferson.

In range.

No more thinking.

Do it.

***

His whole world exploded.

The pain hit like a truck to the chest—brief, but overwhelming.

Something ruptured inside.

He dropped without a sound.

And then—nothing.

***

The police had been watching, but not who they should. Their eyes clung to the wrong doors. That left them free to hunt.

They saw Wang drop, but there was no time to watch the reaction. There were almost certainly witnesses—and very soon, they'd be telling police about the van.

They dropped from the shooting perch and shoved the Barrett into the open Pelican case—no care, no check.

They climbed into the driver's seat as if they could outrun the sound of the shot. They slammed the van into gear and turned north onto Patterson—without even checking for oncoming traffic.

The squeal of tires snapped them back to reality as they headed toward Trotwood.

Mistakes were unacceptable.

It was bad enough the police would soon be looking for the van.

Crashing twenty feet from the scene? That would've been fatal.

Inhaling deeply, they got themself under control and gradually eased off the gas.

No sudden moves. No hard braking. Nothing to draw attention.

Any second the police would be on scene—talking to witnesses, scanning for details. Within minutes, they'd be looking for the van.

They had always known this day would come. That's why the van was so plain. So common.

It would blend in—for a while.

Unless they drove like an idiot. Or unless someone already had the plate.

Fifteen minutes after killing Wang, they were backing the van into the seclusion of the storage unit. They had escaped again, but not clean. Witnesses would talk. Police would circle closer.

Safe—for now—from the eyes of police or nosy civilians.

Time to reflect on the mistakes.

On the arrogance of taking the shot with half the city watching.

They'd made their decision. The mission was over.

With the van compromised, continuing wasn't just risky—it may be impossible.

The plan had always been eight. Eight names. Eight executions, but now it seemed five would have to be enough.

A failure, maybe. But more than that, a betrayal—because Travis Ledbetter, the one who'd already gotten away once, would walk free again.

Damn.

***

Graham and I abandoned our stakeout and rushed toward Patterson. We stepped out of the car into the noise and chaos of a busy downtown crime scene—and knew immediately we had a problem.

I hated leaving Site 1 with nothing to show for it. We'd both felt it—something was off in the last hour—a pressure drop before a storm. Graham kept scanning rooftops, and I'd caught myself checking alleys twice as often as normal. If the sniper was out here, we were in the wrong place. I knew it. But I'd stayed put, hoping instinct was wrong.

There was no question this was the same suspect—the fifth assassination, the one we were supposed to stop, yet here we were.

I moved toward the body while Graham peeled off to talk with the patrol sergeant.

Patrol officers had the scene secured, so at least the crowds were held back—mostly. But they still pressed against the tape, and I had to shoulder through like I was trying to reach the front row at a concert. More than one gawker mistook me for another lookie-loo and tried to block my path. A quick threat of jail usually cleared the way.

The officer by the body looked up as I approached.

"Detective," he said. "This is Zhao Wang. Lived just a couple blocks from here. I'm assuming he was walking home from somewhere—probably a club judging by the heavy stench of liquor."

I looked at Wang, then over to Graham. "Damn, he's on the list. The one we figured was the least at risk."

I looked back to the officer. "Anything else?"

"No, sir. We ran him through LEADS and NCIC, but it all came back clean—no warrants."

"Okay. Thanks, Officer. We'll take it from here."

I took a look at Wang's body—single hole, center chest—the sniper's signature. We wouldn't know for sure until the round was matched in the lab, but for now, everything matched—we had to assume this was number five.

The evidence tech, Sam, was crouched nearby, zipping up his camera case. I stepped to the edge of the scene and called Jenkins who was heading out to pick up Koski and Jeffries.

"Hey, Sarge, it's Angus. We've got number five."

"Son of a bitch! Are you sure?"

"Can't be one hundred percent until the lab gets the round, but yeah—it all looks the same—he's on the list."

"Damn! Okay, thanks. And Angus—before you leave, please let the E-crew know how important the bullet is. Get it to the lab ASAP!"

I hung up and turned back as the coroner's investigator arrived.

"Morning, Angus. What've we got?"

"Another sniper shooting. One shot, center mass."

"What is this—three? Four?"

"Fifth shooting. Six victims. All in under two months."

Sam was finishing up when we walked back over. The coroner's investigator knelt beside the body as I addressed the tech.

"Hey, Sam. We need that round compared to the others ASAP."

"Sorry, Angus. I couldn't find it. May be in the body, but if it passed through? With all this open space and concrete, it could be anywhere."

"It's not in the body," the coroner's investigator said.

Sam and I turned as he gently rolled the victim to one side. The back of the shirt was soaked with blood, a large exit wound gaping in the center.

I hung my head in frustration. The only clue we might've had—gone. How the hell were we supposed to tie this shooting to the others without a round?

I thanked Sam and went looking for Graham.

I spotted him as he stepped away from an older woman pushing a shopping cart filled with what looked like trash—probably everything she owned.

"Witness?" I asked.

"Her? Nah. Just lonely. Wanted to talk." He gave a slight shrug. "But I did find something. Might finally break this thing open."

That got my attention. Without the bullet, we needed a break—bad.

"I hope so," I said. "Sam couldn't find the round, so we've got nothing at the scene."

Graham described conflicting statements from five different witnesses—contradictory and mostly worthless. But then he mentioned one who saw a van.

"Angus, this sounds legit. Sergeant Turner mentioned a van around the El Cuchillo shooting. Now we have one fleeing the scene of this one."

With eyes wide open, I spoke. "Any other details?"

"Yeah, all black, high top, like a delivery van. No windows in the back. And here's the best part – partial plate—last three 847."

"That's outstanding," I said, with a bit of excitement. "Let's keep that to ourselves right now though. As hard as it's been to find this guy, he is probably monitoring our radios."

With the witnesses debriefed, we headed for the car. If anything else turned up, Sam would let us know. In the meantime, we needed to figure out who the hell Zhao Wang really was.

And more importantly, how we'd gotten it so wrong.

We'd been watching the wrong guys all night.

And someone else had died because of it.

***

For hours, they stayed hidden in the corner of the unit.

After parking the van and cleaning the rifle, they sat in a folding lawn chair in a dark corner of the unit and tried to rest for a few minutes. But sleep didn't come. They were convinced the police would be pounding on the door any minute.

Phone in hand, they called off work—no way they could leave concealment today. Then they checked the news. Then the scanner. Then the news again.

Nearly five hours had passed since Wang dropped, and so far… nothing. Could the witnesses really have missed them? Hour after hour, they listened to the radio, scrolled through local news, social media, neighborhood chat groups—anywhere word might've spread. Nothing.

The chatter had been active earlier—scene control, homicide response, crowd management—but now—near silence. No BOLO. No van. No plate. No surveillance image. No "vehicle of interest." Not even a description. Just the victim—they had Wang's name—the chaos—and a mystery shooter they were calling a sniper, who vanished into thin air. Nothing else.

And now, as morning crawled toward mid-day, the radio traffic had all but ended, as if nothing had happened.

They stared at the screen, waiting for the other shoe to drop, but it never did.

They leaned back in the chair, propped their feet on the old metal shelving, and closed their eyes.

It was reckless. Emotional. They knew it.

But maybe… as unlikely as it seemed, they had dodged a bullet. Perhaps they got away again.

Finally, a shallow sleep—but laced with jolts of panic, every creak in the metal unit screaming of boots on concrete. Even in dreams they were running, turning corners, ducking under overpasses, always one step ahead of the flashing reds and blues.

Awoken by hunger, they stood slowly, muscles aching from sleeping in a chair meant for watching children's soccer games, and looked at the clock. 8:45 pm.

They pulled a sandwich from the van refrigerator, unsure how to proceed. They knew they had to make it to work in the morning but felt uncomfortable leaving.

They had fresh work clothes and toiletries in the van, even a small shower—no need to make the trip home. They would stay in the unit until morning, just to be safe.

As they ate the sandwich, their thoughts were no longer on the near disaster, but on the future. The mission was supposed to be abandoned. With yesterday's mistakes, they had accepted it. They had convinced themself the risks were too great, but then…

That was before—

Before the witnesses failed to see them.

Before they remembered the list.

Before remembering—Travis Ledbetter.

As they headed out for the morning commute like all the other common folk in Trotwood, they looked back at the van. Silent. Ready. Waiting. It existed only to fulfill the mission.

No. This wasn't over.

Not yet.

Ledbetter had to die.

Chapter 34
One More Night

Monday morning—straight into slaughter.

Lieutenant Branson's office was quiet when we walked in, but it didn't stay that way for long.

Chief Robertson stood with his back to the wall, hands on his hips, eyes on the TV as if waiting for the news to declare the case closed. Jenkins sat in the corner, head down, eyes tired. The moment Graham and I stepped through the door, the chief turned around—and I knew we were about to take a beating.

"I gave you what you asked for," he barked. "Extra manpower. SWAT. Full discretion. And what did we get? A goddamn corpse downtown—downtown! A couple blocks from the club district and twenty feet from a security camera that somehow didn't catch a single thing!"

He paused, maybe to control his rage.

"I just got off the phone with the mayor. He's taking heat from every direction. Press. Council. Business leaders. They want answers, and all I've got is another name on a list."

No one spoke. The silence wasn't awkward—it was expected.

"I called BCI," Robertson continued. "Official request for outside assistance. But thanks to two police shootings in Columbus and another in Toledo, their critical response team is stretched thin. Closest they can send anyone is next Monday."

A pause. His eyes swept across the room.

I couldn't argue with what the chief was saying. Two miles away, we'd been babysitting a parked van while Wang bled out on the sidewalk. That failure wasn't abstract—it was ours.

Jenkins cleared his throat. "Chief… I know we're losing this case. I know it doesn't look good. But considering the delay—if you'll allow it—I want to propose one more stakeout."

The chief gave him a look like he'd lost his mind.

"One more stakeout?" Robertson echoed.

Jenkins nodded. "There are only three names left on the list. Three possible targets. If we could run surveillance on all of them this Sunday night, I believe we've got a real shot."

"And where exactly do you think I'm getting the bodies for that?" the chief snapped. "You barely pulled this off last time."

"I'll find them," Jenkins said.

I stepped forward. "Sir, we were right about Sunday night—the shooter hit; we just picked the wrong targets. We were right about the van, too: a witness saw a dark full-size van fleeing the scene downtown at high speed. With broader coverage, I'm convinced we'll intercept him next time."

Robertson looked between us. His jaw tightened, then he blew out a breath.

"You get one more night. One. And whatever manpower Jenkins pulls, you coordinate it. At this point, I don't care what you do."

He fixed his eyes on me as he continued.

"I've already had to ask for help. I won't take another hit."

"Yes, sir," I said.

We left the room without another word. The door closed behind us, but it didn't hide the pressure. It followed us down the hall, clinging like the stink of cordite after a shooting—sharp, inescapable, and impossible to wash off.

Within minutes of getting back to the office, Jenkins was already on the phone with SWAT. Morales and his team would help, and we could use the BearCat again if SWAT wasn't deployed elsewhere.

I called Jeffries and Koski. Neither sounded thrilled, but both were in—same rooftop, same plan.

"Whatever it takes," Jeffries said. "We want this guy too."

That left the third team.

"Hey Sarge," I said. "Instead of dragging some random guys in on this, why don't you and the LT take that third site?"

"That's actually not a bad idea, Angus. Let me give him a call."

Graham leaned against my desk, flipping through the printout of remaining names. "We've got Ortega. Voss. Ledbetter. We covering Voss again from the church?"

I nodded as Jenkins hung up his phone. "The LT is in—actually seemed excited to get out of the office for a change."

"Good," I said. "We're set then."

***

The rest of the week passed in fits and starts—paperwork, routine calls, and all the small tasks that piled up while we'd been chasing shadows.

Monday we planned the stakeouts.

Tuesday we got wrapped up in a domestic-related murder-suicide over on James H. McGee.

Wednesday was a stabbing at a barbershop.

Thursday we were stuck in court.

Friday we sat through a search warrant briefing that had nothing to do with us.

By Saturday, the case had become a crime scene gone stale—taped off, untouched, and quietly rotting beneath the surface.

But we knew better.

We weren't drifting—we were waiting.

***

Sunday came slow. The anticipation of the stakeout was agonizing. Moonlight cast an eerie glow as we pulled into the D1 lot at 8:30 p.m. Same teams. Same gear. But this time, it felt different. Heavier. No rain or breeze—just crisp, frigid air and the smell of something burning a few blocks away.

Every road led here. If the shooter moved tonight, so would we.

The other teams were already there. Koski and Jeffries leaned against an unmarked sedan, sipping gas station coffee and going over site sketches. Jenkins stood nearby with Branson. I chuckled—both of them looked as keyed up as rookies on their first field duty.

Empty coffee cups littered the pavement like shell casings from an urban gunfight—spent, scorched, waiting to be swept away. Everyone moved with quiet precision, each gesture loaded with more than caffeine and muscle memory—this wasn't routine anymore. It was ritual.

SWAT's BearCat sat in the far corner of the lot. Dark and silent, ready to roll at a moment's notice, it was always comforting knowing it was there, but it also exposed the danger of the work.

I spotted our SWAT officer stepping out of her car—Morales had reassigned Jenny Harmon to our team. She gave a quiet nod as she approached.

"Ready," she said, not waiting for us to ask.

I nodded. "Church roof, same as before."

Koski and Jeffries were under a streetlight looking through their site file as Officer Lester stepped out of his truck. He carried the same duffel bag as last week and a face that hadn't changed expression in fifteen years. He moved with the quiet ease of someone who'd done this before. Confident. Maybe a little arrogant.

Lieutenant Morales gave final instructions under his breath. "No radio chatter. Confirm visual only if absolutely necessary. And remember, if you need SWAT, identify with your site number and keep the details brief. Jenkins, you and the LT are Site 3."

We exchanged a glance. This was it. One more chance.

"Alright," Jenkins said. "Everybody go dark. Let's move."

Site 1 team headed back to Lamar Street, and Graham and I went back to the church roof—Site 2—same as last time. We knew the angles, knew the lines of sight, knew where to duck if the shooter spotted movement.

There was comfort in familiarity. It was also a reminder of failure.

***

Jenkins and Branson took the new position—Site 3—on the roof of a warehouse in the 200 block of Kiser. The place hadn't seen tenants in a decade. The air up there smelled like wet drywall and cold metal, carrying the decay of a building that had been empty longer than some rookies had been alive.

The roof was a minefield of rusted vents, warped decking, and pigeon droppings thick enough to crunch underfoot, but the view down to Ledbetter's house was clean. If the sniper showed up there, they'd have them dead to rights.

When they first stepped onto the roof, Jenkins scanned the area below and pointed with his chin.

"You seeing this?"

Branson followed his gaze. Three vehicles sat parked along the curb—an unmarked white box truck, a beat-up mid-90s Buick, and a black van.

"All look cold," Jenkins said, kneeling to check the sightlines. "No movement. No driver."

"Could just be overnight parking," the LT replied. "If we weren't looking for a van, I wouldn't have even noticed this one. The dull paint, covered windows, missing plates—it belongs on any street in the city."

Jenkins didn't respond. He settled behind a roof vent, raised the binoculars, and watched.

***

A mile away, I shifted my weight on the cold church rooftop and scanned Helena for the hundredth time.

The first couple hours passed slow and silent. There was nothing moving for blocks, not even a hooker or a crackhead.

By eleven, I'd stopped looking. The streets were nearly abandoned. I'd hear a vehicle drive up even if I were asleep.

Every so often a set of headlights would creep past, but nothing close to what we were looking for.

Graham leaned back against the low cinder wall at the roof's edge, chewing sunflower seeds and spitting shells into an empty water bottle. He hadn't said much—typical—but I could see the hours were grinding him down. The cold air didn't help.

At midnight, a white van pulled into the lot across from our site.

Graham leaned forward. "Here we go…"

We both watched, hands on binoculars, every muscle pulled taut.

The van idled for a moment before the doors opened. Two figures stepped out—middle-aged man and a teenage boy. They carried a case of bottled water and a pizza box, then headed up the walk toward a brick house on Helena.

Graham exhaled. "Late dinner."

I nodded, lowering the glasses.

The van stayed parked.

We kept watching. Thirty minutes passed. No one else exited. No one entered. Just another family, probably finishing off a movie night.

I kept telling myself this wasn't a waste of time. That silence meant we were early, not wrong. But after weeks of chasing shadows, even silence starts to sound wrong.

***

Across town, Koski and Jeffries were watching their block like hawks. Ortega's porch light hadn't turned on once.

"Dead quiet," Koski whispered through the mic.

That changed around 12:45.

A group of teens—six or seven deep—came charging down the street, loud and hyped up. Shoves turned into punches. One kid fell into the gutter.

Jeffries tensed behind the wall. "Jesus. We about to watch a murder?"

Koski scanned through his scope. "We intervene?"

"If somebody pulls a gun, we might have to."

They kept watching. Shouts. Pushing. More shouts.

Then one of the kids threw his arms up, tired of the whole damn show, and walked away. The rest peeled off after him, grumbling, laughing, a few still jawing at each other.

And then, they were gone.

"Test run for our stress levels," Koski muttered.

Jeffries chuckled, then stretched his neck side to side. "Stupid kids."

***

Back on the church roof, Graham leaned in close.

"We got movement across the street."

I raised the binoculars. It was a guy in pajama pants letting his dog into the yard. Not even worth the spike of adrenaline.

The hours blurred. I wasn't sure how long we'd been here.

My legs were stiff. My ass was frozen. And my eyes felt like sandpaper.

But we stayed locked in.

Every shadow got a second glance.

Every passing vehicle was a maybe.

Every creak in the night made me think we'd missed something.

But nothing came.

Not yet.

The rooftops had gone quiet—the whole block sensed a predator. No footsteps. No creaks. Just the faint buzz of a distant transformer and the hiss of blood in my ears. Somewhere out there, someone had a timetable. We didn't know if we were early… or already too late.

My eyes had begun to play tricks—seeing movement in mailbox shadows, shifting shapes behind porch rails. Every blink dragged a little longer. Somewhere in my skull, a voice whispered that we'd missed it again. That we'd failed—again.

I glanced at Graham, then back to the street. If nothing happened tonight—if we struck out again—I didn't know what we'd have left to offer. Maybe the chief was right. Maybe BCI should take it from here.

We'd thrown everything we had at this case. Manpower, instinct, grit. If that wasn't enough—if we'd still missed the mark—I didn't know what else there was to give. Maybe we weren't up against a person. Maybe we were chasing justice itself, stripped of its badge and gone rogue.

***

The shooter's mission wasn't finished. One name sat heavier than the rest: Ledbetter.

Chapter 35
Wrapped in Black

Ledbetter.

They hadn't moved in nearly five hours—Jenkins, Branson, and the SWAT officer—prone on the sagging rooftop of the Kiser warehouse, watching the same black van parked below.

Then Jenkins saw it. A flicker of motion—subtle, but real. "Movement," he said, urgency creeping into his voice. "Something shifted on that damn van."

The SWAT officer swung his rifle across the scene, scanning the area through the scope.

"Confirmed," he said a moment later. "Front roof window, left side. It's open. That's a sniper's nest if I've ever seen one."

He keyed his radio.

"Site 3 to Command—we've got verified movement on the van. Rooftop window has just been opened. Appears to be a shooting position. No shooter visible at this time. No sign of the target."

There was a brief pause on the line.

"Site 3, say again," came the tight reply from Command.

"Movement is verified. Roof window is open—no visual on the occupant yet."

The driver of the BearCat was already moving. D1 was close, and he knew exactly where to go. His job was to roll in hard from the north, turning off Leo St., angling the truck broadside in front of the van, and block any potential line of fire to Ledbetter with its armored hull.

The remaining SWAT officers would respond from Chapel St. to the south, approaching with precision—flanking the van under cover, while the rooftop team maintained overwatch. Everyone had drilled this. Now it was real.

Within two minutes, the BearCat was turning onto Kiser Street, aggressively advancing toward the parked van on the east side of the 200 block—like a steel battering ram looking for something to break.

"Site 3 to BearCat—the van is fifty yards ahead of you on your left. Come in hard and block the line of sight, as well as any escape path north."

"Copy," the operator replied. "In position."

"Site 3 to Command—shooter has no angle. Target is safe."

"You're clear, Site 3," came the response from Command. "All teams—move to the staging area."

The radio came to life with acknowledgments.

"Site 1—three minutes out."

"Site 2 arriving now."

The mobile command vehicle arrived at the predetermined staging area—a vacant lot at the corner of Chapel and Milburn. Close enough to respond in seconds, but far enough to stay safe.

Lieutenant Morales stepped out as officers began to arrive, their movements swift and automatic. Doors popped open. Tactical gear came out in practiced waves—ballistic helmets, shields, Daniel Defense MK18 rifles, and sling packs loaded for whatever might come next.

Nobody said much. Everyone knew what this could turn into.

"Alright, everyone listen up," the commander said, raising his voice just enough to carry over the gear checks and radio traffic. "We've got a shooter concealed in a van one block over on Kiser—east side, about half a block north of Chapel. The BearCat has the front blocked, but the rear remains exposed. I want teams moving fast and silent. Take up covered positions to the rear and west."

He looked to the rooftop units now forming behind him. "Overwatch teams—find elevated positions from the back side. Stay low. Do not expose yourselves to the roofline. Advise when you're set."

A few heads nodded.

"Everyone clear?" he asked.

A chorus of low affirmatives followed.

***

As the teams began to move silently toward Kiser, Graham and I pulled into the lot. The car skidded to a stop on the loose gravel and dirt as both of our doors burst open like the souls of the victims had come back to settle the score.

I ripped off my seatbelt and was out of the car before Graham even realized we were stopped. The moment my boots hit the ground, I was scanning the street. Armored vests, rifles, controlled movements—chaos that only looks calm from the outside. We were a block away from the van. I couldn't see it, but I could feel it.

We were close. This was going to end tonight.

I moved fast. Graham was out of the car now and right behind me.

"Is it him?" I asked the commander. "Tell me it's him."

"Don't know yet," he said. "But it's looking likely. Everyone's in position. We'll deploy the drone shortly. With a little luck, they'll see it's over and come on out."

I hated the odds. I didn't care for the stillness either. The SWAT observer hadn't seen any movement in fifteen minutes. After enough years in this job, you learn to expect certain things. When criminals are cornered, they flinch. They bolt. They beg. But this one wasn't doing any of that.

They were waiting.

And that made me nervous. Made me think they weren't finished.

Before I could respond to the commander, the voice of a SWAT officer rang out through a megaphone, echoing down the block.

"Inside the van! This is the Dayton Police Department. You are surrounded. Exit the vehicle through the rear. Do it slowly, with both hands visible and empty."

Silence.

Then again:

"Inside the van! This is the Dayton Police Department. You are surrounded. Exit the vehicle through the rear. Do it slowly, with both hands visible and empty."

No response.

They repeated the call again. And again. The voice never wavered. The phrasing never changed. The same commands, cycling on loop for fifteen minutes.

Finally, the commander held up a hand.

"Hold the announcements. Let's prep the drone. We need a closer look."

I watched one of the officers in the staging area break from the group and sprint to the command vehicle. He yanked out a large, hard-sided black case and took off toward Chapel St., moving like it weighed nothing.

This was the drone everyone had been talking about.

Inside that case was the latest in law enforcement surveillance tech—just purchased with seized funds. Eighty-five thousand dollars' worth of seized funds. The thing was no bigger than a suitcase, but it cost more than my first house. Damn near twice.

The officer reached a spot of cover near the perimeter, dropped to one knee, and opened the case. With practiced care, he removed the DJI Matrice 300 RTK, setting it gently on the pavement. It was a hybrid of military tech and science fiction—four rotor arms, rigid carbon frame, blinking status lights.

Mounted underneath was our only real chance of seeing inside that van: the DJI Zenmuse H30T—a multi-sensor camera system capable of thermal imaging, laser rangefinding, and low-light optical zoom. Finding a hotspot inside a steel vehicle is tough, but if there were any heat bleeding out… the Zenmuse would find it.

Hope for the best.

The officer began powering it up, calling out as the drone came online.

"Matrice is green. Thermal sensor warming up. Ready for lift in fifteen seconds."

Everyone nearby kept their heads low and their eyes on the van. The drone would fly a tight grid overhead, scanning from multiple angles.

As the drone lifted off the ground with a low hum, rising smoothly into the air like an eagle on an updraft, it hovered for a moment before drifting forward toward the van.

Graham and I trailed the commander across the lot to the mobile command vehicle, where the drone feed would be streamed in real time.

We watched the screen as the drone orbited at about 25 feet, then dropped to just above the roofline. The feed flipped to thermal—Ironbow. Most of the van sat in cool blues; pavement and hood read cold. Then, near the driver's door, a faint orange bloom pulsed at the roofline—barely there, but real.

The operator guided the drone over the open roof window. "Window is open. No signature. No movement."

He circled toward the rear, then swept both sides and back over the top—hunting for bleed-through.

Then the drone stopped behind the driver's door below the roofline. We could see it. Faint. A smudge of yellow-orange at the top corner of the van.

"There's a little warmth there," the operator said over the radio. "But it's small and weak. I can't say it's a person. Could be residual."

I stared at the screen. It told me what I already knew. Whoever was inside knew exactly how to stay hidden.

With a clear sigh of frustration, the commander keyed his radio.

"Retrieve the drone. Resume commands to exit as the forty-millimeter gas is prepped."

As the officers responsible for the next tasks acknowledged their assignments over the radio, the commander and I stepped out of the command vehicle. I had to see the van for myself, so Graham and I moved toward the perimeter as the megaphone instructions resumed.

Same script. Same result.

Nothing.

This continued for nearly fifteen minutes until the radio came to life again.

"Gas is ready. Will deploy in fifteen seconds. Moving now."

I watched as a four-man SWAT element moved from the cover of the perimeter toward the partial cover of the buildings along the west side of the street. With ballistic shields providing forward protection, the officers stayed low and moved in a tight group along the sidewalk, advancing toward the van with practiced precision.

The first two officers carried shields—one covering the front, the other angled toward the van's side as they approached. The third officer carried the gas launcher, cradled across his chest, steady as glass. The fourth was armed with her Daniel Defense rifle, scanning windows, rooftops, and alley mouths—ready to respond to anything trying to spit lead back.

They paused behind a parked SUV about thirty feet from the van. One final radio check. Then the call came through.

"Deploy."

The team shifted toward the van. The first officer stepped forward, shield high. The second dropped back half a step, angling his shield left. The grenadier moved between them, dropped to a crouch, and took aim at the driver's side window—behind the mirror.

He squeezed the trigger.

A sharp *whomp* echoed off the buildings as the CS canister punched through the glass and vanished into the van.

Just as smoothly, the team pulled back—shields up, rifles trained on the van—until they reached cover.

Then we waited.

Seconds passed. A thin coil of white gas began to leak from the broken window, rising into the night like steam off a boiling pit. We waited.

No movement. No coughing. No sound at all.

Five minutes. Ten.

The radio suddenly came to life. "No visible response. No movement."

I didn't need to look at the commander to know what was coming.

"Prep the tri-chamber. We're going in again."

I watched the team move as one—no wasted steps, no hesitation. Shields shifted, the launcher reloaded. Graham muttered beside me, low and certain: "Three bursts instead of one. Keeps the gas thick."

I nodded. "So we're done asking nicely."

"Yeah," he said. "If they're in there, they won't be for long."

I turned back toward the van as the team began moving. Once again, they moved in a tight, four-man formation, protected by ballistic shields and a rear officer with rifle. Approaching within thirty feet, the gas was deployed with a low *thump* as the 40mm launcher sent the canister through the previously broken driver's door window.

As the team eased back to the perimeter, we heard three rapid pops as each chamber detonated. Gas poured from the van, thick and crawling, choking the night air. Every eye was fixed on the rear door, as if they were waiting for Jesus Christ—or the Devil himself—to step out of the cloud.

I don't know how long we stared at that van. Could've been five minutes, could've been fifty. The gas was thick, crawling out through the broken glass like smoke from a chemical fire. We'd hit it with everything short of a flashbang—nothing.

Then the radio snapped alive.

"We've got movement. Rear door movement."

I froze.

"Confirmed—rear door is opening."

Every rifle on the block had the door in their scopes.

The door cracked open. Slowly at first, knowing a sudden movement could be fatal, but the need for air was too strong.

The door swung all the way open, then it poured out—thick, acrid gas boiling from the van, spreading low across the pavement.

A figure appeared in the oppressive fog and stumbled forward, coughing hard, one hand against the doorframe, the other wiping at their mask. All black—jacket, pants, boots, gloves, face wrapped in a balaclava. They gasped, doubled over, nearly collapsed—then took two shaky steps into the open.

"Hands are clear!" someone called out. "No weapon visible!"

The megaphone cracked again:

"Exit the vehicle! Lay face down on the ground! Arms out to your sides—palms up! Do it now!"

The figure didn't speak. Didn't run. Dropped to their knees in surrender, then stretched out on the asphalt—arms wide, chest heaving.

For a moment, nobody moved. Then the four-man arrest team began their approach—shields up, rifle tight, every step careful. They surrounded the body, cuffed them, rolled them over and lifted them to their feet.

Still no resistance. Still no words.

They walked the suspect past me, eyes clenched shut behind the mask, breathing ragged, gas residue clinging to every fold of fabric.

Wrapped in the black of death itself.

And then, it was over.

Chapter 36
Behind the Mask

Wrapped in black, the suspect was led away—no longer hidden by shadows, but by a mask and a haze of gas residue.

Two patrol officers guided the suspect toward a cruiser, the suspect's hands cuffed behind their back.

"Let's get that thing off," one of them muttered, reaching up.

The balaclava slid away, revealing sharp cheekbones, sweat-damp hair, and a face—unmistakably female.

"Holy shit—it's a woman!"

She didn't flinch. Didn't say a word.

"Name?"

No response. Even if she'd given one, it would've meant nothing to them—just another line on the arrest report. One of the patrol officers was female, so she handled the pat-down.

No weapons. No ID. Not even a phone.

The suspect stepped into the back seat without a word, and the door slammed shut behind her.

***

As the uniforms passed by me, disappearing with the suspect among the cluster of police vehicles and SWAT officers, I turned to Graham. "I guess they have to take him to the hospital to get hosed off," I said. "They'll also need to air out the van before we can get inside. Let's head to the ER and see who this guy is."

Graham nodded in agreement, and we began the short walk back to the car near the SWAT command vehicle. We were nearly there when Lieutenant Morales called out.

"Angus," he called. "Hold up."

I turned as he walked up to me. "Hey, LT," I said. "What can I do for you?"

"I know you're anxious to find out if this is your guy," he began. "I don't have an ID yet, but my team's been in the van. Angus—it has to be your guy. Barrett .338 MRAD with a Vortex Razor and a suppressor. No mistaking it. And a notebook. Angus, it's full of names and dates—every hit laid out. But here's the kicker. There's a verse written across the front. Looks Old Testament. From some book I never heard of—Ko-hel-et? Ko-heel-it? Talks about judgment—gave me the chills."

"Thanks, LT," I replied. "That's fantastic news. I can't wait to hear from the lab that it's the weapon from all five shootings." I hesitated, then added, "And the verse…yeah, that's weird. I'd expect something out of the Koran. But a Bible verse?"

"The E-crew is here. He'll get it submitted right away. The lab should have it first thing in the morning."

"Perfect," I said. "The notebook too, and thanks again, LT, for all your help tonight."

I turned back toward my car, walking with renewed energy now that I felt certain we had finally stopped the killing.

***

Graham and I walked into the ER but didn't see the patrol officers lingering around. A nurse sat behind the counter, eating a sandwich that probably came from a gas station instead of a real restaurant. The whole place smelled faintly of disinfectant and damp fabric—a bleach bottle sealed inside a laundromat.

I figured she'd know where they went.

"Hi, I'm Detective MacLaren," I began. "We're looking for the two officers who brought a suspect in a few minutes ago. Where can we find them?"

"Hi, Detective," she said with a smile. "They took her to the shower room for decontamination. Down that hall—left at the end. You can't miss them."

"Okay, thank you," I said, then turned to Graham with a questioning look. "Did she say *her*?"

"I'm pretty sure she did," he replied.

We walked briskly down the hall, turning the corner just as the officers and the suspect exited the shower room.

It was a woman. Lean, olive-skinned, hair damp and clinging to her jaw. Her face was sharp, familiar—high cheekbones, steady hazel eyes appearing red and irritated.

She looked directly at me.

My breath caught. My brain buckled like I'd taken a baton to the temple.

She showed no expression. No emotion

"Daniella?"

My brain didn't process what I was seeing—not at first. I looked at the uniforms, hands spread in front of me in complete confusion.

"Where's the shooter?" I asked.

One of them glanced at the woman beside him, then back at me—like he thought I was blind, or maybe stupid.

"Right here," he said, with enough sarcasm to make me feel stupid.

My heart sank. The edges of my vision went dark. For a second, I thought I might pass out. I felt the whole world crushing down on my shoulders.

I couldn't speak. I couldn't move. For the first time in my career, I was coming unglued.

I'd arrested acquaintances before—for serious crimes. But Daniella? This was different. We'd spent hours together. We'd been intimate.

How the hell did I not see this?

And yet… even through the shock, the old instincts twitched. Little memories replayed—the way she scanned rooms, avoided letting me drive her, kept her phone out of reach. Pieces I'd brushed off as quirks now sat there as blinding neon evidence, mocking me.

I thought it was nerves.

But now I saw it for what it was.

I turned toward Graham, already backing away. "I can't," I said. "You talk to her. I'll see you in the car."

I damn near ran out of that ER. I had to get somewhere I could breathe. Somewhere without those sterile walls and bright lights. Without her standing there—calm as a corpse—turning my world inside out.

With each step, I felt it would be easier to struggle through three feet of snow. My ears were ringing, not from gunfire or sirens—just pressure after my brain turned up the volume on its own confusion.

I could see the car, but it felt the more I ran, the farther it was. My body screamed for relief. I'd stumbled into a burning building and the door had disappeared.

I finally made it after cutting through the sally port, narrowly missing a pair of ambulances as I pushed through the overhead doors. Someone shouted, but I didn't hear the words. It was the tunnel vision we learned about in the academy—except this wasn't deadly force. To me, this was worse.

I fumbled with the door handle, my hands shaking like I was trying to disarm a bomb with seconds left. My stomach was rolling, vomit forcing its way up my throat. I couldn't slow my breathing. Daniella had me spinning, unraveling.

I dropped into the seat, slammed the door, and pounded the steering wheel with both fists. My heart was racing, trapped in my chest, trying to break free.

My mind was flooded with memories. Snippets of our times together. The unexpected meeting in the park. That damn ponytail. The smile that slipped past every defense and stole my heart before I even saw it coming.

I couldn't connect that beautiful, grounded, sharp-eyed woman with the trail of bodies we'd been chasing for weeks.

Was she playing me?

Is that how she stayed a step ahead of us?

Was I the reason she got away with it for so long?

Hell… was I responsible for those men's deaths?

I thought I'd left the front door wide open and gone to bed—while she slipped out and set the city on fire.

I picked up my phone. Lena? Maybe she'd understand. Maybe a text. But nothing came. I started typing, but the words wouldn't come. Nothing felt right.

Frustrated, I tossed the phone onto the passenger seat and dropped my face into my hands. I didn't want to admit it, but it was true. Lena wasn't the one to help. She knew I'd been seeing Daniella—but not how close we'd gotten.

At least, not how close I thought we were.

She wouldn’t be sympathetic. She warned me once—told me I had a thing for women with too much mystery. Said I preferred the ones who seemed strong. Unshakeable. I wanted to see if I could crack them.

I laughed it off at the time.

I wasn’t laughing now.

A light tap-tap-tap on the passenger’s side startled me out of my daze. No cop ever wants to be surprised in his car. I wiped my face and looked up. It was Graham. I wasn't being ambushed. I also hadn’t unlocked the doors. Or even started the engine. I hit the lock button.

Graham didn’t say a word. He just opened the door and slid into the seat beside me. He sat there for a moment, quiet, but staring, thinking I might shoot him if he spoke.

The inside of the car felt too small. Suffocating. The air had turned to mud and I couldn’t breathe deeply enough to move it.

“I don’t even know what to say,” I finally muttered.

Graham leaned back in his seat, stretching his arms above his head. “You don’t have to say anything.”

I nodded, appreciating the silence. I stared through the windshield at the red ambulance lights as they bounced from one wall to the next.

“I thought I knew her,” I said.

“I know,” he said softly. “That’s what makes this so damn hard.”

I dipped my head slowly. My chest hurt. Not in the way you hurt after a run, or a punch. This was a pain that made you think your time had come.

“You ever feel you missed something that should’ve been obvious?” I asked.

“All the time, brother,” he said.

“I feel foolish,” I muttered, head down. "How can I keep working homicides when I didn't see the killer in my own house?"

We sat there five, maybe ten minutes. Two cops. Two brothers. A moment of peace, shielded from the nightmare by a little glass and steel.

Chapter 37
Cold Eyes

We'd barely made it back to the office when Daniella's background check came through. Graham skimmed it first, his brow furrowing.

My gut twisted. Not confirmation. But enough to make everything else feel heavier. If this was the beginning of the truth, I didn't want to see the end of it.

Six dead men on the board. And now, every arrow pointed to her. For the sake of justice, and for the families, we had to land this clean. Each victim had slipped through the cracks on technicalities, loopholes, or flat-out prosecutorial failure. The thought of Daniella walking free on the same grounds wasn't simply ironic—it was unbearable. We'd be trading one broken system for another, like trying to put out a house fire with a bucket of gasoline.

I knew what I had to do. I had to take a step back—recuse myself from all contact with Daniella. We were too close. It didn't matter how impartial I could be. The defense—and the jury—would see only the personal history. That wouldn't only put the case at risk. It would stain everything we'd done to get here. I called Sergeant Jenkins to let him know. He said he would come in to help out. Our odds just got better.

We needed a confession. That would help in court. But we needed more. We needed to know why. We needed to know how. Graham was sharp, methodical, and good on his feet, but closing a suspect wasn't his strong suit. Not yet.

Jenkins, though—he was a master at it. There was a reason they called him in on the big ones. He had a way of wearing suspects down—pretending to be their oldest friend, returned from war with secrets to share. As he stared straight into their souls with his deep blue eyes, never raising his voice, he peeled back the layers until something underneath gave way. As a detective, he rarely let a suspect walk without talking.

We'd wait on him.

***

Graham and I were waiting outside the interview rooms when Sergeant Jenkins arrived.

The weight of the case sat on Graham with the weight of deep water—cold, soundless, and pressing down from all sides.

"Angus, Graham," Jenkins said as he walked up. "Thanks for the call. Stepping back was smart. IA will appreciate it—if they show up."

I pursed my lips and shook my head. "Yeah. I definitely expect to hear from them. This isn't something you can pretend didn't happen."

Sarge nodded. "It'll work out, Angus. Don't lose sleep over it."

He turned to Graham, who was standing by the interview room door. "You ready?"

"Yep," Graham replied. "Let's see what she has to say."

I watched them step inside and close the door behind them. Then I stepped into the adjacent room, pulling it shut behind me. The two-way mirror gave me a clear view. Audio was already live—every word, every breath, every silence.

The interview room was tiny. Three chairs and a small table—but we rarely used it. We kept it pushed aside, close enough to sit shoulder to shoulder with whoever we had in the chair. That closeness made people uncomfortable. And uncomfortable people were easier to crack.

Daniella sat in the far corner, the one farthest from the mirror. She was still dressed in all black. Her hair was dry now, hanging down the sides of her face, uncombed—the cute ponytail only in my mind. Her cuffs were on, hands resting in her lap like she was in a pew at church. No slouch. No fidgeting. Her expression was unreadable—calm, composed. Not blank. Just… closed.

Jenkins leaned over, turned the key, and lifted the cuffs away, setting them to the side on the table—visible but out of her reach. Graham cracked the cap on a water bottle and set it within reach. She took a small sip, then folded her hands again.

"Good morning, Ms. Reynolds," Graham began. "It's good to see you again. I wish it were under different circumstances."

Daniella didn't move. She stared straight ahead—no smile, no frown, no acknowledgment he'd spoken at all.

"It is Monday, March 11, at 0830 hours. My name is Detective Graham MacLaren. Also present is Sergeant Ray Jenkins. This morning we're conducting an interview with Daniella Reynolds in reference to a series of shootings that occurred over the past several weeks."

He paused and gave her space to respond. Nothing.

"Ms. Reynolds, we need to talk about a few things today. Just so you understand, everything said in here is on the record and being recorded—video and audio. Do you agree to proceed?"

Silence.

She sat as rigid as a mannequin in a department store window—too perfect, nothing hinting at the force she truly was.

Graham jotted something in his notebook, then turned to Sergeant Jenkins, who had been silently observing the exchange—or lack of one—between him and Daniella.

"What do we do, Sarge?" he asked. "Can we proceed without her approval?"

Jenkins looked up from his own notes. "She's been Mirandized?"

Graham nodded. "Yes—read aloud. She said she understood and agreed to talk."

"Did she ask for a lawyer?"

"No."

Sergeant Jenkins reached out and gave Graham a light clap on the shoulder.

"Then start asking questions."

"Okay, Sarge," Graham replied, glancing at his notebook before turning back to Daniella.

Daniella sat motionless. Hands in her lap, eyes calm but distant. Graham leaned in, quiet but firm.

"Ms. Reynolds, let's start with the night of January 20th. Do you recall where you were?"

"Yes," she said, her voice low. "In my van. That's where the mission began. *For God will bring every deed into judgment, every hidden thing, whether good or bad.*"

Graham's pen froze. He glanced at Daniella, then at Jenkins. "Excuse me?"

Daniella looked up with a slight smile of contentment. "These men… Dayton was unwilling to punish them for their crimes. I sent them to the one judge who would."

Graham seemed startled but forced himself back on task. "There was a man killed that night. Hassan Al-Khatib. Do you know anything about the death?"

She looked up slowly. "I know him as Tariq Al-Mansour."

Graham blinked. "Come again?"

"Tariq Al-Mansour. Hezbollah smuggler. He ran weapons and girls through the Sinai and up into Lebanon. I served on the border in the early 2010s. We detained him several times but never had a reason to hold him."

"He was younger. So was I."

Jenkins stirred. Graham shot a glance toward the mirror.

"When I saw him in court this winter," she continued, "I recognized him. I remembered my niece—Ayala. Sixteen. Vanished in 2011. Intel back then pointed to a smuggler convoy moving east from Rafah. Tariq was linked. We never found her."

Graham's voice softened. "So you made a list."

"I did. Well… not at first."

She looked up, steady.

"I thought it would stop after Tariq. But the more I researched his case, the more I realized—he wasn't the only one. I started gathering names from court records at work. Then I found a list already posted on a blog."

Daniella paused to get a drink from the water bottle.

"The site's called ThinBlueLie.com. I don't know who runs it. Never met them. Never contacted them. But the names were solid. Cases I was already circling. The blog just got me there faster."

She gave the slightest shrug.

"I verified every one. And once I was sure, I acted."

He flipped to the next page. "February 3rd—Malik Walker?"

"Dayton View gang leader. Killed a child in a drive-by. Judge tossed the gun—bad search. So I ended it."

"February 19th. Miguel Rojas?"

"La Voz del Cristal enforcer. Killed two local kids for making their own meth, but nobody in the neighborhood would testify."

Graham nodded. "February 24th. Christopher Redmond?"

"Redmond tried to appear legit with his car washes, but everybody knew he was shaking down the mom and pop shops. Killed a baker up on Hillcrest when he refused to pay, but his nephew took the blame."

Graham jotted a note. "What changed with Redmond? Someone else died in that diner. He wasn't on the list."

Daniella's eyes flicked toward the mirror—toward me.

"I didn't want that," she said. "But I was running out of chances. Patrols were changing. Surveillance tightening. If I waited, the mission failed. So I took the shot."

Her voice dipped lower.

"Adults who sit beside monsters… sometimes they've already accepted the risk. But I won't shoot when there's a child. That part hasn't changed."

Jenkins finally broke in. "March 3rd—Zhao Wang?"

"Tech predator. Hosted a platform for scam rings—romance, ID theft, elder abuse. Rich and untouchable. But not bulletproof."

"And March 10th?" Graham asked.

Daniella hesitated. Then:

"Travis Ledbetter. I had him in my sights twice."

She paused, jaw tight.

"First time was February 17th. He got off the bus with two kids. He should have been alone. Took them up to his mother's house. I watched as he got back on the bus an hour later. I stood down. I will never endanger a child."

Her eyes narrowed just slightly.

"Second time was last night. I had him again. Perfect angle. No kids. But you got there first. Took away my last chance."

Jenkins leaned back slightly. "So this wasn't revenge?"

She shook her head once.

"Not revenge. Justice—and maybe a measure of prevention. Every name on that list was a failure no one else fixed. But each name also meant a life I might save. Someone else's Ayala. I did what I was trained to do."

As before, Graham seemed stunned. His lack of experience was showing, and his confidence was slipping. He had seen confessions before, but nothing as clinical and cold as he was seeing now.

Sergeant Jenkins moved his chair and sat directly in front of Daniella. He leaned in close and stared into her beautiful eyes, the same ones I had once loved to lose myself in. The silence stretched into something awkward. Then finally, he spoke.

"Ms. Reynolds," he said. "You've been open so far, but we'd like more detail. What can you tell us about—"

She cut him off mid-sentence.

"I already told you," she said flatly. "You know who I shot, when and why. I have nothing else to say."

She looked toward the mirror like she knew I was standing on the other side. With an almost imperceptible nod and the slightest hint of sadness, she stood from her chair.

"Take me to jail. I need sleep."

Graham turned Daniella over to the waiting uniform officers, and we walked back to the office. Just thirty feet—but it could have been miles.

No one said a word as we made our way to our own little spaces. Jenkins went into his office and closed the door behind him. Graham fell into his chair with a sigh—probably louder than he intended.

I found my chair too. I sat and stared at the picture of Daniella I had put on my desk last week.

I wanted to believe it was some terrible mistake. It couldn't be Daniella. No. Not the pleasant and flirty court reporter with the dry wit, the disciplined walk, the habit of scribbling in the margins of her transcript pages.

The woman I used to hold, maybe even loved.

The one I called when the nights felt too long.

Then I heard it—low volume, but unmistakable. Graham had turned on the TV in the corner. Noon news.

I turned toward it. It was like a car wreck on the highway—I didn't want to see it, but I couldn't look away.

The anchor reminded me of Daniella. Young. Attractive. Confident.

Was she capable too?

"We're following breaking news in Dayton, where police have arrested a suspect believed to be connected to a string of unsolved homicides. While authorities are not yet identifying the individual, jail records obtained by our newsroom show that a Daniella Reynolds was booked this morning on a charge of aggravated murder."

My chest tightened.

"Reynolds, a local court reporter, was taken into custody during a SWAT operation in the north side of the city. The arrest appears to be linked to a recent series of random killings that have paralyzed the city. Police are not releasing anything further at this time. News Team 8 will continue to follow this story and bring you any updates tonight at five."

I didn't sit. I stared at the screen. A photo popped up—grainy, old, probably from her ID badge. She looked younger. Softer.

But the eyes. The same cold eyes I saw in the interview room.

I should have seen them before.

Rrrrriiiiinnng! Rrrrriiiiinnng!

The sound cut through the squad room as startling as a siren in a funeral. I jolted upright, heart hammering, still watching the screen. The picture stared back.

I grabbed the receiver—nearly dropped it—then managed to get it to my ear.

"Detective MacLaren," I said. "Homicide."

"Angus," the voice said. "It's Ben. Ben Levine."

"Hello, Ben. What can I do for you?"

"I saw it on the news," he said. "Angus, is it true? Has Daniella really been arrested?"

I gripped the phone tighter and pursed my lips. My throat tightened, but I didn't answer right away.

I didn't know Ben well. Daniella had introduced us once, a few weeks ago, when we bumped into each other at a restaurant. All I really knew was that he was her ex-husband. I didn't feel like saying much. But the news had already spilled the biggest secret—her name.

"Ben," I said. "I really can't say much, but yes—Daniella has been arrested. It's complicated. And it's serious."

"They said she's the sniper killer," Ben began, his voice quivering. "Angus, I'm so sorry. I should have said something earlier, but… it makes so much sense now."

"What does, Ben?" I asked.

"Daniella hasn't been herself for months. I thought it was the stress of this new… thing between you two, but I guess it wasn't."

I didn't have a response for that. I just listened. I let Ben talk.

"I know you two have gotten close," he continued, "but what do you really know about her?"

He didn't give me a chance to answer. Maybe he could tell I wasn't going to.

"Daniella hasn't always been a court reporter. Before we got married, back in Israel—she spent more than six years in the military. Everyone serves in the IDF, but Daniella was different."

That got my attention.

"Different how?" I asked.

"She re-enlisted. Multiple times. She was a long-range marksman."

I sat back hard in my chair.

A sniper.

With the jolt of hearing it confirmed—my stomach dropped like a lead anchor.

I leaned forward, switched the phone to speaker, and motioned for Graham to come closer. He caught the look on my face and sat down without a word.

"What did you say?"

"She was in the Caracal Battalion—Israel's co-ed border unit," Ben said. "She worked the border—regularly engaged with traffickers. Drug runners, smugglers. Iranians. Syrians. Hezbollah."

"Hezbollah?" I sat up straighter. "The first victim was Hezbollah. Holy shit. That's the motive."

It was all becoming so clear. Every crime scene. Every angle. Every impossibly clean, calculated shot—the damn precision of it all.

It wasn't just skill. It was discipline. Experience. Cold, practiced calm.

The kind you only learn under fire.

I looked over at Graham, and for once, he didn't say anything either. He didn't have to.

Ben's voice kept coming through the speaker, but part of me had already stopped hearing it. I was somewhere else now—somewhere darker, deeper. Connecting dots I didn't want to believe.

Chapter 38
The Fallout

Tuesday. I walked into the office with a 42 oz Yeti of Devil's Tears—Pitch Black roast. After hearing Daniella confess to everything yesterday, I didn't get a bit of sleep. In my mug wasn't merely coffee—it was the jet fuel for what was sure to be a hell of a long day. And I needed it. The sharks were circling.

The office felt different. Not quieter—it sounded the same. Not busier—just the homicide crew. No brass. No admin. Phones were already ringing. Maybe that was it.

I couldn't put my finger on it, but something was off. And I'd learned to trust that feeling.

I stopped to speak to Jenkins, but he wasn't in yet. Strange. He was always in early—especially after a high-profile arrest. Maybe he'd stopped for donuts or got stuck in traffic.

Graham was already at his desk, staring into a half-empty mug, trying to remember where the coffee had gone. I offered him a refill from mine, but he pretended to gag and waved me off. I laughed. He couldn't handle real coffee anyway.

Across the room, Chris from the firearms lab was waiting with a folder in hand. No smile. No small talk.

"Angus," he called as I crossed the room.

He raised the folder like a surrender flag—but there was nothing in his face that said retreat.

"You need to see this."

I took the file. A single glance was enough. The ballistics were in.

Five bodies. Four slugs. One rifle.

The Barrett MRAD .338 Lapua from Daniella's van.

"Damn," I said, looking back at Chris.

Chris gave a short nod and walked off.

I didn't sit. I stood there with the report in one hand, coat over my arm, as the weight of it settled in. She'd said it was her. But now the evidence said it too.

Then the door opened.

Major Trammell and Assistant Chief Carpenter walked in. Desk jockeys, both of them. Neither had been on the street in years. They sure as hell didn't come upstairs unless something was wrong. Or about to be spun into something else.

We all stopped talking mid-sentence and looked toward the office door. Graham raised an eyebrow at me across the desk.

"Morning, detectives," Trammell said. He gave a professional nod, trying to smile but couldn't quite remember how. "Mind if we interrupt?"

No one answered. There was that loaded silence that says everything. I guess that counted as consent, because they both walked in with the arrogance of the new owners of our old space.

He continued. "Guys, listen—we wanted to take a minute to personally thank all of you for your persistence and overall outstanding work on the vigilante case."

The word *vigilante* hung in the air. No one liked it. I sure as hell didn't like it. But it was the word the press had chosen, and now we were stuck with it.

"You closed a case that's terrified the city for weeks," Carpenter added. "Six murders. No evidence. Just good, old-fashioned police work. A solid arrest. No casualties. Even the biggest departments in the country usually botch cases with half the complexity."

I have a deep distrust of praise from the first floor. I wasn't sure whether it was genuine. Were we getting a slap on the back or being prepped for slaughter? Maybe both.

I listened with skepticism.

Trammell went on. "The mayor's office will release a statement this morning. There'll also be a press conference later today. This unit will be recognized. All of your hard work, the countless hours, the frustrations. All of it. You are all encouraged to attend the press conference to be recognized in person, if you'd like. You've earned it."

Graham gave a polite nod. I didn't move. I didn't wear a brass shield. I wasn't going in front of a camera. Hell with that.

Behind them, I saw Jenkins step through the door, a file tucked under one arm and a look on his face that said it all.

He had not been at the Donut King.

"Sergeant Jenkins," Trammell said with a hint of irritation at his lateness. "We were thanking your team for their hard work."

Jenkins gave a stiff nod. "Appreciate that, sir."

The whole room seemed ready to explode.

Trammell offered a few more scripted atta-boys, then Carpenter spoke again—something about coordination between departments and thanking the lab team. I'm not really sure. I had stopped listening.

Then they left—no handshakes, no small talk. Just a few nods and two pairs of polished shoes disappearing down the hall.

Once the door clicked shut, someone finally exhaled. I think it was Chris.

"That was intense," he said. "I'm going back to the lab where I can breathe."

We all laughed and thanked him for his work. I chuckled to myself at the thought of Chris being in the same elevator as those clowns.

"Jesus," Graham muttered. "That was a weak pat on the back. I thought I was back in the principal's office in third grade."

I didn't answer. I was eyeing the spot where Trammell had stood, but I was thinking about the word *clean*.

But it was never that simple. And maybe I'd been too willing to believe it could be—I'd also been too willing to believe Daniella was only who she said she was.

Jenkins crossed the room slowly, like a man walking toward the electric chair. He didn't say anything—to anyone. He kept walking until he disappeared into his office and shut the door behind him.

I knew that look. That wasn't the face of a man feeling great about a job well done. That was the look of someone about to take a hit for somebody else's screw-up. And I had a pretty good idea whose name was on the line.

Jenkins didn't call us right away—he let the silence in the room settle. No one moved, until finally the door creaked open, Sarge barely sticking his face through the gap.

"Angus. Graham."

No yelling. No request. It was a tired command, heavy enough to sink us.

I grabbed my coffee. Graham also stood, sliding in behind me, holding his empty mug. Jenkins had already closed the blinds, and I closed the door before anyone said a thing.

Jenkins didn't sit in his chair. He sat on the front edge of his desk, hands gripping the manila folder. His expression looked carved from stone.

He waited a beat. Then another. Then he let loose.

"What the hell were you thinking?"

Neither of us said a word. He wasn't done.

"You didn't think this might come back on you?" His eyes gaze looking straight through me. "Someone from downtown already called me this morning—asking how the hell you didn't know she was the shooter when you've been spending weekends with her."

There it was.

Sarge stood, walked slowly behind his desk, and rubbed the back of his neck.

"I told them this unit got the job done. I told them you're the best, most ethical detective I've got. I told them none of us had a crystal ball. But Angus—" He leaned forward, staring me down. "I also told them I didn't know you were sleeping with the goddamn suspect. And dammit, Angus, please tell me you didn't know either."

I didn't flinch. Didn't confirm or deny it. Graham stayed quiet too, gazing at the floor.

"I had to stand there while the command staff shook our hands and slipped the knife in with the other."

Graham and I said nothing, and Jenkins let the silence hang.

"I defended you, Angus. But you have to understand—they are coming for you. And once the press conference is over and the cameras are off, they're gonna want someone to answer for this. And Angus—you better pray to whatever god you believe in that the media doesn't find out."

I nodded once, slow.

"Yes sir."

Jenkins sat back down, leaned into his ragged office chair, and pushed his hands through his hair. Then he finally looked at Graham.

"You didn't know either?"

Graham shook his head. "Not until after the arrest. We all loved Daniella. There was never anything to raise suspicion about her."

Jenkins looked between the two of us. He didn't say *I believe you*. He didn't need to.

"I'm not going to micromanage your personal lives, but please—try a little harder to vet your flings. And if a situation like this ever happens again—you say something. Early. We handle it in-house if we can. We can't get blindsided again."

Neither of us replied. There wasn't anything left to say. Sarge looked back down at the file in his lap, and flipped through it mindlessly.

"Go get some work done. Expect to be hearing from Internal Affairs soon."

Graham and I turned toward the door and walked out together, returning to the squad room as if nothing had happened.

But something had happened. Everything had changed.

Graham and I had barely taken our seats again when the phone on my desk rang.

Not my cell. The desk line.

I picked it up.

"MacLaren."

"Angus," the voice said—gravelly and low. "It's Frankie Calloway."

Of course it was.

"What's up, Frankie?"

"Off the record," he started. "I just got off a call with a guy from one of the downtown papers. He's asking questions. The kind that make great news—but can also destroy lives."

I didn't say anything.

"He's chasing a rumor. Says one of the detectives might've been screwing the suspect. Wants to know if it's true. Wants to know if the department's circling the wagons."

"You calling to confirm or to warn us?"

"Both," he said. "I told him I didn't know anything about that, but if I were him, I'd be digging too. You know how this city is.

They love a scandal more than a conviction—and if it jams up a cop, even better."

I had nothing to say.

"I'm not asking you to tell me the details, Angus. I'm just saying—if it's true, it's only a matter of time before it's confirmed. And once it's out, the first version will always be the one remembered."

"Appreciate the call," I said.

"You good?"

"I'm fine."

"You sure?"

"I said I'm fine, Frankie."

"Angus, please call me if you hear anything. Okay, brother?"

"Thanks, Frankie."

Click.

Graham looked over at me. "That the press?"

I nodded, giving him a thin smile. "Frankie," I said. "The friendliest we've got."

***

The rest of the day crawled by. Nobody said much. The squad room felt wrong but I wasn't sure why.

Graham buried himself in old case notes. I sat through a call with an assistant prosecutor on a case headed for trial—gave a summary they already had and pretended it felt useful. Jenkins stayed in his office with the door closed.

By mid-afternoon, the news stations had started circling.

They'd named her. Daniella Reynolds. Local court reporter. Israeli military veteran. Six confirmed kills—maybe more. Channel 8 ran old courthouse footage. Her face was clear enough—and so was that faint, sniper's composure that never really left her.

And so was mine.

They didn't have a motive yet—not one that made sense. But they were guessing. They'd figure it out soon. One station even tossed in a line about "federal agencies monitoring possible overseas connections," just to stir the pot.

Around four, Graham looked over from his desk.

"You okay?"

"Hard to say," I said. "With that video of Daniella and me, it won't take a genius to put a name with the rumors."

He nodded and left it there.

By five, most of the squad had cleared out. Jenkins walked past without a word, just a glance that felt like a goodbye. I stayed behind, letting the headlines pile up.

Eventually, I stood, grabbed my coat, and reached for my keys as the desk phone rang again.

"MacLaren."

A woman's voice. Clipped and direct.

"Detective MacLaren, this is Captain Reese from Internal Affairs. You're to report to Room 412 at 0800 Monday morning for a formal interview regarding your connection to the suspect. This is a mandatory appearance. Do you understand?"

"Yes, ma'am."

A beat of silence.

"Be sure to bring your union rep. Have a good weekend, Detective."

Click.

I hung up, slipped my coat on, and didn't say goodbye to anyone. Didn't need to.

She was behind bars. The rifle was gone. But her aim? Perfect—every shot had landed.

By Monday, I'd be answering questions under fluorescent lights, with nothing but a tape recorder and a closed door for company.

And this time, there wouldn't be a case to solve.

Just me.

No longer a detective. Just another story.

Epilogue
The Quiet End

Saturday morning. No alarm, but it didn't matter. I hadn't slept.

I'd spent most of the night staring at the ceiling—it had been the same all week. If I closed my eyes, there was Daniella. First—the glorious ponytail, the smiles and mimosas; then she was in that van, surrounded by gas, walking out with her hands up—silent as a ghost.

My phone lit up with an app notification. 5:43 a.m. I gave up.

Dragging myself out of bed like I was nursing a hangover—I shuffled into the kitchen and poured a half cup of bitter coffee that had been sitting in the pot since last night. I made the call.

It rang three times before a voice picked up. Groggy. Not thrilled.

"Yeah?"

"Mike. It's Angus."

A pause.

"You good?"

"No. That's why I'm calling."

I heard whispering, the soft rustle of papers.

"You need me Monday, right?"

"You're the only one I trust, Mike. Room 412. Eight a.m."

"Okay, brother," he said. "I'll be there. And Angus—you sound awful. Get some sleep."

Sleep. I wish it were that easy.

Tossing the phone on the table, I went to my room and threw on some clothes. I filled my water bottle and my coffee cup and headed to my truck. I didn't know where I was going—I just drove. I got on I-75 South and found the highway empty. The sky was dark, a reminder of how I felt about my life. I continued for several miles and exited in Miamisburg. A few more miles and a couple of random turns later, the sign for Germantown MetroPark appeared—back to where Daniella and I had started. Maybe my brain knew before I did.

I hadn't been back since that morning.

The place looked the same—early light slipping through bare trees, the lot half-muddied from melting snow. But it didn't feel the same.

Not even close.

I parked my truck in the same spot as before and sat for a few minutes. There were no tears, but I couldn't deny I was sad. I missed Daniella, and I knew she was gone forever. I climbed out of my truck and started walking the orange loop like I had that day. I knew she wouldn't be here, but part of me hoped she might appear.

Looking back, when I first saw her by the bench, I felt something. Something hiding under the surface. I couldn't name it then—hell, I didn't even try.

She was so calm. Collected. Confident. But there was tension behind her eyes, like she was running from something she couldn't leave behind.

We talked about hiking. Escaping the city for a few hours of peace. Life.

I stopped at the clearing. I sat on the same bench, elbows on my knees. My body starting to feel the cold air.

There'd been signs. Not obvious ones. Nothing I could write in a report or testify about. But something in her posture, discipline, behavior. The way she watched the world—like she was waiting.

Cops are always taught to trust their instincts—those gut feelings. When something feels off, it usually is. But I didn't trust mine. Because I didn't want it to be true.

I liked her. Since Lena, I hadn't liked anyone. I might've even been falling in love with Daniella.

Smart. Beautiful. Stronger than she looked. Sharper than anyone gave her credit for. And maybe part of me wanted to believe we were just two tired people, finding something quiet in the middle of the noise.

But it wasn't that simple. She was carrying something heavy—too heavy to leave behind.

I leaned back and looked up at the brightening morning sky.

The department would do what they always did—issue a statement, tighten policies, blame someone lower on the ladder. IA would ask their questions. The press would run their story. Eventually, something else would knock it out of the headlines.

But for me, it wouldn't go away.

She'd confessed. Clear. Controlled. No tears. No excuses. She had owned it and seemed proud. And I believed her.
But that didn't make it easier.
Didn't make it right.

I wasn't grieving what she did. I was grieving who I thought she was.

The wind shifted, bringing different smells. Wet, muddy smells that were a refreshing break from the stench of the city. Somewhere in the trees, a woodpecker hammered away at a trunk—relentless and unseen. A barred owl lifted from a dark limb and slipped deeper into the trees—silent, certain, gone before I could track it.

I sat there awhile, watching the sun rise. As it cast its light across the frost-covered trail, the quiet surrounded me like fog on a cool spring morning.

I stood, took a drink from my bottle, and headed deeper into the forest.

At the far bend in the trail, I stopped and pulled a folded piece of paper from my jacket. Penny's drawing—me, her, and a giant smiling sun. The edges were worn from living in my pocket for weeks. I smoothed it out against my thigh and looked at it until the cold bit my fingertips.

I smiled and texted Lena.
Me: Can I grab Penny for pancakes?
The bubbles blinked.
Lena: Of course.

For all the noise, all the politics, all the damage—this was the part that mattered. This was the part worth walking back toward. Justice wasn't perfect, and I'd never kid myself into thinking it was. But as long as Penny could draw smiling suns, there was something left to protect. Something left worth standing in the line of fire for.

I slid the drawing back into my pocket, took one last look at the trail ahead, and kept moving.
I didn’t look back.
Didn’t need to.

ABOUT THE AUTHOR

Scott Lawson is a retired Dayton police sergeant and current inner-city schoolteacher. The son of a Dayton homicide detective, he accompanied his father on his first late-night homicide callout at the age of fourteen. Through high school he witnessed several more investigations, gaining an early, inside view of how homicide cases unfold—from the crime scene to those first critical hours of chasing leads.

That early exposure grew into a lifelong career in law enforcement, where he responded to countless murders and violent crimes. Now, as a teacher, Lawson brings the same commitment to truth and human stories into the classroom. His decades of experience—first as an observer, later as the police—bring grit, realism, and humanity to his debut novel, *Silent Justice*.

www.ingramcontent.com/pod-product-compliance
Lightning Source LLC
Chambersburg PA
CBHW020913310726
48980CB00011B/869/J